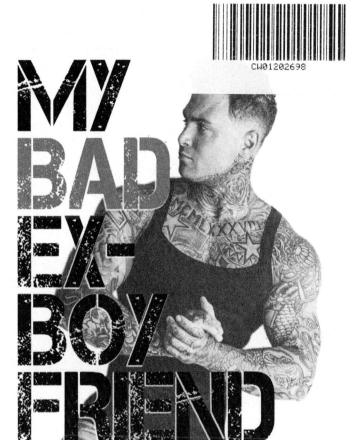

MY BAD EX-BOY FRIEND

a hot & hilarious M/M romance

by

Daryl Banner

Author of Bromosexual, Hard For My Boss,
Raising Hell & the Spruce Texas Romance Series

My Bad Ex-Boyfriend

Cover Photography
Golden Czermak / FuriousFotog

Cover Model
Alex Michael Turner

Cover & Interior Design
Daryl Banner

I dedicate this

to all the single lads & ladies out there

who just can't cut a damn break.

xxoo

Daryl

Other Work by Daryl Banner

Male/Male Romance

- Hard For My Boss
- Bromosexual
- Getting Lucky
- Raising Hell

The Spruce Texas Romance Series

- Football Sundae
- Born Again Sinner
- Heteroflexible
- Wrangled
- Rebel At Spruce High

Boys & Toys (serial novella series)

- <u>Season 1:</u> Caysen's Catch / Wade's Workout / Dean's Dare / Garret's Game
- <u>Season 2:</u> Connor / Brett / Dante / Zak

The Brazen Boys (stand-alone novellas)

- Dorm Game
- On The Edge
- Owned By The Freshman
- Dog Tags / Commando: Dog Tags 2
- All Yours Tonight
- Straight Up
- Houseboy Rules
- Slippery When Wet

Male/Female Romance – A College Obsession Romance

- Read My Lips
- Beneath The Skin
- With These Hands
- Through Their Eyes: *Five Years Later*

The Beautiful Dead Saga (a post-apocalyptic fantasy saga appropriate for all ages)

- The Beautiful Dead
- Dead Of Winter
- Almost Alive
- The Whispers
- Winter's Doom
- Deathless

The OUTLIER Series (an epic dystopia saga in six large multi-perspective novels)

- Rebellion
- Legacy
- Reign Of Madness
- Beyond Oblivion
- Weapons Of Atlas
- Gifts Of The Goddess

Kings & Queens (an OUTLIER companion novella series, stand-alones)

- The Slum Queen
- The Twice King
- Queen Of Wrath

My Bad Ex-Boyfriend Chapter List

MY BAD EX-BOY FRIEND

Chapter 1.
Evan's bad ex-boyfriend.

Deep breath.

Check your perfect part of russet hair a seventh time in the rearview. It's fine. Stop fussing.

Notice those strands that keep falling by your ear. Fix them with an agitated sigh, because you're always overly critical of yourself and it's your mother's fault.

Did you put on enough deodorant?

Deep breath again.

You can do this. You can totally do this. You got this. He's just your ex. You have a few, right?

But Dane Cooper is not just any ex. He's your bad *ex. He's the one you swore you'd never talk to again. He's the one who made you swear off boys for good. The only ones that'll satisfy you now are in your imagination late at night when you slip a hand down your pants and rock your eyes back.*

Realize how pathetic that sounds. But also applaud yourself for your honesty and keeping it real. Then sigh and convince yourself you're better than this.

I'm better than this.

You wonder what he's been up to all these years. Is he a completely different person now? He didn't sound too strange on the phone, other than his initial surprise at your calling him at all, as well as your own surprise (and slight relief) that he has the same number.

You wonder if he is curious about who *you* are now. Will he be impressed with all your accomplishments, or think you've become a totally self-inflated tart?

Maybe driving out all this way was a mistake. You could be home binging the rest of that crime show with that one hot actor whose name you keep forgetting.

Maybe the name starts with a D. Derek. Davy. Don. *Dane ...*

Close your eyes and—despite everything good and holy—remember vividly the last time you saw your ex's ripped body, so muscled it looked like he *eats* gyms for a living. Go ahead and think of the way your own body reacted every time he touched you, turning your helpless limbs into silk and your heart into a drum. Imagine his brawny, handsome face, his sharp, strong jawline, how manly the stubble on his cheeks was, the pinched look in his eyes that was so intense, you felt like he knew your every dirty thought when he looked your way.

Ignore that boner swelling between your thighs right now.

Dane ...

And you absolutely must envision the unexpectedly slinky way his body moved when he crawled over you atop a bed, then dove with his lips for that place between your ear and your neck he knows makes you squirm.

Then snap the fuck out of it.

Remember why you're here.

Step out of the car. Slam shut the door too hard on accident, causing you to jump. Fumble with your keys until they're shoved away into a pocket somewhere.

Pause just outside the door of this out-in-the-middle-of-nowhere Texas country bar you'd never in a million years *deign* to catch yourself in, yet you're standing there about to cross the threshold of noise and jeering and smoke and beer, and damn it, you hate beer, you hate beer so much, but this is where he said to meet up, and here your gay ass is, nearly an hour away from home.

Maybe five years ago when you were with Dane, you might've come to a bar like this, and it would've been an adventure. Back then, you were a different person. You were impulsive, and his bad boy antics excited you.

It's one of the reasons you're terrible for each other.

But you've since reinvented yourself. You're such a hot shot now. You live on a street called Figaro Lane in the middle of a safe, prestigious community, and you got there by your own hard work. You've earned those specialty brew lattés you grab hurriedly on the way to your posh salon every morning where you work. You've earned picking the more expensive entrée on the menu when you go to a restaurant with your friends. This is who you are now: crisp designer shirts and hair styling paste that costs more per jar than your electric bill.

Don't let him get to you. Be strong. Be smart.

But most importantly: Be sexy as hell—*because what's the harm in showing him what he's missing out on?*

Another deep breath. Close your eyes.

Then push through the door.

I open my eyes and stand there scanning the room of bikers and leather-clad men.

Okay, it might be my imagination, but I feel several eyes on me and my mauve button-up at once, the sleeves folded precisely two cuffs, worn just half a size too small because how else do I show off my three days a week at the gym? (Not that it does anything to my skinny shape except give me a pair of modest pecs and a couple laughable bumps for biceps.) I decided to dress down today with a pair of brown boots and jeans, as opposed to my usual fitted pair of butt-hugging skinny-leg dress pants and designer shoes. *Somehow, it still doesn't seem I dressed down enough.*

I knew where I was coming tonight. I knew who I'd be facing. *And I want him to see how far I've come without him, how hot I've gotten, what a* catch *I am now.*

Cross the smoky room, despite the glances and loud snorts and quizzical stares.

Keep your posture as stiff as a king's, and your eyes forward and focused.

Bump into a chair. Apologize, then back into a pool table where three burly men with beards glare at you. Apologize again, then rigidly make your way on through a haze of country rock music and smoke.

Don't let it shake you. You're totally rocking this. Just a few minor jitters, that's all. You'll be your fierce and flawless self from here on out.

Deep breath. Deeper breath.

You got this.

But after my third circling of the place, I still haven't found him. I stop by the only tall table that's empty, lean against one of its stools, and fold my arms, then wait some more.

A table bursts into laughter somewhere, startling me. People at the bar cheer and scream when a football team scores on the TV. All I hear are the cracking of pool balls and loud chatter. All I see are words turning into swirls of smoke before people's faces.

I check my phone with a squint. It's ten past nine.

Of course the bastard would keep me waiting.

Three very long minutes tick by. Then eight more. Soon, all my uneasiness from earlier is gone and I'm just plain pissed now.

It was already a stretch to expect him to be on time. But to totally stand me up like this?

I come to the decision that I'll have to deal with my pressing matter some other way. I don't need him or his help, right? I'll figure something else out.

But what?

I close my eyes to think. My eyes, even closed, sting from all the cigarette smoke. My ears are clogged with the noise of clinking glasses and distracting laughter and that annoyingly catchy country song.

"There you are, cupcake."

My eyes flap open and I jump with such force, my elbow knocks into the table behind me and causes a loud clatter. I look up, wide-eyed.

Now you're staring into the eyes of Dane Cooper.

And you shit yourself.

What you did not expect to discover is that your hot ex-boyfriend has gotten even hotter.

He's gained about ten pounds of muscle since the last time you saw him, easy—not that he needed it. He's got on a sleeveless denim jacket, which shows off his guns in a devastatingly sexy way. You also didn't expect him to have decorated his whole arm and shoulder in a spread of tattoos that scream: *"Fuck off, I'm dangerous."*

He was a bad boy before.

Now, he is as intimidating as he is hot.

And you'd be absolutely remiss not to mention his distressed jeans—skintight—and the way they glue to his big muscled thighs and round, firm, perfect ass, like they are just another tattoo on his smooth, taut skin. They're torn at the knees and bunch up at his meaty calves where a pair of thick black boots house his big, wide feet.

He's grown a beard, which only further accentuates the intensity of his eyes, the chiseled Romanesque fall of his nose, and the slight pinch of his full, kissable lips.

Dane props an elbow up on the table, bringing his whole muscled body far closer to me than I was prepared to handle. His face is so crushingly handsome.

Really, it's annoying how hot he is.

It's certainly not helping me maintain any confidence.

"Cupcake?" I manage to throw back.

"Old habits." He looks me over with that sly smirk of his, scratches his beard in thought, then nods at my shirt. "So what's with the fancy getup? Is your cute ass going to bible study after this?"

I frown. "I'm not *that* overdressed."

He lifts a blunt eyebrow. "Do you have eyes?"

My gaze drags down his body in frustration. *Yes, I have eyes, and they're doing nothing useful right now except to drink in every inch of you.* "Some things *never* change. You were always quick to criticize my taste in clothing."

"I never criticized it. I'd always said your ass would look good in anything. You'd even rock a giant teabag."

"I recall many *immature* mentions of *teabags*," I reply, "but they weren't referring to what I was *wearing*."

A humored smile spreads across Dane's face.

7

There is so much history between us, even a simple smile says much more than words do. Has it really been five years already? I could just as easily imagine it's been five days, if it weren't for all his tats, and that messier, sexier hair he's rocking tonight.

Even the glint of appreciation in his eyes that seems to twinkle every time he looks my way is the same.

Just like the old days.

He swats my arm, then pushes away from the table. "C'mon. Let's have ourselves a game."

Without waiting for my response, Dane turns and heads off, giving me an unfortunately timed view of his plump, muscled butt in those jeans, shadowed barely by the back of his denim jacket which comes down to just the top of his *shelf* of an ass.

I could bite my fist and cry.

"Dane, I don't have time to play games," I protest as I follow him through the crowded room. "I have ..." My words are interrupted as he gets too far ahead of me and I find myself squished by a couple I'm trying to move past. I excuse myself, despite the hairy, leather-clad pair of them doing nothing to move out of my way. "I have things I need to do after this!" I call out at him as I catch up after stepping over a spilled drink on the floor. "I'm ... *ugh, what is that?* ... I'm very busy."

"Is that so?" he calls over his shoulder as we make our way. "You a big hotshot interior designer now?"

I fret. "I ... well, no, I'm not, but I—"

"You're not?" He stops to face me, brow furrowed. "But it was your dream. I figured by now you'd be one."

"It ... isn't practical." I stiffen up with pride. "I own a full-service men's hair salon. I'm a celebrated stylist."

"A ... celebrated stylist." He looks me over critically.

If there's anything I don't need, it's his opinion on what I've done with my life. "Not everyone needs an interior designer. You hire one once, maybe twice. But everyone needs a haircut, mani-pedi ... some more than others," I add with a sidelong glance at Dane's untidy mess of hair—which even I have to admit is a little sexy.

Dane doesn't seem satisfied with that answer. After a moment's deliberation, he shakes his head. "Sounds like good ol' Mom and Dad's words coming out of your mouth, not yours. I know your dream, and snipping hair isn't it."

I gape. "A trip to the salon is a lot more than just 'snipping hair'. Excuse me," I say to another person I accidentally bump into. "Dane, I don't have time to—"

"If you want my help," he calls over his shoulder as he walks on, "then I think the least your tight ass can do in return is play me a round. For old times' sake."

We arrive at an unoccupied pool table where three men are gathered at a corner, one of them sitting on its edge, none of them actually playing. I wouldn't have dared bother them, but when Dane approaches, the three men take notice of him, one of them tipping his hat with a, "Evening, D," for a greeting, then all three respectfully vacate the table. I quirk an eyebrow, watching them go, then look at Dane as he calmly racks up the balls.

Apparently people know him here.

And respect him like some kind of bearded-man celebrity.

I stand at one end of the table and cross my arms. "And what's so great that you're doing with *your* life?" I ask him. "Living out your dream as a police officer still?"

"I quit the force over two years ago."

That catches me by surprise. "Why?"

Dane shrugs carelessly, still racking up the balls. "It wasn't a good fit for me. I work better alone."

And now I'm not so surprised. Ugh, that's such a *Dane* thing to say. "I don't know why I'd expect you to have committed to that path, even after all the schooling and training you did while we were together. You can't even commit to a denim jacket with sleeves."

"I've got my reasons."

The balls clack together and roll as he tightens them up into a perfect triangle, then lifts away the rack.

"So what you're saying is ... you can't help me?"

He peers at me. "You seem to *really* want me to help you. I'm the only one you can trust, huh?"

I smirk. "Don't go getting a big head about it."

He jerks back with half a chuckle. "Damn, boy, who squirted the Sriracha up your tushie?"

I'm not making the mistake of looking into his eyes again. And I'm deliberately not going to take note of the way his strong, sharp jaw tenses cutely when I sass him.

And I am one hundred percent *not* acknowledging how many references he's made to my ass already.

Four. It's been four.

"I never agreed to a game," I lightly remind him. "I told you I've got a lot of things I need to do. And now that I discover you're not even a cop anymore, I don't—"

"I'm not with the force anymore. It doesn't mean I can't still help. I'm a private investigator now."

I blink. "Like … a detective? A private eye?"

"Want to break?" He goes to the wall and fetches a stick, then lays his eyes on me, heavy and hard and full of innuendo. "Or … you want me to?"

I wish he wouldn't look at me like that. I peel my eyes away from him to glance at the triangle of balls on the table, then peer at the sticks on the wall.

I eye him sternly. "One game. I'll break."

Dane cracks a smile. "Good boy."

I ignore his words—and the fluttering of excitement they cause in my chest that's not unlike a puppy wagging his tail—then snatch a stick from the wall. Coming to the head of the table, I carefully apply chalk to the tip so as to not get any on my hands or shirt.

"Don't go breaking a nail," taunts Dane, watching from the side and leaning on his stick.

I ignore him yet again, then bring my stick gently to the table, carefully preparing to shoot. I pull back with precision, calculate my angle, then let it fly. *Crack!* The balls go speeding by in a traffic jam of bright colors and geometry. Two solids are sunk as well as a stripe.

I lift my face to Dane. "You were saying?"

He nods approvingly, then crosses his big arms, half-hugging his stick like a lover as he studies me with those bottomless, hungry brown eyes of his.

And that *look*.

That look that rips all my clothes off and slams me to a bed whether I'm ready for it or not.

I force my attention back to the table. "I'll be solids," I decide, since I earned the choice, then position myself for my next move. Before I shoot, however, I throw a question his way: "If I'm staying awhile, you plan to buy me a drink or what? I did drive nearly an hour to get to this damned place."

He snorts. "Sorry to tell you this, cupcake, but they don't serve fruity drinks with cute umbrellas here."

My eyes narrow to slits. "Don't be a prick, Dane."

"But wasn't that your favorite thing about me?" He reaches down and grabs a big hearty handful of his crotch in those torn jeans of his. "My *prick*?"

My heart jumps excitedly.

All breath is stolen away. In an instant, every speck of progress I've made over the years is gone, and I'm that horny, dumb, love-struck eighteen-year-old again who'd dance in clubs every night with Dane at my side.

Sense slaps me hard on the face, shaking me awake. I roll my eyes hard and scoff, feigning indifference. "Ugh. Predictable." I pull back my stick, then strike.

The ball misses its mark. Nothing goes in.

"You distracted me," I point out.

"How?" He grabs himself again. "With my prick?"

"Still mature as ever, I see. Remind me again why I'm playing pool with you?"

"Because you need me." He struts right up to his end of the table, gripping his stick like it's his five-foot-long cock, and eyes me. "Though I gotta admit, I didn't really get all that clear a picture from you on the phone of what your big pressing problem is, exactly. Something about a pink mailbox ...?"

When Dane leans over the table, I can't help but watch his arms flex and bulge as he aims his stick. No matter how hard I try, I can't look away.

I bite my lip. My breathing changes.

Crack! A striped ball goes into the corner pocket.

Dane rises and moves around the table, coming right up to my side. "Pardon me," he grunts as he bends over to take his next shot.

And now his ass, tight and firm and hugged by those ripped jeans of his, is in full view next to me. With just a sweep of my hand, I could spank him or grab a hearty handful. It's literally an invitation, the provocative yet effortless way he bends over like that and shows off his goods, like he isn't even aware how sexy he is.

Bent over like that, he's got me *thinking things*.

Crack! In goes another ball.

"Too bad this isn't strip pool, huh?" he remarks with a breathy chortle. "We'd have each other naked already."

"Three balls, I'd have your jacket, shirt, and pants," I point out. "That leaves you in your underwear."

"It would, if I was wearing any."

I blink, then glance at his ass again, as if to check.

Just then, he slowly rises and saunters around the table like he owns it. Of course, my eyes are trained on his ass, doomed now to picture him—and it—completely naked, which I'm certain was his plan, the tease he is.

Then he throws over his shoulder: "You're checking out my ass, aren't you."

My eyes flick up to his indignantly. "No, I'm not."

"Whatever you say, cupcake." He stops and bends over to take his next shot.

I move in front of him and grab his stick. "Can we stop all this game-playing? I came here to ask for your help, and I feel like you aren't even taking me seriously. It's more than just my mailbox, which was painted pink overnight. *Hot pink*, at that. More's happened. There's ... clearly some gay-targeting vandal in our neighborhood, and the ... the police aren't doing a thing about it."

Dane stands up straight and digs his stick into the floor by his feet. "So you want me to sniff out some silly vandal in your neighborhood? That's it? Really?"

He's always been so infuriatingly difficult. I sigh, then throw him a tired shrug. "I know it doesn't sound like that big a deal. Maybe it isn't. But I thought it might—"

"Escalate?" he offers.

It's my heartbeat that *escalates.* Ugh, how does Dane make just one stupid little word sound so sexy?

"I could easily help you out. That's not my holdup." He leans against the edge of the table and looks me over. "I just can't help but feel like you ... came to me for *another* reason." His full, kissable lips purse suggestively. "A reason you're too chicken shit to admit."

I swallow as my eyebrows pull together. I stare him down quizzically.

"You could've asked a hundred other people to help you," Dane points out. "You could even grow a pair and be more of a dick to the cops, who I can tell you right now won't lift a finger except to file some report that'll get shoved under another stack somewhere, forgotten, unless blood is spilled. And *that's* being optimistic. And so I circle around to my point." His intense stare bears down on me as he leans so closely, I can smell the heat of desire coming off his body—*or is that my own?* "You came to me for another reason, and I think I know what it is."

"What?" I ask challengingly, daring him to say it.

He grins. "You want me back."

"Nope," I answer at once.

"Yep."

"I said nope, I meant nope. I'm not getting back with you," I tell that beautiful, bearded face of his.

His eyes shine with longing. "I don't believe you."

"I don't care if you do or don't. That's *not* what this is." I swallow again, privately acknowledging the sweat forming in my pits. "Can you step back a bit, please? I'm smelling your sex. I-I mean your cologne."

Fuck, that slipped.

Dane grins, not missing a thing. "Yeah. You've been unsatisfied since we broke up, haven't you? I can tell."

"I've been *perfectly* satisfied."

"By who? I can also tell when you're turned on." His voice grows deeper as he takes another step toward me, nearly putting his big, muscled pecs in my face. "Your cheeks flush and your right foot taps impatiently."

I stop tapping my right foot at once.

I didn't even notice.

"Or maybe I'm just *actually* impatient," I point out, flushed face and all, "because you won't answer a simple question. Are you going to help me out or not, Dane?"

He smirks. "Win this pool game, and maybe I will."

To that, I slap down my stick on the table and face him with frustration. It doesn't faze him at all; he just stands there staring me down, amused by my reaction.

"This," I tell him with a gesture at him, then at our scattered balls on the table, "is what's wrong with you. All the *games*. You're just a boy who never grew up, who grabs his junk in public, who ... dresses like the missing lead singer to a death metal band no one's heard of."

He brings his face so close, he could kiss me. "And don't forget that all three of those reasons are also why you fell in love with me, Evan James Pryor."

I find myself trapped by his intense stare. It's like an insect in a dish of honey; no matter how strongly I pull, I'm helpless to break free.

Which is why it's all the more amazing that I find it in myself to say back to him: "On the contrary, it's why I dumped your ass."

Dane's face tightens.

"You're just a man who clearly can't learn from his mistakes. And ... clearly you're someone who can't help me. Maybe this whole thing *is* stupid. Maybe you think it's a silly little problem and not worth your time. You won't find out either way, because I'm leaving."

"I'm gonna prove you wrong about me," he vows.

"Have fun playing with your *balls*," I throw back as I turn away and head for the door in a swirl of cigarette smoke and sticky footsteps ...

And desperate, yearning heartbeats.

Chapter 2.
Evan and the scandal with the vandal.

I wouldn't have humiliated myself by going to Dane Cooper if it wasn't for waking up last Sunday morning to a mailbox spray-painted hot pink. *My* mailbox.

This kind of shit just doesn't happen on Figaro Lane.

I mean, our community is regularly patrolled. Isn't *security* the point of that? All our streets are named after famous operas. All our backyards have privacy fences made of stone. We even have a lake.

And now I have a pink mailbox. *Hot pink.*

"Oh ... muh ... *gah.* Who did this?" asked my wide-eyed, white-shirt-and-khaki-wearing neighbor that same morning while sucking down a Caramel Mocha Frap like he was trying to impress a casting director. If he isn't loitering around somewhere sucking on a straw, he doesn't exist. His name is Stevie.

All I could do that morning was bite my lip and shrug. "I'm still trying to figure out whether it's an act of vandalism or a free paintjob."

Stevie made a slurping sound, then gave me a lift of one arched, over-plucked eyebrow. "Question of the day is ..." *Slurp.* "... a paintjob courtesy of *whom?*"

That would be a question still left unanswered half a week later when Josiah across the street woke to discover one giant word written in baby-blue and bubblegum pink paint across his driveway.

H-O-M-O, it read.

The word isn't all that scandalous. Or news. I mean, everyone on this long and winding cul-de-sac is a homo.

It's like Sesame Street, except everyone's Bert and Ernie and drives a Mercedes.

"Well," I mumbled, Josiah at one side and Stevie on the other, as we stared down at the decorated driveway, "at least they have nice handwriting ...?"

Josiah shot me a look.

Stevie kept sucking his straw—new day, new Frap.

By the time the third vandalism happened—a glitter and rainbow confetti bomb exploding in Marcellus and Vinnie's car—I knew I'd have to do something about it. The bomb wasn't particularly explosive or dangerous per se, but Marcellus's black poodle apparently made a lunch out of some of the glitter, and an emergency trip to the vet was soon required—you know, before the poor doggy started shitting rainbow sprinkles or something.

The police aren't taking us seriously, since no one's been hurt (*except little Madonna*), and nothing *especially bad* has happened yet. So before this neighborhood turns into a real operatic tragedy of Figarian proportions, I decided something needed to be done.

I grabbed my phone, bit my lip, and called the last person on Earth I swore I'd ever speak to again.

My ex-boyfriend Dane.

And, well, we know how *uselessly* that went.

"*Vandal!*" states Raymond grandly to the room.

Please step back for the indubitable queen bee of Figaro Lane: Raymond Havemeyer-Windsor III.

Don't you already hate him by his name alone?

Add to that the crisp-ironed white pants that are so tight, they leave nothing to the imagination. Add to that the white sweater he wears tied over the shoulders of his sea foam skintight polo, collar popped. Add to that the fact that this man is thirty-eight, yet tells every single newcomer to our street he's still in his "tragic twenties" because he uses some special face cream from Italy.

"We need to protect our *neighborhood*," he announces to those of us gathered in his palace, which is the only word I can think of annoying enough to dignify his obnoxious spread of real estate. "For now, it's mailboxes, driveways, glitter bombs ... but what's next? A *real bomb*? The vandal broke into a car, but will he break into one of our houses while we're sleeping? How far do we let this vandalism go until we're the next *scandal* on the news? Is that the kind of reputation we want for us here?"

Feet shuffle uncomfortably as each face turns to the other. Each person wonders if someone else will reply.

"What if it's just bored teens from the high school?" puts in Will in a speculative tone, adjusting his too-big sunglasses—yes, even wearing them indoors, likely not taking them off so as to maintain the complement they give to his perfectly-fixed wave of blond hair.

When Raymond looks at him down the length of his perfect, unblemished nose, his stare is long and cold.

Will, after a second of discomfort, flinches and looks away. "Well, I ... suppose not," he backpedals, takes a sip of his martini, then shrugs and peers at Josiah across the room. "Handwriting on your driveway was too *neat* to belong to any *high-schooler*, anyway," he jokes.

No one dares dignify him with even a chuckle.

The thing about Raymond Havemeyer-Windsor III, head of the HOA, is that no one dares to defy him. No one dares to even *annoy* him. He can make your life hell with just a single letter slipped into your mailbox. On account of an unreturned smile or nod, he can decide he doesn't like the color of your front door and write you a sweet little letter, ruining your week. He holds all the cards, always, and no hand you could possibly play will ever outplay his.

Raymond's word is, and always has been, the final one on anything and everything that goes on in this prestigious neighborhood—*and especially this cul-de-sac.*

"I still think it's a hate crime thing," says Marcellus with one hand drawn to his chest and the other holding his little black poodle, whose name is Madonna. "It can't just be someone's disgruntled nephew who didn't get his Xbox for Christmas. Raymond, shouldn't we—?"

Another withering look from Raymond, and now it is Marcellus who retreats into his poodle's curly black hair with a fretful, humiliated shutting of his lips.

"What if it's Old Man Hanson?" blurts his short twink husband Vinnie at his side who can't be more than twenty-two years old—ten and a half years younger than him. People talk. "That man—"

"Oh, way to *stereotype*, Vinnie," Marcellus spits back at his husband. "Pick on the new-money redneck down the street and pin him for a homo-hater."

"But he *is* a homo-hater! He *eyes* me contemptuously whenever I walk Madonna past his house!"

"Honey, you're worse than little Madonna, barking at anyone who walks past *our* front porch. The vandal is *not* Hanson. He's just a misunderstood old man."

"First things first," interrupts Josiah by the couch, "but are we going to hire a crew? I've been trying to scrub 'HOMO' off my driveway for two days, and—"

"Um, *we* have glitter all inside our brand new Lexus, which Madonna ingested, lest I remind you," Marcellus spits back while stroking said poodle with mounting agitation, "and unless *your* works-from-home lazy tushie has tried vacuuming glitter *embedded* in carpet and leather car seats, I'd recommend making like a whore on Halloween and *closin' them haunted house lips.*"

Then, quietly, the stiff-necked fellow with a tight, tucked-in dress shirt named Preston mutters, "*Why's it always have to be 'whore this, whore that' all the time? Ugh.*"

Things are getting rather touchy and roll-your-eyes dramatic here in Raymond's living room. It's only eight of us who've gathered here today, like some impromptu clubhouse meeting. We all have better things to do with our Sunday. We all wish this would just end. Yet here we are, putting on our best.

"I know a good power-washer who'll get those words right off your driveway," Will says, his eyebrows lifting over his big shades, "and that *isn't* a sexual euphemism."

"*For once,*" mumbles Arry with a roll of his eyes.

I find myself staring off toward the window. Despite all that's going on around me, it feels like I still haven't left that smoky bar from last night. Every time I blink, I see Dane by that pool table in his torn jeans and cut-off denim jacket, his eyes on me and his firm grip around that stick of his.

Pool stick. Not his *other* stick.

Which I'm totally not thinking about right now.

Maybe I shouldn't have been so pigheaded about him helping me. Enduring a little flirting from my ex isn't so awful, is it? Maybe it isn't such a bad thing if Dane takes one little step back into my life, just to help catch some pesky troublemaker on our street.

Just one step couldn't hurt, right?

The next moment, the front door swings open, and the midday sunlight is eclipsed briefly by the shape of our ninth unexpected member to the meeting.

It's Xavier, the newest guy on our street—*and Lord help him*. He's got a spread of spiky black hair that's so circa 90s alternative street kid, he looks like an MTV reality show reject. His face is plain, his eyes are beady and black, and his lips—interrupted by a ring piercing—are pulled into a permanent, unimpressed smirk.

Raymond gives the newcomer a steely look. "What are you doing here?"

Xavier lets the door shut carelessly at his back, struts into the room, and shrugs. "Coming to a neighborhood meeting I wasn't invited to, I suppose."

Raymond's reply is even and quick. "You were not invited because you haven't been a target."

"Neither have you," points out Xavier.

The tension in the room is wire-taut. But instead of dignifying Xavier with any reaction at all, Raymond merely turns his cold eyes my way, and his voice is soft as mango gelato when he asks, "And what do you think of this, Evan?"

All eyes turn my way.

Great. The spotlight. Exactly what I wanted.

"I ..." I clear my throat. "I guess I ... can see Xavier's point. Only four of us have been vandalized, yet all of us were invited here to figure out a plan for how to—"

"I meant of the vandalism itself," Raymond clarifies with steely resolve, lifting a tall glass of vodka tonic to his thin lips, his posture bone-rigid and his chin lifted.

I blush. *Oops.* "I ..." I give a shrug, then cross my arms. "I'm not sure I know what to make of it at all."

Raymond gives me the faintest of smiles. "Oh, you sweet thing," he nearly coos, as if poking at a baby in a crib, then lifts his eyebrows. "Not even one thought?"

He has an odd and uncharacteristic soft spot for me ever since I moved here. I can't explain it. Maybe we hit it off when he learned I had an eye for interior design and asked my opinion on a mauve dresser. Though I'm a hairstylist, he has yet to actually visit my salon.

To be honest, I'm relieved he hasn't. Ugh, can you imagine if he didn't like the cut I gave him?

"I mean, you were the first one vandalized, darling," Raymond points out. "I just wonder if you've had any special thought as to why they might have targeted you first, whoever our *ballsy* culprit is."

Preston next to him quirks an eyebrow, curious, too.

I give it a moment's thought. I have no answer.

Come to think of it, why *was* I the first target?

"Why haven't the police done anything yet ...?" asks Will and his perfect, blond wave of hair.

"Ugh, girl, who you kiddin'?" comes the dry voice of Arry by the drink cart, pouring another bourbon at half-past noon on a Sunday, but who's judging? "These local cops don't give a *hooker's left shoe* about us."

"They're probably busy on the *other side of town* with *actual crimes*," insists Josiah with a sigh. "We'll be buried in glitter and pink paint before they bother with us."

"Cops here aren't like they were in Belleview," sighs Marcellus in sad agreement, stroking his poodle. "There, half the force was gay, it seemed like. They'd be out here in the drop of a *fancy fascinator*."

"I could use some hot gay cops in town," mutters Josiah, making Marcellus laugh—the only thing the two quarrelsome neighbors can agree on, apparently.

"What about Evan's ex-boyfriend?"

The question comes from Stevie, who has been aloof all this time, standing so still by the wall that he nearly blends right in with it. For once, he does not have a straw or a drink at his mouth, but instead a finger, and it's on the tip of it that he absently bites, wide-eyed and awaiting a response.

I flinch at the sound of Stevie's question.

Yet again, all eyes fall on me.

"No, sorry," I say right away. "He won't help us."

"*Who's his ex-boyfriend?*" Vinnie quietly asks his husband Marcellus, like I'm not here, "*and why did we all go weirdly quiet at the mention of him?*"

"*He's a cop, isn't he?*" hisses Marcellus, then turns to Arry. "*Or a martial artist, or an assassin, or ...?*"

"*An ex-cop,*" whispers Arry dryly, eyes me, then asks much louder, "He's an ex-cop now, right? Isn't that what you told Josiah this morning? Some *big scandal* got his badge taken away?"

"*I didn't say anything about a scandal!*" hisses Josiah, eyeing me worriedly. "*You made that part up!*"

"You said that *he* said his ex isn't a cop anymore."

"*But I didn't say anything about—*"

"I mean, otherwise it sounds like you're trying to imply that I'm a *gossip* or a *liar* or *something* ..." Arry goes on flippantly, eyes half-lidded as he turns away.

"*You're making* me *sound like I embellish, or lie, or—*"

Whether out of pure insanity or just to get the two of them to shut up, I set down my glass of wine, clear my throat, and state, "He isn't a cop anymore, it's true. He's a private investigator now, and he—"

Then I shut the hell up. And so has everyone else.

Fuck. I did *not* mean to let that last part out.

"A private investigator ...?" says Preston, eyes wide. He exchanges a startled look with Raymond.

"That's perfect!" exclaims Marcellus, patting his tiny poodle's head with excitement, annoying poor Madonna. "You can get him to help find out who glitter-poisoned my sweet puppy!"

I try to say something, but then Josiah cuts in with,

27

"I wanna know who did it, too. I've given lots of thought to what words I'll paint on *their* driveway."

Again, I attempt to protest, desperate for everyone to *not* jump on the Let's-Hire-Dane Train, but in seconds, the room is aflutter with excitement and relief.

My stupid ex-boyfriend just became their answer.

It's Raymond who keeps every inch of his cool, his stare finding me through the noise of the others. His eyes narrow as he studies me, and when he speaks, the room falls silent. "Is something wrong, Evan?"

Everyone turns to me, curious.

I bristle. "I ..." I clear my throat. "I'm just ... It was just that I've ... I-I've already gone to him. And ..." My eyes meet Josiah's hopeful ones. Then Marcellus's and Vinnie's. Even the poodle's. "And ... he can't help us."

The whole room fills with thick, hot, armpit-sweat-inspiring silence.

Raymond's eyes turn to needles. "Is that so?"

The thing is, when Raymond Havemeyer-Windsor III asks something, you don't actually have a choice; you answer, or you oblige, or you agree.

Every scrap of freedom you think you have is an illusion. Your gay ass is *owned* in this neighborhood.

"It's ... It's so," I finally manage to say, my mouth so dry I could spit sand. "I'm sorry to let you all down."

Raymond lets out a sigh that fills the room. "Don't worry, Evan," he says. "We wouldn't want you to feel ...

put out. If you don't want to help us by involving your ex-boyfriend, then ... we won't."

My eyes flit between each person's face, all who look away in discomfort, feeling the cold water of Raymond's unspoken threat wash over the room.

"I ... I *want* to help," I insist in my defense. "It's just that ... I mean, when I talked to him last night, he ..." I close my eyes. It's not like this is easy for me. "He's just *impossible* to work with. He's being difficult. I-I mean ..." I feel my cheeks flushing—and this time, it's certainly *not* because I'm turned on. "We wouldn't want him to help us anyway, trust me. Really, I'm sure I can think of some other way, or someone else who—"

"I understand," states Raymond crisply, cutting me off like a hot knife through butter.

While that sweet spot Raymond has for me might come with its occasional advantages, it also has its cold, hard limits. I know when to fold my hand.

Again with that whole thing about not really having a choice when Raymond wants something.

I close my eyes, defeated. Then I let out the next words with a smile on my face. "But maybe I can suck it up and ..." *Oh, God.* "... and talk to him again, and see if he'll ..." *I might be sick.* "... see if he'll ... help us anyway, despite being a difficult, obstinate, pigheaded ... *man.*"

Raymond gives me a cold, approving nod.

Goddamn it, Dane.

Chapter 3.
Dane and the big prick.

"The big prick isn't cheating on you."

The woman slaps a hand over her mouth in surprise, tears swelling. "R-Really?" she moans past her fingers.

"Really," I assure her. "He isn't cheating." We are seated across from each other at her dining room table. She offered me a cup of tea, which I've taken a courtesy sip of and set down in front of me, untouched since. You can say a cup of tea *isn't my cup of tea*.

"What a relief!" she exclaims.

"I'm afraid the truth of why your big prick husband comes home late every evening is ... worse."

The woman's face collapses from relief to dread all over again. "It's ... It's worse?"

"Much, much worse." I lean over the table. My eyes turn serious. "Your husband plays *Dungeons & Dragons*."

She acts as if she didn't hear me, stunned. Then she tilts her head. "Dungeons and what-now?"

"Dragons. It's like a card game without cards."

She is thoroughly confused, her eyes searching for the punchline of a joke I'm not trying to tell.

"He gathers with friends at a house off Maple Road. All male friends. Sometimes they dress up. He's a Lawful Neutral Halfling Geomancer, whatever the fuck that is," I go on, reading from my notes. "He plays until 8:30, sometimes 8:45, curses about having lost track of time, then races home to you while swiftly getting out of costume on the road. One night, he almost hit a cat."

"Oh, no!"

She sounds more concerned for the cat's welfare than her or her husband's. I flip the page in my tiny notepad. "Also nothing to worry about with your teen. He's not—" I make a gesture of taking a toke with two pinched fingers at my lips. "—with his friends from school."

"Oh, thank God. The Devil's Lettuce took over my brother's life, and I—"

"But he *is* flunking geometry and doesn't wanna tell you or your husband."

The woman sighs. "That boy. I'll have to get a tutor. Oh, what a relief! I've been *dreading* this day, and now it's come and gone and everything's fine. You've been so great, Mr. Cooper. Thank you, thank you, thank you!"

When I first decided to be a private investigator and flip the bird to my former chief of police, I'll be honest, I kinda was hoping for more exciting clients. I was picturing *Mission Impossible* shit. *James Bond* shit.

Instead, this is my life, and it is what it is.

She hands me an envelope of cash—so there's no paper trail. Then with a, "Have a great day, ma'am," I see myself out before her family comes home.

In my car while watching the sun fall behind a row of houses and set the shingles afire, Evan's face surfaces in my mind—and that last lingering look in his eyes before he effectively told me to fuck off and left the bar.

To be honest, the last damned thing I expected to get Saturday was a call from my ex-boyfriend.

The one who got away.

For a second, I seriously thought I was being punked.

But there he was at the bar, waiting for me hours later, right on time. I had to stand back awhile and just stare at him. I knew I'd feel something when I saw him after all these years, but I didn't know it'd be this.

It was like love at first sight all over again.

See, the day we first met, it was in some entry-level psych class. He was going for a minor in it, and I just needed a social science elective. I was bored out of my mind that first day, running on two hours of sleep after a binger with my buds the night before.

And just before I thought I might nod off, in walks a cute motherfucker—*ten minutes late*—in a pair of low-rise jeans and a t-shirt with an open plaid button-down over it. His russet hair was swept to the side, and he had this clueless sparkle in his eyes like he thought he was lost.

It was instant. I knew I wanted him the second I saw him. "Right here," I called out, interrupting the professor and slapping the empty seat of the desk next to me.

The psychology professor frowned at me and cleared his throat, but I wasn't paying attention. My eyes were caught on that cute-faced boy who'd just walked in. And now his eyes were on me, eyebrows slightly lifted, blood rushing to his cheeks at the attention I just gave him.

Then I had the pleasure of watching him cross in front of the classroom, take a short walk of shame down the aisle, and plant himself in the desk next to mine. He had all these whispered apologies on his cherry lips, and kept sneaking glances my way as he pulled out his laptop and got settled. I just kept grinning, watching him being all shy and bumbling and shit.

Immediately after class ended, I was on him. "You wanna grab some lunch?"

He looked like he might've shit a brick in that seat, his face blushing at once. "I ... I've got another class."

"I'll walk you, then."

He blushed even more.

The two of us crossed from one end of the campus all the way to the other where a giant building loomed in the distance. "Architecture, huh?" I blurted, surprised as we approached. "Wanna design buildings for a living?"

"The insides of them," he was quick to clarify. "I ... I want to be an interior designer."

I nodded. We were walking slow. "You got an eye for interior design or something?"

"It's fascinating to me. You know, you can tell a lot about a person just from the layout of their furniture."

"That so?" I grunted.

His arm kept brushing up against mine. Or maybe it was me who was doing the brushing, I couldn't tell. It was giving me wood all the way down that long road and was distracting in the most pleasurable way.

He frowned. "But it's just my freshman year. Who knows. Maybe I'll realize I hate it and pursue some other thing. Business school. Marketing." His eyes flicked my way nervously. "Are you studying to be a psychologist?"

I snorted. "Me? Nope. I want to put bad guys away for a living."

His face scrunched up, confused. "Like, you mean a judge? Or a lawyer?"

"A cop." I beat a fist into my palm. "I'm gonna take down baddies and make this world a better place."

He nodded slowly. "That's really great."

"And you're really cute," I threw right back at him.

That made him stop in place, as if the road beneath our shoes became a glue trap. "W-What?"

In retrospect, maybe it wasn't obvious at first that I was attracted to men. I wasn't all bulked up and tatted back then as I am now, but I was still fairly intimidating. "Why else do you think I'm walking you to your class?"

He stammered: "B-Because it's the first day of the semester and you're looking to make a new friend."

The next instant, I felt a jolt of misgiving. *Fuck. What if* he *isn't into dudes?* For some reason, I'd never considered that option. I just saw a hottie, wanted him, and went for it. "Look, if you don't swing my way, fine, sorry I barked up your tree. I just thought—"

"You can bark," he blurted.

I looked at him.

He pulled on the straps of his backpack, dropped his anxious gaze to my chest, swallowed hard, then repeated, "Y-You can bark up my tree." Then his eyes met mine.

My heart danced excitedly. "I'm Dane."

"Evan," he said back, soft and sweet.

I was smitten from that day forward.

Buzz! I nearly jump out of the memory at the sudden vibration in my crotch. I look down and fish my phone out from between my thighs where it fell, then bring it to my face.

I smirk.

I'll be damned.

I slide my finger along its face to answer, then slap it to my ear. "Sorry, buddy, but I'm super busy over here playing with my balls, and I'm afraid I can't—"

"I'm sorry I was a prick to you."

I bite my lip to keep from grinning like a dumbass. *Evan is so much fun to play with.* "Big prick," I correct him.

I hear his signature sigh of surrender. "I'm sorry for being a *big prick*. Whatever. Don't press your luck, Dane, this is hard enough for me as it is."

I snort and shake my head. "Oh, boy. Some things never change."

"Maybe no one's dead," Evan starts. "Maybe there's no reason at all to be worried. Maybe it's just some idiot having fun at our expense. Whatever the reason, all of my neighbors are freaking out, the head of the HOA is up my butt, and no one feels safe."

I lean back in my seat. I could easily be a jerk and tell my ex no. I could play with him for days, really draw all this out, and make him squirm with frustration.

But what's the fun in that when I already have the cute bastard in my palm? "You still single?" I ask.

"I—" He sputters, caught off-guard, then asks, "How is that relevant at all?"

"I take that as a yes. I'll see you tomorrow."

"W-Wait. Does that mean you're going to help us? Where are we meeting? What time?"

I grin. "Guess you'll know when I'm at your door."

"But—Wait a sec. How do you know where I live? I have a private address. It isn't listed anywhere."

"Have you already forgotten what I do for a living?"

I hang up before hearing his reply, toss the phone in my lap, chuckle, then crank the engine and burn rubber.

Chapter 4.
Evan's got the tea.

"Okay, okay, so give a bitch the tea on the new guy," demands Arry, curled up on my couch with a cup and saucer in his hands. "I'm *ever so thirsty.*"

"No!" protests Stevie in my rolled arm accent chair. "It isn't *becoming* to talk about people who aren't here!"

"Bullshit, *girl*, you're an expert breed of *gossip monster* and you know it," Arry fires back in his deadpan voice. "Now dish! What's the tea on this Xavier? Something's up with him and you know it. Is he a drug dealer?"

"Oh, I don't know. I couldn't possibly." Stevie sucks on the straw of his berry-mango tea in a red lidded cup because he's really a twenty-two-year-old two-year-old.

"You *can* possibly. You live by him. C'mon. Dish."

Stevie glances between Arry, Josiah, and myself— the only ones who came to our fancy little after-work Tuesday Tea thing this week—and says, "Okay ... maybe I heard about a ... *tiny* thing Xavier does on the side for money. Not drugs. Don't ask me how I know, I just do."

"A tiny thing ...?" Arry and Josiah share a look.

"Ugh, you guys and your *gossip*," I sigh as I reach for a fat-free strawberry tart off the platter I set out earlier.

I also sneak a peek at my phone. Still nothing. Typical Dane. The unreliable bastard probably had no intention of meeting me today at all.

Just another promise he couldn't keep.

Arry rolls his eyes at me. "Oh, come on. Don't you go acting like you aren't interested in what Xavier *does on the side for money.*"

"I'm interested in *actually* getting to know the guy," I say, "and not *gossiping* about him like a bunch of mean girls at a slumber party." I gesture with my tart as I talk. "He seems nice to me. Maybe a little standoffish, but—"

"You want to fuck him, huh?" asks Arry.

I roll my eyes. "Just because I said Xavier *'seems nice'* doesn't mean I'm attracted to him."

"You haven't been attracted to anyone on our street. I've noticed," says Arry. "I notice everything."

"*He notices everything*," agrees Josiah in an aside.

I shake my head at Arry. "You and Stevie are so in everyone's business, you two would play matchmaker with Vinnie and Marcellus's *poodle* if you could."

"I'm just saying, you're totally boyfriend material," Arry points out. "Stevie here's a bit young for you. I'm just, well ... not right for you at all by any stretch. Josiah is playing the long-distance thing with a Navy boy."

Josiah lets out a wistful sigh and a smile, clutching a necklace his boyfriend gave him that falls to his chest.

"So maybe this Xavier guy—?" Arry starts again.

I lean forward. I haven't even taken a bite of the tart I grabbed yet. "I'm not interested. Sorry, I know that it *bores* you that I don't—and haven't—had a love life for you to dissect and amuse yourself with during my time here on Figaro Lane, but I just prefer to keep to myself. Love only ... complicates things." My eyes drift away.

My words do nothing but spark further intrigue into my life—the opposite of my intention. "Is it your ex?"

For a split second, I want to indignantly, furiously, vehemently say no. I mean, how dare he ask something as ridiculous as that, right?

And then I see Dane Cooper's ass as he bends over to take another shot with his pool stick. I feel the same jolt of excitement inside me as if that sweet and delicious moment is happening all over again.

Except this time, in my mind, I don't just stand there like a paralyzed piece of meat.

I grab a handful of his firm, tight ass, and I squeeze it like a goddamned lemon.

He looks at me over his muscled, denim-jacketed shoulder, then grins that knowing, devilish grin of his. Even with that dark beard he's grown, I recognize it.

Then he ditches his stick, rises up from the table, and his lips descend towards mine.

"Well?" interrupts Arry, yanking me right out of my thoughts the moment *fantasy-Dane* was about to kiss me.

I cross my legs, suddenly aware of all the blood in my body rushing somewhere inconvenient. I glance at my phone sitting on the end table next to me. *Still nothing*, I note with frustration. "I ... well, I mean ..." I choke and set down the tart I never ate. "I don't know."

"You've checked your phone a lot," Arry notes.

"So?"

"Expecting someone to text you back?" he taunts.

I roll my eyes. "Arry, oh my God, you are *impossibly* nosy, and my singleness has *nothing* to do with my *stupid ex*, other than literally."

"Jeez. What'd he do to you? He break your heart?"

His words make my gaze drop to my finger foods platter. "I ... think I broke his."

With those few words, now I have the full attention of every guy in the room.

It only now occurs to me that no one really knows a thing about me and my ex. It has never been something I've felt very comfortable talking about.

A direct result of that secrecy, apparently, is earning everyone's undivided attention at the mere mention of some minor detail about him.

Not that breaking Dane's heart is a minor *anything*.

"Look, it's just easier to be by yourself," I tell their wide-eyed faces. "I mean, it's such a chore to ... to make sure you *look* good all the time for someone else. Or to *worry* about what another person thinks of you. Or to go to all these insane extents to be *sexy* and *hot* and ... *sexy*."

"Honey, you do all those things already," Arry says. "We all do. It's called being a single gay man."

"But what about the stress of worrying whether your boyfriend's being honest to you?" I go on. "Every time he goes out to do his own thing, you're left wondering if he'll meet someone hotter. You've seen enough romance movies where someone's boyfriend or husband turns out to be living a double life. You know how it works."

Arry scoffs. "Girl, you are *paranoid*."

But I barely hear his remark. "And when you go out together and some hot guy walks by, scoping your man without even a *glance* of acknowledgement your way ..." I shudder. "I'm tired of the constant doubts. Oh, and all the anniversaries ...? Ugh, love is just this big, *exhausting*, useless effort. It's so *draining* to have a boyfriend."

Arry and Josiah and Stevie all exchange looks.

Maybe I went a step too far.

I lift a hand to their silent faces. "You can save your judgment, kindly, for when you're *out* of my house and talking about me behind my back like normal neighbors. Just let me be miserably single awhile longer."

"That's what my uncle Carl said once," Stevie puts in, taking a break from sucking on his straw. "He lives with seven cats and a cockatoo now."

There's a knock at the door. All four of us turn to it, surprised. Only the soft beat of the music playing from my smart house system fills our ears.

I didn't invite anyone else. *It couldn't possibly be ...*

I peek at my phone once again. No messages. No missed calls.

"Well? Are you gonna answer the door, or should I?" Arry looks at the others, as if asking for some support in wondering what the hell has gotten into me.

I grab my phone off the table and hurriedly cross the living room to the foyer. I regret at this specific moment that my front door is perfectly visible to every single person I've invited over for my Tuesday Tea gathering. Every one of their eyes is on my back (and the door) as I stand here, dreading terribly the man on the other side.

My phone buzzes in my hand. I look down.

DANE

u gonna let me in, cupcake?

Oh, God.

The three sets of eyes on my back eagerly await my opening the door, not knowing what they're in for. And I'm standing here thinking that this is certainly *not* how I wanted to introduce my ex-boyfriend to the Three Queens of Figarian gossip.

Come to think of it, I'd rather not introduce them at all.

After much deliberation and an inward sigh, I decide to just crack open the front door a couple inches so only I can greet my visitor.

Dane Cooper stands there on my front doorstep, and boy is he one thick *mountain* of hotness. Distressed jeans. A plain black t-shirt that his sculpted body turns into artwork. Tats dripping down his muscled arms. Messy, dark, overgrown hair that casts a slight shadow over his penetrating kill-me eyes. Beard dressing his face and making his lips so crushingly kissable.

To all that mad sexiness, I just glare and hiss: "*What are you doing here??*"

He shrugs. "Said we'd meet today, didn't I?"

"*Yeah, well, perhaps a little* notice *would have helped, as I am currently entertaining a few* guests *and am* occupied," I sternly whisper back.

"Perfect. Then I can start my work now," says Dane, giving me a wink.

I don't follow. "Your work? What? How?"

"Mmm," comes Arry's dry voice over my shoulder.

I nearly jump out of my skin as I shriek and slam the front door shut on Dane's face.

Arry is flanked by both Stevie *and* Josiah, all three of whom brought their nosy selves out of my comfortable living room and right up to my back.

"And who was that hottie?" asks Arry suspiciously.

"Your secret squeeze?" suggests Josiah.

"Midnight booty call arrived early?" suggests Stevie before taking a (loud) suck from his straw.

"And why are you hiding him from us?" coos Arry.

I sputter and gape at each of them, unsure of whose question to be more annoyed with. "He ... It's ... He got the wrong ... He's just a—"

"I'm Dane," my ex helpfully calls through the door.

My eyes roll back and I shut them. *Motherfucker.*

Arry purses his lips. "Dane ...?"

Josiah cranes his neck, as if looking around me might get him some magical view through the front door itself. "Wait. Do you mean—?"

"Evan's ex-boyfriend!" Dane is then quick to answer.

My face is so fucking red right now, I could be a thermometer. "And ... he was just *leaving*," I call out over my shoulder with force, back still pressed to the door.

Arry, Josiah, and Stevie collectively gape at me.

I realize I'm on the losing side of the battle here.

"Not before I get some of that tasty tea," Dane calls out through the door at my back.

Arry inclines his head toward me. "*Honey, let the man in and give him some of your dang tea,*" he whispers.

Tonight may be the night I murder my ex-boyfriend. Mark my words.

I surrender my life to whatever might happen in the next five minutes—*fuck it, next five* seconds—and turn around to pull open the door.

Dane Cooper takes one step inside. His eyes are on me, and he looks positively proud of himself. "Well, that wasn't so hard, was it?" Then he turns to my neighbors and gives each of them a curt nod, but not quite a smile. "Afternoon, fellas."

So ... Arry looks like he can't breathe suddenly.

Josiah clutches his necklace and turns to stone.

Stevie, wide-eyed, is sucking on his straw with such intensity, his lips might collapse into a black hole.

Not a single one of them says a word.

"Didn't mean to interrupt your tea party," Dane says for an apology, his voice low and deep and dripping with something between sex and courtesy. "I just thought I'd drop in and say hi to Evan here."

"Oh ... oh ... it's nothing at all." Arry bites his lip and lets his eyes drag all the way down my ex's body. "We can always use ... an extra guest."

"The merry, the morer," agrees Josiah, frets, shakes his head and corrects himself: "The ... *more* the *merrier.*"

I bring myself right up to Dane's side and give him my hardest look. "Dane. A word."

I don't give him time to respond as I slap a hand to his back and guide him down the hall while throwing an apologetic look over a shoulder at my friends, who stare quizzically back. "Fancy pad ya got here," mutters Dane along the way, eyes flitting from my couch to my TV to a painting on the wall. "Is that a painting of a dick?"

I pull him into my room and shut the door. "I would have preferred we met in *private*, and *not* where I *live*."

"Seriously, I think that was a painting of a dick."

"Dane," I warn him.

He struts around my bedroom, drinking in the sight of each and every little thing: my desk in the corner that holds my tablet and laptop, my walk-in closet with its door slid wide open and showing off my gazillion shoes and designer clothing, my bay window with turquoise throw pillows, and my matching bedspread, at which he stops and presses a palm into. "Mmm, soft," he grunts.

Just those two words are so fucking sexual, I fight an inward squirm. Instantly, he has me hallucinating the sound of bedsprings, heavy breathing, and the rustling of clothes slipping off our bodies.

Why do I let Dane have so much power over me? "Dane," I try again more sternly.

He turns and eyes me innocently. "It's important I get to know the neighbors, isn't it? Especially if you're looking to have me help fix your little problem here."

"It isn't a *'little'* problem."

"Compared to what I've seen ...?" He offers me a superior smirk. "Besides, isn't it nice to work together on this? You and I ..." He bites his lip and glances down at my chest. "I like the sound of that ... *'You and I'* ..."

I bristle under his heated stare, then squint at him. "I think you just like all the attention."

He knows exactly what I'm talking about, yet lifts a blunt, dark eyebrow and goes, "Attention?"

"Just like when we were together and you'd—"

"Oh yeah?"

"—and you'd strut around every room, knowing full well that everyone was staring at you. You *loved* it. You *loved* being the hot one. You had no idea what it did to me, how it made me feel so ..." I can't find the word, so I just replace it with a scoff. "Well, congrats, Dane. All my neighbors want you now. Take your pick."

"Great. I pick you."

I roll my eyes and turn toward the desk. Sunlight from the bay window glares off the screen of my laptop. "Isn't part of your job to *not* be seen, anyway? I figured with investigative work, staying out of sight is sort of rule number one."

"It's rule number two, and besides, you know I've never been one for *rules*." He moves to the other side of the desk I stand at, then leans his ass against it and crosses his tatted, muscular arms. "I get the job *done*. It isn't in my nature to ... *not finish* something I've started."

I keep staring at my laptop screen, blinding myself, as I try desperately hard not to draw a double meaning from his words.

I draw it anyway. "Well, sometimes something isn't worth finishing." I lift my face to his. "Sometimes you need to know when to call it quits."

He eyes me so hard, I literally feel the heat coming off of him. "I'm not a quitter, Evan."

"Maybe, maybe not. But you're sure not a good boyfriend, either." I muster up a stroke of boldness. "I don't even have to hold some long, meaningful chat with you to tell—without a doubt—that you are still the same immature *boy* I knew back then."

He looks me over. "Yeah, well, you got a stick up your ass."

I scoff. "Excuse me?"

He loves working me up. It's his favorite thing in the world. "You were obsessed with rules back then, too. What we shouldn't do. What we should. And now look at you. The Evan Pryor I knew wouldn't be caught *dead* wearing ... *what is that, even? Cashmere?* ... and here you are, hosting a tea party." He lets out one jerk of laughter.

My face burns red. "I ... *love* ... tea. It's delicious, in fact. And it's *classy*. And it's *healthy*. And it's—"

"Boring," he finishes for me. "Evan *hates* tea."

I scoff, about to disagree, then edit my words. "He ... *used* to dislike it. He was also younger and less refined. You can say he's been *shown the way* ..."

"And now we're hiding in your bedroom. This Evan you've become, he's so afraid of how he looks like in front of his neighbors that he—"

"He values *image!*" I exclaim, then blink, annoyed. "Why are we talking about me in the third person?"

"Because that's what you are now, cupcake. A third person in this room. Give me back the old Evan, not this new one who's got a stick up his butt."

"I've got nothing up my butt!"

Dane slides across the desk, bringing himself right up to my side. "*Well maybe that's your problem, then.*"

I shut my eyes, my face going red again. I walked right into that one. "*All the ass jokes in the world and you go with the most obvious one?*" I groan under my breath.

"You've been working out."

That came out of nowhere. I open my eyes and face him. "W-What?"

"I can tell." He observes my whole body without reservation, like a judge at a dog show. "Your arms look bigger. Chest, too. Not to mention ..." He leans back to get a look, then meets my eyes with a smirk. "... *your ass really fills out those pants.*"

For a moment, my heart flutters excitedly.

The next moment, I frown at him. "It's not gonna happen, Dane."

He lifts his eyebrows innocently. "What?"

"We're not gonna ... do whatever it is that's on your dirty mind right now." I fold my arms tighter and shrug away from the desk, putting at least a few feet of distance between me and his scorching hot gaze and his thick, sinewy arms that simply *pour* out of the sleeves of that tight black t-shirt.

Oh my God, listen to me. Pathetic.

"You said you'd help us," I remind him. "And you're taking this as seriously as the police are: *not at all*."

I watch the way the features of his face tighten, just the way they used to when—finally—he stopped playing around and started to focus.

There are only three things Dane Cooper ever takes seriously: beer, sex, and police work.

Just then, I hear a shout outside in the street. Dane and I exchange a look before rushing up to my large bay window to investigate. At first, I see nothing, until a swat on my arm from Dane brings my attention to the garage door across the street and down a few houses. All three of my tea party guests are standing at the end of the driveway of that house, staring at a painting across the whole width of the garage door.

An obscene painting.

"Is that a—?" Dane starts.

"Yep," I answer, then glance his way with narrowed eyes. "Looks like you got the painting of a dick you were looking for."

Chapter 5.
Dane is a dick painting connoisseur.

"Oh my *God* that's a big dick," blurts the one named Stevie with a cup and a straw, his eyes wide and wet.

It's his garage door, according to Evan.

No one is standing too close to the giant dong that's staring all of us in the face like some horror porno flick. We're all at the end of the driveway under the faint cool-white light of a nearby streetlamp that just flickered on, as the sun is starting to set. Some others have come out of their houses and gathered to witness the spectacle, too.

Evan is right by my side, which is the first and last thing I notice.

It's also the first and last thing my dick notices.

He could've chosen to stand with his little tea party friends. Instead, he planted himself right next to me. His hand is dangling so close to mine, I might mistake it for an invitation to hold it.

I've nearly forgotten how soft and silky his skin is.

I'm kind of dying to be reminded.

Right in the middle of all of us staring intently at the garage door painting like it's a fucking Van Gogh, there is a chuckle from far off. Heads turn, and we all see the figure of a punk-ass-looking twenty-something with his arms folded, eyebrow quirked, and he's laughing.

"It isn't funny, Xavier!" shouts Stevie. "That's *my* garage door, not yours!"

Xavier stops laughing, looks from face to face, then gestures at the house. "C'mon. Not a single one of you thinks this is at least *a little* funny?" He glances between us all again. "It's a giant dick. It's a giant fucking dick the size of your neighbor's Lexus."

"I'm so glad you're amused," Stevie spits back. "And unless you're planning to pay to have my garage door repainted, then maybe you should keep all your laughs to yourself." With that, Stevie grabs the straw of his drink and furiously sucks away with more force than ever.

Xavier just snorts, shakes his head, and saunters back into his house, throwing Stevie—and perhaps all of us—the double-bird over his shoulders as he goes.

That dude's not winning any best neighbor awards.

Minutes later, we're back on Evan's doorstep. One of his friends—Arry—is lingering in the lawn. "Really," Evan tells him, "I think it's fair to declare this Tuesday Tea a bust. I think we ..." Evan sighs and puts a hand to his forehead. "I think we need to let all of this ... *activity* on our street settle down before we do tea again."

Arry, eyes half-lidded, smirks. "Fine, fine. If you say so." Then he brings his gaze to mine, winks, and in his deadpan monotone goes, "It was a pleasure to meet you, lover boy Dane," before spinning on his heel and trotting off to his house.

Evan shuts the door behind us, then says, "I have a feeling it was Old Man Hanson," before turning and heading to the kitchen.

I follow him. "Old Man Who?"

"Everyone already thinks it's him. He's a big homo-hater who lives down the street—*allegedly, allegedly a homo-hater.*" Evan pulls open a cupboard, then glances at me over a shoulder. "Want a shot of Jack?"

I lift an eyebrow. "Seriously?"

"I sure am tonight." Evan pulls out a bottle and two shot glasses, quickly fills them both, then slides one over the counter to me. Without even waiting for me, he kicks his back and slams the glass onto the counter.

"Uh, cheers," I grunt, watching him warily before finally kicking back my own.

He pours another for us both. "This was a bad idea."

"What was?"

"Going to you for help. What was I thinking?" Evan shakes his head, downs another shot, then slams it down on the counter again. His eyes are watery as he blinks. "Ugh, I haven't had Jack in years."

"My name's Dane, not Jack."

He glares at me, not appreciating the joke.

I smirk, come around the counter, and lean against the island next to him. "Well I'm glad you came to me, Evan. It's a good thing, in my opinion."

"Is it? How?"

"I miss spending time with you."

For a moment, my words stir up something in his eyes. Even through the little haze of alcohol, I can see it.

Then, as quickly, Evan brushes it off like a fly. "You are only here to entertain yourself."

"Remember the summer between our freshman and sophomore years? When we went out to your parents' lake house and were just two lazy motherfuckers for weeks and weeks and weeks?"

Evan's face tightens up, fighting the memory. I'm not sure if it's the whiskey, but something lets go in his eyes, and I watch a faint smile appear on his lips. "My mom was *not* your greatest fan."

"Neither was your dad. They hated me."

"Hate is a strong word." He eyes me. "And it still isn't strong enough to describe what they felt for you."

I laugh at that.

Evan does, too. He's about to go for another shot, then rethinks it and looks my way. "Why'd you bring all that up?"

"It was the most fun I think I had during my college years. Hell, and we weren't even at college."

"The summers were longer back then," Evan notes with a slow, subtle nod. "But ... what's your point?"

It's too early to dive all in. I can't just throw myself at the guy, no matter how badly his ass is screaming for my hand to reach out and grab it, no matter how badly I want to tear off his pants and suck him off, no matter how hard just the thought of touching my lips to his makes me.

Evan's got this whole new life now, but underneath those designer clothes of his, the old Evan is crying out for me to save him.

That's the real reason he called me up when things got tough for him out here in snobsville.

He needs me.

"My point ..." I lick my lips, then shrug. "... is that sometimes we just need to ... kick back. Just like the good ol' days. We have to let our brains go blank, worry about nothing, and just remember what it means to be alive and *fuckin' free.*"

I have Evan caught under my spell for exactly four and a half seconds.

Then he snorts and shakes his head. "Well, must be nice to live a life with no responsibilities. The rest of us actually have to worry about things."

"Worry is a choice."

"Tell that to me when *you* have a hot pink mailbox and a giant penis painted on the garage door across the street from you."

"It's only a matter of time before we solve this thing. The vandalisms are just a temporary distraction that will end when someone gets bored or outed. But you and I?" I wag a finger between us, then tsk-tsk at him. "We aren't solved, cupcake."

"Call me that one more time and I'll shove a cupcake into your face," he promises, lifting a warning eyebrow.

I catch myself smirking. "I'd be lying if I said that very image doesn't turn me the fuck on." I edge a bit closer to him. "What else do you wanna shove in my face, Evan?"

He looks at me, and his eyes are hard as crystal. His jaw is tightened up, too. I love the way that makes these dimples pop out in his cheeks, and I especially love how they flush when he's angry.

And turned on.

While maintaining our intense stare-off, I reach and grab hold of the bottle of Jack he ditched on the counter. Then, our eyes still locked, I pour another shot.

My eyes are on him tauntingly as I grab that shot and down it in one strong, audible gulp.

He watches.

He doesn't move a muscle, seemingly not even to breathe.

Then his lips part.

Thirsty?

I lick the rim of the shot glass when I'm done, then set it down on the counter with comical daintiness. With that, I flash him a cocky, lopsided smirk.

His hard, watery eyes fall onto my lips now—right where I want them.

My heart jumps unexpectedly, just from that subtle flick of his eyes to my lips. I feel so connected to him, like I know exactly what he's feeling.

Like I know exactly what he wants.

And I want the same fucking thing.

Just kiss me, Evan James Pryor. Snap out of that daze of yours, stop second-guessing, stop weighing all those pros and cons in your head and kiss me.

His head, ever so slowly, starts to move.

He inclines his body my way.

Holy shit. He's about to do it.

He's really about to do it.

He closes his eyes.

I part my lips for his.

DING-FUCKIN'-DONG.

His eyes flap open at the sound of the doorbell.

We're between an inch and nothing-at-all from each other's faces. Neither of us move. Neither of us breathe.

"You're *not* letting a *doorbell* cock-block us," I state.

Evan pulls away, stares at the counter for half a sec in horror, takes a breath, then forces his way out of the kitchen and into the foyer.

I sigh and throw my hands onto the counter to brace myself. I could break this pretty marble edge right off if I wanted.

Motherfucker.

"Why, hello," comes an airy voice.

"Raymond, hi, I'm sorry, I just had to cut Tuesday Tea short on account of the—uh, the garage door thing—and I just—"

"I heard your ex is here. The one investigating all of our recent vandalisms. Is that true?"

A steel-cold button of silence fills the foyer. "Y-Yes. He's ... just leaving, sadly. We were discussing—"

"Have you been drinking? Never mind. I would like to meet him."

A set of footsteps tells me this Raymond character invited himself in. When he appears at the entryway to the kitchen, I'm met by the sight of the biggest, gayest douchebag I have ever seen. And I've investigated an Ivy League fraternity for fuck's sake.

He flinches when he sees me, as if my appearance somehow electrocuted him for half a second.

Evan rushes in behind him, then stops, his eyes on me. "This ..." He clears his throat and tries again. "This is Dane Cooper, a ... private investigator."

"It's good you're here," Raymond seems to decide. His posture is so stiff, it's like he's got a bustier on under that popped-collar green polo of his. "We can't have any more of these *occurrences* on our street. I am Raymond Havemeyer-Windsor III, head of the HOA here. Have you made any discoveries yet? Anything to report?"

I glance at Evan a moment, if anything but to assess his state of mind, then decide to address this Raymond character directly. "I've—"

"It's much too soon," Evan suddenly answers for me. "He only just got here today. He hasn't really begun his work in finding the vandal, per se. He—"

"Yes, I have," I cut him off.

Evan shuts up, and then the two of them cock their heads in unison, surprised.

I shrug at them. "Isn't it obvious? We already know five people it isn't." I lift a hand and tick off a finger for each name: "Your three friends who were here tonight— Stevie, Arry, and Josiah. And Evan. And myself."

Raymond lifts an eyebrow. "Oh? You mean to say you believe it's someone on our street who's the vandal? It's one of our own?"

Evan's face flushes at once. "H-He isn't saying that. Why would he say that?" he asks rhetorically, throwing a look of contempt my way.

I shrug. "I have a sense about these things. And the sorts of things that have happened thus far seem a bit ... *directed*. They're too intentional. They aren't the random acts of some bored street punk, and I used to see shit like that in my old line of work. Saw it all the time."

To Evan's apparent surprise, Raymond gives me one tight nod. "I think you're absolutely right." He shoots Evan a smirking look. "He's a smart one."

Evan only stares at me, eyes half-lidded, and silent.

Raymond lifts his face to me. "So it's someone on our own street. Very well. You can tick me off your list too, for obvious reasons, as *I'm* the very one who had to push your stubborn little boyfriend *Evan* to get you out here and solve this thing in the first place ..."

"*Ex*-boyfriend," mumbles Evan miserably.

"... and why would I vandalize my own cul-de-sac? You can also eliminate Preston, Leland, and Thomas off your list, because they were with me at my house tonight working on plans for my Valentine's Gala. Oh!" He lifts a hand and gestures at me. "You should come to my gala. It is my most favorite party that I throw all year long, even better than New Year's and Christmas."

"That's kind of you to invite him," Evan cuts right in, "but I'm sure he's busy with his other obligations—*he has so many clients, he was just telling me*—and can't really neglect them in order to—"

"I'll be there," I interrupt him, giving this Raymond a firm nod.

Raymond returns my nod with a rigid one of his own. "It is a formal event, by the way. I recommend a tuxedo, black, perhaps with pink accents. Hmm ... Don't you think that'll make him look lovely, Evan?"

He then turns to Evan, whose face has flushed like a cherry. Evan's eyes work me over like some confusing math problem. Then I see a flicker of anxiety play across his face as his lips part.

I wonder if he's picturing me in that black tuxedo with a cute pink bowtie and cummerbund right now. I wonder how soon that tuxedo will drop off my body in his mind and he starts picturing ... other things.

"Yeah," Evan finally agrees, though his voice is far away and dreamy. "He'd look ..."

Then his gaze flicks up to meet mine.

I give him a pompous smirk.

Evan's eyes narrow. "... *dashing*," he finishes with far less grace.

Raymond doesn't seem to notice. He merely smiles stiffly at me, then turns away. "Well, I must return to my guests. Thank you for your hospitality, Evan, though I must say *alcohol* is not very becoming on you. I trust you're in good hands here with Mr. Cooper. Do mention my suspicion with certain faces on our street and ..." He shoots a look my way. "... their inability to *cooperate* with the HOA's strict standards of living. I think they have *prime* motive for doing what they're doing. Goodnight."

The Douche Queen sees himself out. Evan, looking less than thrilled, follows to close the door behind him. Then he stays right there, as if lost in a thought, hand on the door handle and head bowed.

I've come up behind him. "I ... *do* believe we were interrupted."

Evan pulls the door right back open. "I ... *do* believe you were leaving."

I frown playfully at him. "Really, cupcake? Not even a blowie before I go?"

"I can't believe you invited yourself to the gala."

"If memory serves, it was Ray-Ray who invited me."

Evan rolls his eyes. "Well, *Ray-Ray* is going to be *pissed-pissed* if you don't find out who's drawing dicks all over our cul-de-sac."

"I like the way you say that word," I say as I come up close to him, making the space in this doorframe feel even smaller. "*Cul ... de ... sac.*"

"I figured you were referencing my saying the word 'dicks' instead."

"I like how you say every word."

"Well, then I have a few more for you: *Leave. Go home. Stop trying to seduce me. It isn't working.*"

I bring my face right up to his. Desire is rippling through my body and it's getting harder and harder to deny it. "But it *is* working, isn't it?" I lick my lips with one drag of my tongue, bearing down on him. "I can still tell when you're hot for me. I can see it in your eyes as easily as I see your cheeks flushing, or thighs clenching together, or hands fretting anxiously. Your heart's racing right now, isn't it? You're breathing quicker, too."

He slaps a hand to my chest and pushes me away. "Of *course* I'm turned on," he exclaims suddenly, "but I have different needs now, Dane. Life isn't all about who we fuck and how hard we make each other. Sex is just *sex*." He folds his arms, furious, then unfolds them right away. "And even *if* I let you have your way with me, what then? What comes after? You'd finally be satisfied, got what you came here for, and you'd strut off to your next conquest."

"No, I wouldn't," I fire back. "I'd never be able to get enough of you, Evan."

He gives me a stern look. "Dane, if you're looking to win me over, you've got to rely on more than just those looks of yours. They'll get you far in this world, sure, but only so far, and if you don't have that *something-else*, then you're nothing but a big, sexy waste of my time."

With that, the door closes on my face.

Chapter 6.
Dane's something else.

I park my truck, step out onto the smoothest paved parking lot the soles of my boots have ever kissed, then walk toward the front glass doors of the fancy building.

When I push it open, a clean digital chime rings over my head like a fairy fart. I look up for a second, confused by the clatter.

"Hi and welcome to *Blown Away Salon*, where you'll be blown away by a cut, color, or styling today," recites the pencil-thin snooty forty-something receptionist with a clean, tight parted look and glasses. "Appointment?"

He hasn't even looked up from the computer in front of him, clicking his mouse five times a second. "Nah," I answer. "Thinking you might be able to just fit me in."

"We're way super booked today," he drones on while he types something, then clicks some more—and still not looking up. "Is there a stylist you're hoping to schedule?"

"Yeah. Evan Pryor."

"Mmm, he's booked until next Tuesday. Sorry."

I smirk. "I'm fairly certain he's got an opening. Tell him Dane Cooper's here."

The man snorts. "Honey, I don't care if your name's *Bradley* Cooper. We don't have any—" He looks up.

Insert: longest gay gasp in history.

I flash a cockeyed smile. "I'm just here for a quick cut, anyway. Surely you got a five-minute spot to just ... fit me right in?"

The man collects himself in the space of two seconds by quickly adjusting his little nametag, straightening his posture, then tapping a shit ton of keys on his computer. "I'll check the system. Maybe I'm mistaken. Oh, look, I'm mistaken. He has an opening right now."

"Dane?"

I turn at the sound of Evan's voice. Goddamn, he is a piece of work in a pair of black dress pants and a cute, form-fitting white dress shirt, just the top button popped open. His sweep of russet hair is pristinely parted today, a bit more styled and managed than usual.

I give him a smile. "I hear you have an opening."

He frowns, not following. "You're here for ...?"

"A cut. I'm a bit overdue, and with that Valentine's Gala coming up in a couple weeks, I thought I'd—"

"I'm fully booked," he cuts me off.

Helpfully calling out from behind me, the front desk man cries, "Your next appointment isn't until two!"

Evan closes his eyes, grimacing.

I lean in. "Looks like you're ... *fully available.*"

After a microscopic scowl at me, Evan walks away. I grin, satisfied, and follow him to his station, which is in the prime location in the center of his salon.

We need to take a moment here to acknowledge how fucking incredible this place looks. I'm not really all that into color complements and shit, but even I can tell when every chair, countertop, and wall seems to coordinate in some kind of eye-pleasing symphony.

Do you hear that shit? I don't talk like that.

And yet here I am, drawing circles with my eyes around this place, floored by how pristine, royal, and yet welcoming the atmosphere is. Sure, I also feel a bit like I want to punch a trust fund baby's face from here to the kingdom next-door with all the pretension that floods this neighborhood, but coming from Evan's clear vision and obvious *love* that went into this place, I'm impressed.

Evan slaps at his chair. "Giddy-up," he says dryly.

The second I take a seat, he fixes a soft sheet of paper around my neck before flinging a giant pink-and-black zebra-print cape over my front, then snapping it in place on top of the paper. Normally these things strangle me, but with Evan, it feels strangely comfortable.

Except for the color. "Pink?" I grunt.

"It's what I give my younger, fussier clients. You know ... the ones who are *difficult.*"

I shoot him a look in the big mirror before me.

He shoots back the fakest smile. "And isn't that your best accent color for the gala, didn't your buddy Ray-Ray tell you? Pink?" He comes around to the front and leans against his workstation, facing me. "Now what kind of look are we going for? Inverted Mohawk? Mullet? Shave every bit of it off? Dye it lilac?"

I give him a smart, quirky look of my own. "Y'know if I don't like my cut, I *will* complain to the manager."

"I'm counting on it."

I can't help but smile when Evan tries to antagonize me. It's so fucking cute, really, when he thinks he has the upper-hand and toys with me like this.

"How about," I start, lifting my chin, "I just trust you to give me whatever you think fits my head shape?"

"Nothing fits the shape of an *egg*," Evan sasses.

I frown. "I don't have an *egg-shaped* head."

He shrugs, then waves his hand at me. "So you want me to do ... *whatever* ... to your hair?"

"You're the expert."

With that, Evan goes for the clippers. He comes up to my side, murmurs, "Hold still," and then flicks it on, filling my ear with soft-yet-certain buzzing.

When he touches me, however, I instinctively close my eyes, and I'm in heaven.

Despite all the provoking and attitude, Evan handles me with the utmost care. I feel the sensitive way his fingers caress the side of my head, bracing as he gently yet firmly runs the clippers across my scalp. There is confidence in his every stroke, but also sensitivity. I know without a doubt that in his hands, I won't suffer as much as an ill-timed cut or abrasion of the razor.

Then he gets closer, repositioning himself, and I feel the front of his thighs gently touch the side of my arm. As he slowly works his way around my head, his thighs press more firmly against me.

I feel his crotch right there against my arm, too.

Fuck. Is this deliberate?

I don't know what Evan is feeling right now, but this experience for me is becoming downright erotic—*and fast.* I'm fighting some serious *wood* right now, and even with my pants and this flowy pink zebra smock-thing, I'm fairly certain it won't stay hidden for long.

"So ..." I make myself talk because if I don't, I'll lose my mind in this fucking chair. "Nice place you got here. I love the layout especially. How long have you—?"

"We're fast approaching our two-year anniversary of our grand opening, actually."

"Two years already? Wow." I'm trying not to notice how deeply his crotch is grinding into my arm. It's not every day you get your side dry-humped by your hot ex-boyfriend and hairstylist. "You opened your salon about the same time I left the force."

"Stop moving."

"I'm not."

"Unless you want me buzzing a *landing strip* up the back of your head—"

I lift my hands in surrender, then place them firmly on my armrests and keep perfectly still.

Evan smirks, satisfied, as he continues buzzing and gently dragging that electric monster up and down my head like a scalp massage.

And his crotch keeps grinding against my arm.

It's like he's jacking himself off with my biceps.

That is so fucking hot.

After some time, he repositions himself on my other side, and then my other arm gets some loving from his subtle dick-bumping as he works.

"How's Anne Boleyn?" I ask.

"She still has her head," answers Evan, "as well as all her whiskers."

"I still think you need to get a dog called Henry."

"That's an ill-fated relationship right there."

"But it's also entertaining and a sure conversation starter," I am quick to point out. "Besides, maybe they'll rewrite history. Your Puppy King Henry doesn't have to take Kitty Queen Anne's head."

"Is that what you're trying to do here with me?" asks Evan lightly. "Rewrite history?"

He grinds against my arm, finishing up a last little bit near my ear before the buzzer flicks off and my ears are granted their first mercy.

I turn to him. "I didn't say—"

"Face forward," he tells me as he goes to his station to trade his clippers for shears.

I face forward, and my eyes are on his cute butt in those dress pants while he stands at that station awhile, preparing whatever he needs to. It isn't long before he turns back around and I have to feign like I was looking at myself in the mirror.

And then I'm *looking* at myself in the mirror. "Holy shit that's short."

"Keep still," he tells me, then starts to squirt my hair with a water bottle.

I oblige.

Then I can't help it: "I ... *did* say I'd trust you ..."

"Yes, you did." Evan squirts, squirts, squirts that cold water at my head. "And you're also quite terrible at keeping your promises."

"Am not!"

"Hold still."

He brings a comb to my head—which he must have pulled out of thin air, because I didn't notice it before—and starts gently cutting the top of my hair with skillful, pinpoint precision. I observe him working in the mirror, admiring his artistry.

"Tell me one—"

"Hold still," he repeats.

"I *am* holding still. Tell me one promise I broke."

Evan smirks, then flicks his eyes at me through the mirror. "You said you'd never call me 'cupcake' again."

"That's nothing. I'm talking a *real* promise. One that counts."

He snip-snip-snips a bit off the top, flicks it away, then continues to work without a response.

"Exactly," I mutter.

Evan takes a breath, snip-snip-snip, and then lets it out with, "Don't mistake my silence, Dane. I just don't feel like having this *particular* conversation in my salon."

I watch him awhile in the mirror, nearly forgetting that I'm getting a haircut at all. '*If you're looking to win me over,*' he'd said, '*you've got to rely on more than just those looks of yours.*' The more I hear his words replay in my head, the more determined I am to prove him wrong.

Meanwhile, two female hairstylists are not lost to me in my peripheral view, sitting at their stations and staring at us with wide-eyed interest, now and then leaning toward one another to whisper something, which almost always inspires a gasp or a titter before they return to watching us.

Either they—like the front desk man—have figured out who I am and are making their judgments, or Evan shaved the word "PRICK" into the back of my head.

That's probably exactly what he did.

"Y'know," I start as I watch him in the mirror, "it's been a long time since you cut my hair."

"It's been a long time since you let me. Of course ..." For a second, it looks like Evan's about to sass me with some snide remark. Instead, his voice turns soft. "... I *did* appreciate you volunteering to be my 'haircut guinea pig' when I first started out." He teeters his head side to side, weighing it over. "Though you were also at other times stubborn and did *not* want your precious hair touched."

I shrug. "I liked my hair long and unruly back then."

"It wasn't *too* long. Kinda ... surfer-boy long. It got in your face a lot, but ... well, I guess it wasn't bad."

"You've always had perfect, cute hair." I sigh as I look him over in the mirror. "You'd roll outta bed first thing in the morning, it's all cute and swept with those one or two cowlicks in the back, and it looks like you meant it to be exactly that way. Styled. Messy where it needs to be, and perfectly-in-place everywhere else."

Evan doesn't respond, carefully cutting away. I keep watching my hair drift past my face like long wispy strands of black snow falling.

"What your salon needs is better music."

He shoots out a breath of a chuckle. "No one ever agrees on what music to play. It used to be Adele in here on loop until *Hello* became the new *Let It Go*."

I furrow my brow at that. "You're the owner, aren't you? You say what plays. You pick the music. You're the big boss."

He shakes his head. "I'm not that kind of boss."

"Maybe that's the problem. You don't assert yourself enough."

His lips purse in annoyance. "Nice. Criticizing me in my own salon while I'm cutting your hair."

"Hey, it isn't criticizing. It's ..." I gesture toward his reflection in the mirror. "... giving you an unasked-for piece of wisdom. Hell, if I hadn't asserted myself at the station, I'd have been walked over every day. There were some really great men in that department, but fuck, there were a bunch of assholes, too."

Evan cuts awhile longer in silence, then something seems to make his face tighten. "I can ..." He picks and chooses his words. "I can tell you've ..."

"I've what?"

He stops and looks at me in the mirror. "You aren't so much of a pushover anymore."

I lift an eyebrow. "Is that how you saw me? You saw me as a pushover?"

"You lacked ambition, Dane. You ..." He bites his lip as he runs his comb through my hair, searching for a spot. Then he starts clipping. "I mean, you wanted to be a law enforcement officer. I knew you did. You were committed to the training. You worked out, like, a ton."

"But?"

"But you wanted it *easy*. You expected everything to just ... happen. I kept trying to impress on you the value of hard work and commitment, but—"

"Hey, I worked damn hard," I blurt out.

"—but it always led to a fight. It just seemed like whenever life got hard—and it always did—you gave up or ran away or ... or *sulked*."

"Sulked? I never sulked."

"I can't tell you how many times I came back to our dorm room and found you gnashing thumbs into your Xbox controller, scowling with your big headphones on, blocking out the world, spending *hours* shooting random strangers in that loud, gory game you always played ..."

I watch Evan in the mirror. Even while he talks, he is focused hardcore on his work—combing and clipping, combing and clipping, over and over, always with expert precision and care, perfectly confident. He could do this work in his sleep.

"And I could never get through to you," he goes on. "I'd have to wait until your mood passed—hours later— to get the story. And no matter what happened, I always found myself thinking, '*Why doesn't he just try a little harder? Why doesn't he exercise patience?*' Over and over."

I remind myself that this whole spiel of his started as a compliment. "So ... you think I commit now?"

He shrugs. "Haven't quite decided. I mean, you quit the force, but I don't know why. Maybe you needed to. Or ... maybe you're still the old you, running off when things get hard."

"I guess that depends on *what's* getting hard."

Evan's comb and shears freeze as he eyes me. "Was that a dirty joke?" He tsk-tsks me. "And you were doing so well."

I chuckle dryly, then eye him. "Do you really think that about me? ... That I run away when life's tough?"

He doesn't respond, but he doesn't look away, still watching me through the mirror, his hands frozen.

"Or," I go on, "maybe it's easier to think that about me, because it makes the blow of our last argument five years ago that much softer for you. To have someone to blame for our breakup."

Evan's eyes falter.

"I forgive you, by the way," I add.

His eyes meet mine again and turn indignant right away. "For what?"

"What you said that fateful night so many years ago. Before you kicked me out of our apartment at two in the morning and tore my favorite shirt in half. I remember. And I forgive you."

Evan bristles, looking positively vexed, yet he says nothing. After a moment of mental jujitsu, he decides to resume his work on my hair.

He doesn't work much longer before he removes the giant pink-zebra cape off me. "Hair-washing station," he states, gesturing for me to get up. "Come on."

I climb out of my chair, giving myself a quick glance in the mirror before I go. "Wow, you did a number."

"Shorter than you expected?" We cross the salon—amidst three other customers and those pair of stylists who watch our every move—and arrive at the hair-washing station where a chair and a little bowl-thing await me. "Sit down."

I sit. Evan starts to wrap a towel around the back of my neck as I quietly mutter, "A *lot* shorter."

"Lie back."

His fingers, soft and gentle, cradle my head as he guides the back of my neck to the bowl where I settle into position. Soon, a spray of warm water slowly works across my head and hair.

Evan's fingers work through my hair, massaging into my scalp and neck. I try to look at him, but he's too far behind me, and every now and then a rogue droplet of water splashes at my face. So I keep my eyes closed and succumb to the hypnotic white noise of water.

"*You* certainly committed," I tell him. "Hell, owning your own salon? In this part of town? At your age? Shit, that's fucking impressive, Evan."

"Well, without all of my dad's investments in the business, it wouldn't have happened so quickly."

"Of course ..." I shrug. "I was expecting you to have your own design firm by now. Not a salon."

"Really? We're going there again?"

"Hairstyling, it was always your backup plan, not your *main* plan. I mean, nothing against what you do, or the art of ... hairstyling and cosmetics in general. But it just isn't you."

"And how would you know what's me?"

"Because something tells me that the *real* passion in opening this place came to you when you got to design its interior." I open my eyes despite the splashing water and glance up at him as best as I can. "Do you still have the same love in your heart now? Or do you find ..." I lift an eyebrow. "... something lacking?"

Yes, the question is loaded.

No, I don't care.

The water shuts off abruptly. For a second, I think I've stepped over the line and pissed him off, but then Evan brings his fingers back to my hair, this time working in the shampoo. I feel it tingle and hear it froth as he works it deep into my scalp.

He still hasn't replied. This is the part where I break the tension by making a joke about Evan fondling my head. It's also when I spring a big boner and somehow direct Evan's attention to it in a less than subtle way.

But I fight those instincts.

See? I can be mature around him. I'm not always so sexually-oriented. Sometimes, I can go to the salon and just get a haircut.

Though, honestly, I was hoping with a name like *Blown Away Salon* that he'd give me another reason to feel *blown* by the time I leave.

Wishful thinking or some shit.

The water squirts on again, and slowly the shampoo is washed out of my hair—or whatever's left of it. Then he applies some fruity-smelling conditioner shit on my head—again working it in—before rinsing it out as well in a gentle spray of warm, tingly water.

Nothing else is said as he brings another towel to cover my hair, dries it, then guides me back to his station where a few fingers of "hair styling paste" is applied.

"Holy shit-fuck," I blurt. "Is that me?"

Evan's arms are folded as he stands back, observing his work. "You like it?"

He gave me something of a low-fade cut with the top just long enough to be a mad combination of messy and neat. I didn't even know my hair was capable of that.

"I can guarantee you I'm not washing or *touching* my hair for a month," I tell him.

One breathy chuckle shoots out of him.

I look up at Evan. "I didn't mean to piss you off with all of that crap I said. But ... I'd be doing you a disservice not to say how I feel."

Evan gives me a slow nod, then quirks his head. "Well, you went and said how you feel."

"Yeah?" I gesture at him. "And ... any response?"

He purses his lips, then shakes his head no.

I guess I won't press it. "You realize there's no way I'll be able to make my hair do what you just made it do."

He studies me awhile. Then, in a voice too soft for anyone else to hear, he says, "Well, I guess you'll have to come to me ... whenever you want it styled this way."

My gaze lingers on his. My heart picks up pace.

Evan swallows, then lets his eyes drift down to my lips, which I just involuntarily licked, as if preparing.

Something's happening between us right now.

He knows it.

I know it.

Do something!

"Evan ..." I start to say, lifting a hand toward his.

He takes a step back and, quicker than a sneeze, says, "The cut's on me. You don't owe me anything."

"Evan," I try again.

"Might want to drop by my neighborhood sometime in the morning," he goes on, oblivious, "if you're hoping to catch the next act. We don't know when the next thing will happen."

"Right."

Evan meets my eyes briefly, then looks away with a tightened smile. "Thanks for stopping in, Dane," he says too quickly.

I've risen from the chair. "Evan ..."

He disappears into his back office, the door shutting softly behind that cute, tight tushie of his.

Chapter 7.
Evan is full of fucking questions.

I don't want to jump to any conclusions, but I'm lying here in the dead of night, can't sleep, with a giant erection under my bed sheets.

And every one of my thoughts is Dane Cooper.

Is it possible that I'm still in love with him?

Yes, it's very possible. I have to face that fact like a grown-ass adult. It's possible that I'm discovering, in my little spurts of time spent with him, that the feelings are still there, and maybe I wouldn't be terribly opposed to rekindling that wicked, wicked flame.

Also, it's possible I'm *not* still in love. It could be a passing wave of loneliness. After all, I haven't been in a serious relationship with anyone since him. I've been pouring every bit of my soul into making something of myself in this town that I haven't had time (or patience) to let anything meaningful with anyone else develop.

Apparently, neither has he.

I wonder if that's total bullshit.

Well, if there's anything you remember about Dane, it's that he isn't a liar. In fact, he's honest to a fault. Half your arguments came from him being a touch too honest about what he thought of your clothes, or your friends, or your parents.

Something about his honesty is infuriating.

And something about his honesty is infuriatingly sexy.

The thing about Dane Cooper is, I always feel safe when I'm in his presence. It's totally natural—downright *fateful* if you ask me—that he became a police officer, sworn to protect the lives of his fellow man and woman. He was always a protector, even during our college days. Every time I was upset about something, his first response was, *"Is there someone whose ass I gotta kick?"*

His strength has manifested into a rippled, muscled body he's built over the years. I mean, he was pretty hot back then, too. But now he's just ridiculous.

I close my eyes and bite my lip.

I still haven't seen him with his shirt off.

But behind my dreamy, restless eyelids, I can.

My right hand slips under the sheets like a bad, bad boy. I take my time and make the journey really, really leisurely. My left pec is teased and cupped. I fondle my nipple, giving it a coaxing pinch until it hardens between my fingertips. *Good boy.* I let my hand travel farther, its fingers sliding down my smooth abdomen until they are caught in the tiny hairs of my happy trail.

Did I mention I sleep naked?

When my fingers reach my swollen, throbbing cock, I let out a sigh of delight.

And interrupting my sigh, a chorus of digital tones fills the room. It's like I just won an arcade game by at last reaching my cock.

Ding, ding, ding! Dick achievement: unlocked!

Then I turn my head, confused, and realize it's my phone going off on my nightstand. *Ugh, at this hour?* I frown and prop myself up on an elbow to get a look.

My eyes flash.

Dane Cooper, calling me at fifteen past midnight.

I grab the phone off the nightstand with my free hand, awkwardly swipe my thumb across its face, then lift the thing to my ear. "Dane?"

"Hope it isn't too late," he replies.

"Is everything alright?" I ask quickly.

I'm still very, very hard, by the way, throbbing and flexing in the curled fingers of my other hand, which still dwells down there.

"Yeah, everything looks alright so far. I just—"

"Looks alright? What do you mean everything ...?" It clicks. I glance over at my window, eyes wide. "You're in your car right now watching my street?"

"It's a truck, and yes. I thought I'd keep an eye out tonight. The vandal can't be too smart. I'm bound to catch the dumbass in the act."

"How long are you ... keeping an eye out?"

"Until it feels right. I have a pretty good sense about these things."

Absently, my fingers that are wrapped around my swollen cock twitch, and I'm reminded what I'm still holding.

I let out a tiny gasp, then give myself one miniscule, experimental stroke.

My gasp becomes audible as I add a brief moan into it, then bite my lip to shut myself up.

"You alright over there?"

I nod, then realize my nod can't be heard. "Yep," I squeak. *His deep, brawny voice is not helping ease my boner, for the record.* "I'm ... just ... surprised you're gonna be out there all night."

"It's the least I can do to try and find out who this creep is. Y'know ... by turning into a creep myself and staring at everyone's front doors." He chuckles deeply.

I close my eyes, really *hearing* the depth in his rich, manly chuckles. *Ugh, listen to me, I'm so pathetic.* But it isn't long before my own judgments of myself fade away and all that's left is my hand, my naked body, my giant throbbing dick, and my sexy ex-boyfriend's voice against my sensitive ear.

I give myself another stroke. *It feels so fucking good.*

"So," I make myself say in the silence, "are you ..." I give myself another stroke. *Oh, God.* "... are you looking at Hanson's house especially ...?"

"Sure, yeah, I'm seeing it." *Fuck, his voice is so hot and dripping with masculinity.* I start jerking smoothly, slowly. "But I'm still keeping my eyes open. Never know."

"Who else do you ..." I suppress a grunt and try not to breathe too erotically, despite how desperately horny I've become since I picked up the phone. "... think might be our devious culprit?"

"I dunno. What if it's Raymond himself?"

I cradle the phone against my shoulder and ear, freeing my other hand, which I let slide down my body. "Really?" I breathe. "You think it's the head of the HOA himself? That's ..." My other hand reaches my balls. I cup them and swallow another moan. "... ridiculous."

"Nah. It's just a motive away from making perfect sense. Though, he *was* with friends who might be able to vouch for his whereabouts the night of your tea party. The *dick* wasn't painted when I arrived at your house ..."

Just the way he says the word "dick" makes my own jump with excitement. I could come right now all over the inside of my sheets.

"... so it had to have happened sometime between the time I came ..." he points out.

Came. Oh, God, his use of that word ...

"... and the time you and I were in your bedroom and heard the shout in the street," he finishes.

Bedroom. You and I. I'm jerking with more speed now while fondling my tightened-up, sensitive balls with my other hand. I haven't closed my mouth since answering the phone. I feel like I need to bite down on something.

"You alright, Evan?"

"Just keep talking," I blurt out, jerking faster.

"About what?"

"Your thoughts." My words are out of breath as I jerk harder listening to his voice. I picture his handsome bearded face, yearning eyes, and full, heart-shaped lips.

"Alright. Well, I've been taking notes all day, kinda figuring out the daily routines of all your neighbors ..."

It's such sweet torture, to know he's in a vehicle just outside my house somewhere down the street.

"... funny habits, that Stevie guy, who always ..."

And I'm jerking off like a madman in this stifling bedroom, too proud and shameful to invite him in.

I could do it. I could invite him inside.

"... Vinnie watering his garden when the husband ..."

I could tell him I'm desperate for him, that I don't want to play it safe anymore, that I need him to come over right now, bust through my door, and have his way with my body. He can do whatever he wants to me.

"... ran up a tree, that tiny furry thing, which killed me because I could easily have gone and ..."

Thinking about surrendering to Dane's every desire got me so close suddenly. I'm riding the edge, drunk on my ex-boyfriend's voice, playing out some abstract hot fantasy in my head that doesn't even have a shape.

"... which drives you crazy as I reach down and suck you off so hard ..."

I'm out of breath as I race toward my inevitable climax. My toes curl beneath the sheets. My jaw drops and my eyes rock back and my legs tighten, fighting it off to the very last second.

"... and then you blow your wad down my throat."

I blow my wad.

The orgasm is so intense that I can't help but let out a whimper as I thrust and thrust my cock into my fist. My whole body squirms and melts into the sheets as I calm down and succumb to the aftershocks and warm, delightful waves of pleasure that swim around my body.

A drunken smile breaks over my face. I haven't felt this relaxed in years. *Maybe five years.*

"Well?" asks Dane.

I haven't even been listening to him. "Sorry, what was that?" I'm so fucking happy right now.

"Was it as good for you as it was for me?"

I freeze in place, breath held. *What?*

Dane lets out a breathy chuckle. "Some things never change. You're still cute as ever, trying to hide that dirty side of you from me. *But I know you better, Evan Pryor,*" he growls tauntingly.

"I ... I wasn't ..."

"Sweet dreams, cupcake." Then he hangs up, leaving me holding my dick in a bed with wet sheets.

Chapter 8.
Evan's got a stick up somewhere.

First, I reach for a tin of shaving cream instead of my styling paste, then apologize to the irked-yet-patient customer in my chair.

Second, I forget to let the water get warm and end up spraying an ice-cold stream over some poor guy's hair I'm trying to shampoo. "I'm so sorry," I mumble for the fourth time today.

Then I catch myself staring off into the nothingness while holding a hairdryer as I recount every mistake I've ever made on account of my own insatiable horniness.

Every mistake begins and ends with one name.

My ex-boyfriend's name.

Dane Fucking Cooper.

"You're not yourself today," notes Gary, my front desk guy who really needs to work on his stiff demeanor. Remind me why I hired him as my receptionist? Was it a favor to someone or something?

I eye him. "When is anyone actually themselves?"

Gary's face wrinkles up. He's about to answer.

But I answer myself, cutting him off. "It's a rather profound question, when you think on it. Are you really yourself when you're around your clients? No, you're a version of yourself you want them to see. How about in front of your parents? Nope, you're hiding your flaws and putting on your best so they stay off your case. Your best friend? Nope, you just need to impress them and make them go 'ooh' and 'aah'. How about when you are home alone, all by yourself, with no one left to impress?" At that, I give the biggest scoff of all. "Even then, hell-to-the-fucking-no, you aren't yourself. Even when you're alone, you're performing in front of mirrors and telling yourself you're totally *not* masturbating to fantasies of your ex-boyfriend. No way, you're not still desperately hung up on him—*why would you be??* You do anything to avoid the truth, ignoring your petty stupid problems, like your *hot* ex-boyfriend who won't let you go, and then you wonder if *you're* the problem or if it's *him*, and—"

"Are we still philosophizing, or mourning the loss of love?" asks Gary carefully. "Because your next client is here, and he's staring at you like you're a Martian."

"*I must be a Martian, then,*" I fire back. "It's the first *reasonable* thing I've heard all week." I face my client, a sweet man who looks temporarily horrified. "Please, this way," I direct him, heading toward my station.

No, the rest of my day does not improve.

By the time I turn onto my street, I'm just plain over it and ready to throw myself into a big sudsy bath with a glass of wine.

Instead, I find Dane sitting on my front doorstep.

"Not today," I beg him as I slam shut the door to my car. "Tomorrow, maybe. But not today."

"How about tonight?" he offers as I approach.

I stop in front of him and stare down at his devilish eyes. "Tonight? What the hell's going on tonight?"

"Are we just gonna ignore our little midnight phone call?" he asks.

"You're blocking my door."

"I know I've gained some mass over the last five or so years," Dane replies, "but I wouldn't say I've gotten big enough to *block your door*, per se."

"Oh? 'Gained some mass'? Is that how bodybuilders say it? Because somehow 'gaining weight' is somewhat less self-flattering? Excuse me." I squeeze past him and pull out my front door key.

He rises off my step and faces my back. "What's so wrong with us having a little fun while I'm around?"

"I'm not in the mood for fun," I state, still fumbling with the front door. *Why the hell isn't this stupid key fitting into the lock?*

Then Dane comes right up to my backside. I feel his firm, strong hand cup my ass and give it a squeeze. The heat of his big, muscled form towers over me.

I feel his breath on my neck as he says, "Now *that—I know, and you know*—is a bold-faced *lie*."

"Yeah?" I throw over my shoulder. "Then watch me as I get this door open and shut it yet again in your sexy, handsome face."

"So you still think I've got a sexy, handsome face?"

My cheeks flush. *Damn it.* I give up on my front door and turn around to glare at him.

Big mistake. Now I've basically put my face right in front of his muscled chest and parted lips framed by his strong, dark beard.

I'm out of breath so fast, I can't even say anything as I stare at him. After so many years together, I should be used to Dane and his bold, seductive antics.

Why does it feel like he's a new, beautiful stranger I've encountered?

But if he was a new, beautiful stranger, would it make this any easier?

"I think you're pretty," he tells me softly, and I can't tell whether he's taunting me with the word "pretty", or if that's genuinely the word that comes to his lips at the sight of me. "And while it has been my intention—for days—to respect you and your space ... I'm finding it harder and harder to do so."

I lean toward him and take his lips with my own.

I don't even think.

My heart slams against my chest as I kiss him.

I've touched a few lips over the years. Some Tinder match four years ago with peppermint breath whose lips were slippery and strange. A guy from OkCupid who I was so relieved to drive back to his place to end the date, and then his lips crashed into mine (uninvited) before he got out of the car, leaving me with a parting gift of his garlic breath to remind me of the awkward Italian dinner we just shared. There was also a stupendous guy I was tricked into going on a date with through a mutual acquaintance at my salon as recently as nine months ago, and his lips were so dry and chapped that it was literally a slow-motion horror movie as he opened his mouth and summoned his Loch Ness Monster tongue out for a kiss. I couldn't get the mouthwash in my mouth quick enough the second I got home.

And then there's Dane Cooper.

I kiss him again and again. His soft lips smack as they caress and touch mine.

There is a certain confidence in his lips, like there isn't a place on this whole, lonely planet he'd rather be than right here, right now, arresting me with this kiss.

My hand grips his shirt and pulls him all the way against me, flattening me to my front door.

There is deep, unquestionable trust in his kiss, too, that allows me to say without a doubt that there isn't an ulterior motive behind it. He merely desperately needs the touch of my lips against his.

And nothing else can possibly satisfy him.

This is the kind of kiss that made me fall in love with him for the first time.

"Goddamn, Evan," he breathes between one kiss and the next. "You're so ..." Another kiss interrupts him, and the pair of us are out of breath again.

Then I can't stand it. I pull away at once, produce my key, and thrust it into the door as fast as I can.

This time, it opens on the first try.

"I-I'm sorry," he blurts out at my back, devastated. "I went in too strong. I should've held back. I—"

"Shut up and kiss me." I grab hold of his shirt, yank him into the house, and slam the door before our mouths crash into one another's again.

Chapter 9.
Dane gets busy.

I want to say Evan and I made it to his bedroom before we got all nasty.

We barely made it through the door.

The pair of us fumble backwards while we kiss. I have no idea where we are until the back of my heel kicks into the couch, and then down we go.

Evan straddles me, his mouth covering mine as our lips lock in a heated, breathless embrace.

My hands slide down the sides of his body, which shudders with anticipation at my touch. His dress shirt is so soft as I gently untuck it from his tight, belted dress pants, teasing the material out one little tug at a time.

He moans and gasps when my fingers slip under the bottom of his shirt, caressing his smooth, bare abdomen.

I smile against his lips. "You are *so* horny for me."

"*Shut up*," he breathes, then dives in for another kiss.

I unbutton his shirt from the bottom as slowly as I'd savor each bite of a rich and succulent dessert. Each kiss we give one another while I slowly strip him is more sensual and careful than the last, inspiring countless waves of chills and excitement down both our bodies.

Or maybe it's my fingertips as they dance their way up his abs from the inside of his soft shirt, now opened completely. When they arrive at his nipples, Evan stops kissing me and freezes right there in front of my face, eyes shut, lips parted and breathless.

If that's not an invitation, I don't know what is.

Inspired, I give both his nipples a gentle pinch, just to amuse myself. Like clockwork, Evan's mouth parts even more and the slightest of anguished winces crosses his face—a beautiful, pleasurable agony.

I fucking love this guy.

I apply just a little bit more pressure with a cruel bit of torque, and Evan's eyes rock back as he gasps, his lips refusing to close.

I own this boy just by his nipples alone.

"Mmm, I see your kryptonite hasn't changed."

Evan's eyes flap open with a furrow-browed scowl. "You'd better—"

I knead his nipples a little more, then watch as his eyes rock back—again—and he squirms with pleasure.

"You realize I'm never letting go of these puppies," I tell him. "Seems like I've got you in quite a predicament here. You're all mine to play with, Evan."

"S-Stop ..." he moans.

I give him another squeeze of my fingertips.

Evan moans like some kind of feral cat, succumbing to another fit of inner squirming.

In an Olympic-wrestler-caliber maneuver, I flip us around so that it's me on top and a startled, wide-eyed Evan on the couch looking up at me with all the wonder of the world in his eyes.

I grin down at him, then descend my lips to his chest where I plant a firm, meaningful kiss.

Evan sighs against me, having no choice but to trust me with whatever devious things I want to do to him.

I kiss again, traveling across his chest slowly.

"*Dane ...*" he breathes, like a warning.

Or a pleading.

Or a begging.

I let out my tongue and, ever so gently, drag it over his hardened, sensitive left nipple. Evan lets out a sound that lives somewhere between a sigh and a whimper. *He is so fucking sexy when he makes those noises.*

He spends so much of his life being responsible for things. Managing things. Worrying over this or that. Being the boss. Being in charge. Calling the shots and expecting his employees to fall in line.

But when I have him underneath me, all of that goes away, and he's not the boss of anything.

He's my cute little bitch.

And I'm the boss.

I give his nipple another firm lick, then draw circles with the tip of my tongue, torturing him.

When Evan is underneath me, every bit of pleasure he experiences is because I'm giving it to him. That fact makes me feel fucking sexy.

It also gives me one hell of a power trip.

"*Don't stop* ..." he whimpers, out of breath.

I grin up at him from the smooth valley of his chest. "Or what?" I goad him.

With that, Evan brings a hand to my hair, in which his fingers get tangled, then presses my face against his nipple forcefully.

I take the hint, part my hungry mouth, and bite.

"Oh, *GOD!*" he cries out.

I suck hard on that nipple and play him like a drum set, nibbling, then releasing, then nibbling again. I lick, I suck, and I surprise him with my cruel nips. He never knows when they're coming.

And each time: "*FUCK ME! Mmmph, oh, GOD!*"

I hope his stick-up-their-asses neighbors hear all this.

Before he can come down from the high I just sent him into, I switch to his other nipple, causing him to buck desperately under me, throwing his body against mine as he dances.

"You just can't get enough," I murmur, grinning, as I lift up from his nipples and come in for another kiss.

He looks at me, puffing, and says, "*You're the worst.*"

My hand slides down his body, right into his pants, and grabs hold of his steel-hard cock, making him gasp against my face.

"And *you*," I say back to him, "are fucking *boned*."

I slide my body down his, kissing a trail down the middle of his chest until my face hovers over his crotch.

"Oh my God," he moans. "What are we *doing?*"

I pop the button of his pants. "Giving in," I answer, then yank them—and his underwear—down.

Evan lifts his head up, eyes wide and mouth parted, as he watches me drag my tongue up the length of his cock. "*Dane* ..." he whispers, and that's all he whispers before he just stares, breath held, not moving a muscle.

Except for his hard dick, which bobs with his racing heartbeat.

My tongue reaches the tip where I give it a kiss, meet Evan's eyes with my own, then grin.

"Tell me something." I tilt my head while gripping his dick, aiming it tauntingly for my parted lips. "How long have you been dreaming about this exact moment?"

"Dane ..."

"How many loads have you shot thinking about my mouth ... and what it used to do to your body?"

Evan doesn't answer. He just gulps with intensity and stares, cock throbbing in my firm, powerful hand.

A bead of pre-cum dances at its tip.

I smirk. "Someone's ready to play."

"Tons."

I lift an eyebrow. "What was that?"

"Tons. I've ..." He can't seem to find his breath. "I've ... shot tons of loads. Tons ... thinking about you."

"Yeah?" I give his cockhead a lick around its entire breadth, taking up that tasty bead of juice with it. Just the unassuming touch of my soft tongue running across the slit of his dick makes him squirm, sensitive as it is. "Was I sucking you off in these fantasies of yours?"

"Yes."

"You want me to suck you off right now?"

"*God*, yes."

"How badly?" I give his dick one teasing lick up its length, causing Evan to roll his eyes back and squirm.

"B-Badly."

"What was that?"

"*BADLY*."

Without warning, I close my lips around his whole cockhead.

Evan gasps, does half a crunch, then grips my hair again, staring at me with wide, eager eyes.

I half-smile, his cockhead in my warm, wet mouth. Then I let my tongue play with it, teasing the end of his hard cock as I slowly let my mouth slide down its length. My speed is so slow, it must be torture for him.

Evan throws his head back with a moan, then brings it up again to watch, his mouth never shutting.

I come up to the tip again, eye him knowingly, then descend once more down his length, taking even more of his dick in than before. My tongue flutters all along his meat as I go, giving him all the love I can give with my skillful mouth.

This torture must go on for longer than he thought he was capable of handling, because it isn't long before I feel his legs flexing and tightening underneath me.

I pop off his dick, then bring a hand to the base of his tightened-up balls. They're so smooth and sensitive that the second I touch them, Evan gasps and his whole body flinches.

"Damn," I say up to him, tsk-tsking. "You can't let yourself go this long without any loving. It's downright cruel. Look at how you're reacting to me."

I give the base of his balls a loving little doggie lick, which makes Evan rear and moan like a spooked horse, like the sensation is too much to endure.

"Downright cruel," I repeat, then chuckle.

Evan scowls at me with this look that's so defeated, yet turned on, and reveals how little he can do about his situation but endure it and accept every bit of pleasure I give him without complaint.

I can say just about anything right now and get away with it. I can sass him, torment him, and mock him for hours while I lick and toy with his cock and balls, while I torture his poor, sensitive nipples, while I kiss him.

He won't do a single damned thing about it, because he knows he's never felt pleasure this deeply in years, and he needs me to experience that big and explosive release he's long craved. He *needs* me.

That's how badly he wants this.

I give his balls another lick, firmer, as my hand that grips his cock starts slowly jerking, slick from my saliva after blowing him. My rate of stroking him is clearly too slow for him, considering his grunting and all the scowls of frustration he throws down his body at me.

And no matter how much he scowls, I won't give in. I'm the one in charge here. I'm the one who says when he gets to come. *And he knows it.*

"Dane, you're killing me."

Still licking his tight, smooth, perfect balls, I don't answer, but I grin as I look up at him across the silky, cascading flesh of his abs and chest and two reddened nipples. My hand slowly slides up and down his slippery dick, which is so unrelentingly hard, I feel like half a pole dancer right now, gripping it.

"Please ..." he nearly begs. "F-Faster ..."

I don't speed up one bit as my eyes are on his. I just keep torturing him with my little licks, and the dragging of my soft, wet tongue across his sensitive skin.

This has got to be driving him insane.

"Is ... Is this payback for something? *Ughn* ..." His eyes rock back as I twist my grip around his cock, giving it a little rotation right at the cockhead, which makes his whole body tense up. "*You fucker* ..." he breathes.

"You're so sensitive right now," I murmur between my licks. "Your cock's like a joystick that controls you."

"Not everything's a *game*," Evan groans.

I twist my stroke right at his cockhead again.

Evan sucks in air, his eyes shut, his lips part, and his eyebrows shoot up in sweet, delirious agony.

I grin. "Tell that to your schlong."

"This *is* payback," Evan decides as he lifts his head and shoots me a glare. "You're driving me crazy to ..." I twist again at his cockhead. He bucks in reaction, then resumes his glare uninterrupted. "... to teach me a *lesson*."

"Am I?"

I switch my hand for my mouth, wrapping my lips around his dick and swallowing it all the way down to the base. Now it's my mouth that rotates each time I come up to the cockhead, making his whole body dance.

I come off his dick again. "Or maybe I just love you enough to torture you the way you like."

He lifts his head up after having rocked it back, and his eyes are on me.

The look in his eyes tells me I'm right.

It also tells me something else. "And I think you still love me, too," I hear myself saying.

Evan opens his mouth to say something, but doesn't, staring at me in wonder.

"Probably not the ideal time to have this revelation, huh?" I taunt him, then lick the end of his cock where another desperate bead of pre-cum has appeared. "While I have you dangled ..." I give him five firm strokes. His jaw drops and his eyes flash. "... right on the edge."

"Damn it, Dane," he growls.

I drag my tongue around his swollen cockhead one last time, then eye him. "How does coming all over my face sound?"

Evan gawps.

That's his answer.

Then I grab his slippery cock and start jerking with no mercy or pause. As I watch that hungry, desperate, crazed look on Evan's face, I bring my own right up to his dick and part my mouth just a little, tongue on my bottom lip, out just enough to tease the end of his cock.

"I LOVE YOU, DANE!" he cries out suddenly.

I lift my eyebrows, still jerking, tongue still teasing, eyes on Evan.

"I FUCKING LOVE YOU! I—"

Then Evan comes, shooting all over the side of my cheek, my parted lips, and my flicking tongue. I close my eyes and bask in the wet, warm glory as he bathes me. It seems to go on forever, one shot after another. His cock pulses and throbs and flexes in my slippery grip as I continue to stroke him, milking him for all he's worth.

I'm literally dripping from my chin and mouth.

Evan collapses in a fit of heavy panting and sweat.

"Oh my *God* ..." he breathes, then looks up to meet my gaze, as if checking to see if I wasn't blasted away by his orgasm.

I let go of his cock and bring my sticky hand to my lips, giving two of the fingers their own five-second blow jobs. "*Fuuuck*," I moan, a satisfied, broad smile over my face. "Damn boy, you're tasty."

"I ..." He's still catching his breath. "I can't believe ... we just ... *did that*."

I grin at him. "I can't believe you just told me you still love me."

Evan's face freezes. He looks to the left, then the right, then straight back at me. "I ...?"

"That's alright. Pretend it didn't happen." I chuckle as I rise to my feet. I kick off my shoes, unbuckle my pants, then let them drop to my ankles.

Evan's eyes follow, zeroing in on my dick.

"Meanwhile," I go on, gripping my shirt and peeling it off in one quick pull, then pitching it aside, "I'm gonna go make love to your shower."

Evan's eyes are on my chest. And then they're on my face. "W-What?" he murmurs distractedly.

I shake my head, unable to wipe off my smile, then turn to grace him with a view of my bare, muscled ass as I strut off toward his bathroom.

Chapter 10.
Evan obviously follows him in.

I'm still in shock at how fast things happened.

But maybe I shouldn't be.

Maybe it was inevitable that Dane and I crashed into each other's lives again.

We had a dynamic back in the day. It was something of a *sexual* dynamic.

When either of us got horny, this other side of Dane would come out—a dominant side. And something in me would eventually let go, giving in to whatever he wanted to do with me. I don't want to call it submissive, because I always pretended to fight back and resist—and even hate it, scowling at him. Whenever I finally gave in to Dane's dirty desires, I acted like it was some kind of defeat for me, like I'd lost the game and was suffering the pleasurable yet humiliating consequences.

But really, I was getting exactly what I wanted. And so was he.

Even if my prize was prolonged, agonizing, sexual torment.

After hearing the shower turn on, I get right up off that couch and stare at the trail of his clothes leading down my hall.

For a second, I'm petrified. Did I just make a huge mistake? How long will this go on before those old and terrible habits of his kick in that used to annoy me to no end? How long will this supposed bliss carry on before I start seeing all of those little things that made me so fed up, I finally called it quits after roughly four years?

And let's be adults about this. What about *my* habits that Dane couldn't stand? He's probably humming to himself in that shower right now, washing all my funk off his face, thinking he's in heaven, but he's going to wake up eventually, too.

Or maybe I'm underestimating what time has done to us both.

Maybe we really are two different people, who have grown into mature adults during our time apart.

Maybe it isn't so crazy to think this could work.

When I reach the bathroom door, which he left wide open, I see his broad and muscled backside through the steamy glass doors of the shower. For a second, I'm just taken by the glorious sight, leaning weakly against the doorframe as I stare in.

What a fucking beauty Dane Cooper is.

Then he turns around, eyes me through the glass, and says, "Hey there, jizz bomb. You getting in?"

And then he goes and says that.

I narrow my eyes. "I much prefer *cupcake*."

"Alright, jizz cupcake. Get in before I use up all the hot water."

I peel off the rest of my clothes, then slip into the shower, wide and deep enough to house us both with room to spare. I'm assaulted by a near-burning wash of steam over my body the second I get in, and I growl. *I forgot how miserably hot he takes his showers.*

"Sorry," he blurts before I even have a chance to complain, reaches, and twists the knob a bit. "I'll cool it down for you."

It's a little nothing detail about me, but witnessing his remembering of it makes my heart swell as I look up at his face. I can't even think of anything to say.

Dane helps me by taking the soap and bringing it to my chest where he gently starts to lather it. His eyes are on me the whole time while he washes me.

"I know what you need," he tells me softly.

Steam swirls around us like a warm, slow-motion tornado. "Yeah?"

"You need this." He tilts his head. "A man who will be rough when you want it. A man who might even be a little mean sometimes, in the right context. A man who can fulfill all your high-school-bully fantasies ..."

Then Dane puts a dainty kiss on the end of my nose and flashes me a heart-crushing smile.

"... and then care for you like a lover afterwards," he finishes.

I bring my hands to his body. His thick, rippled abs. His sculpted pecs. His broad, round shoulders. His big arms, sinewy with cords of muscle, dressed in beautiful, exotic tattoos. *God, this man is built of fucking stone.*

"Doesn't it sound like some kind of dysfunctional, codependent, psychosexual nightmare?" I throw back.

He chuckles. "Maybe." He runs a hand through my hair. "But it's ours. Our special little thing."

I bring my hand up to his, stopping it.

He watches.

I pull his hand to my face, press my cheek against his wide, warm palm, then incline my head to place a kiss right there where his palm dimples by the thumb.

His fingers gently curl under the touch of my lips, innocent, vulnerable.

"And I still love you, Evan Pryor."

My eyes meet his. All of those misgivings rush up to the surface at once, pressing against my tongue, against my lips, against my eyes, daring to be voiced. I always voice them. I always speak my worries. I always exercise caution, the one to tell Dane to slow down, the one to say, *'Take it easy'*, and *'Wait, wait'*, and *'Are you sure?'*

But something in me today is made of diamond, and despite all my fears, I look Dane in the eyes, brazen as a storm, and say, "I still love you too, Dane Cooper."

Our bodies come together, and we kiss in the swirls of steam and the rushing noise of shower water.

Today might've just become the best day of my life.

Moments later, Dane is dressed and stewing over something in the living room while I'm still putting on a shirt in the bedroom. The sunlight through my large bay window is waning as evening approaches, and I have a stray thought or two about what to get for dinner. *Maybe Dane would like to stay for a bite.*

But when I come up to the door and watch him for a bit, I find myself curious—and maybe a touch worried—about what's going on in his mind. He's staring out the front window with a faraway, pensive look in his eyes. I hope the flood of doubts I had earlier haven't hopped out of my brain and made a nest inside his.

Before I can ask anything, he spins around, notices me, then shoots me a grin. "Ready for seconds?"

I lift an eyebrow. "Dane, I've barely recovered from the first, and we just showered."

"I don't mean that." He taps a finger on the window. "I'm gonna get nice and up-close in my *investigative work* tonight."

I don't think I like the sound of that. "Uh, how?"

"Do you know your Hanson character hits up the bar every night from now until near ten o'clock?"

"Well, I know he's a drinker, but I—"

"He just stepped out." Dane wiggles his eyebrows.

I don't follow. "So ... he's not our guy?"

"We don't know yet." He purses his lips and nods at the door. "But we will tonight."

I glance at the door, then him, then the door again. It clicks—*I think*. "You mean you're gonna sniff around his house while he's gone ...? You're ..." I lower my voice. "*You're gonna trespass on his property??*"

"I was thinking a bit more *Mission Impossible* than that." The corner of Dane's lip curls up in that way that can only mean trouble. "You in or out?"

I take a step back and lift my hands. "Oh, I'm ... I'm one-hundred-percent out. No way. I am *not* ..." I scoff and shake my head. "No, I'm not gonna do it. And to be frank, neither should you. What if he comes home? I bet he owns shotguns. Like, a ton."

"So do I. Hey, you remember that time junior year," Dane starts, strolling right up to me, "when you forgot to include photos on your final project you'd just turned in, and we had to sneak into Professor Towson's office to paperclip them to your report so you wouldn't flunk?"

I narrow my eyes. "That's *hardly* the same."

"Isn't it, though?" He pokes a thumb at the window. "It's just another office we're sneaking into. All we're doing is having a little look-poke-and-pick for evidence."

"No."

He swats me on the arm. "Wasn't it fun? Don't you remember how fast your heart raced?"

Vividly. "We're not breaking into his house, Dane."

"Man, when we got back to the apartment that night, we must have fucked for *hours.* Who knew breaking into your prof's office would be such an aphrodisiac!"

"Well, you seem to remember it differently, because *I* remember wanting to barf all the way home. I kept thinking, *'Oh my God, were there cameras? We didn't even check for cameras! Oh my God, I'm going to be expelled!'* Oh, but of course," I go on, squaring off with him, "I guess it didn't mean as much to you as it did to me, the threat of having my career thrown down the drain on account of a very bad idea—*your* idea, I might add."

"If you'd flunked that class, it would've been down the drain anyway. C'mon. Don't you wanna come and have a little fun with me tonight?"

"No." I move away and sit my little ass on the arm of the couch. "You and I are gonna order ourselves some dinner, chat about the good times over a light movie and wine as we await our dinner, then eat while we eye-fuck across the table. *We are not breaking into Hanson's house.*"

To that, Dane just chuckles, shrugs, then turns away with a, "You're missing out," thrown over his shoulder as he pushes through my front door.

I sputter, wide-eyed, as he struts off across my lawn like he's magically become some kind of invisible-to-the-world superhero. "*Dane!*" I hiss from the couch.

He doesn't hear me, strutting across the street.

I fold my arms. *Yeah, about that whole waiting-for-his-bad-habits-and-traits-to-appear-and-ruin-my-fantasy thing.* I huff, scowl, and glare at my left-wide-open front door.

He's just testing me.

That's what this is.

He isn't really going to do it.

Then I think about that fateful night, years ago. We were in my apartment, about to play a game on Dane's Xbox with a giant bag of Doritos for our dinner, when the sight of my photos left on the dining room table hit me harder than a bag of bricks. *"My photos!"* I cried out.

The next instant, we were in my professor's office. Dane talked me through each step, telling me all these little tricks and secrets no one's supposed to know. I felt like his little bandit apprentice, learning the darker side of the law. *"The trick is,"* he told me, *"you gotta think like a criminal ... without someday becoming one yourself."*

The irony of us having broken into my professor's office at the time of him saying those words never truly hit me until now.

I lift my face to that door, then let out the world's longest sigh. "Dane, you motherfucker." The next thing I know, I'm off the arm of the couch and pulling the front door shut behind me, cursing under my breath as I hurry down the street after him.

Chapter 11.
Dane is always full of good bad ideas.

I slip through Hanson's gate and into the backyard, where I draw right up to the back door and crouch. After a moment of working my tiny tool into the lock, the door pops right open, and I slip inside.

The back door opens into the dining room, where the man's table has no room even for himself to eat; the whole fucking thing is covered in toys, creepy doll parts, tubes of paint, bottles of glue, and yarn. *The fuck?* I peek around the table, curious, until I find a framed picture propped up on a shelf nearby. The picture is of Hanson and a little girl, who I take to be his one granddaughter. I already got a good look into Hanson's records, so I know very well what he looks like up-close, as well as the fact that his record is squeaky clean if you ignore one arrest for disorderly conduct at a bar in '97, but that's nothing to give yourself a wedgie over.

I smile with a new appreciation at the doll parts. *So what? He loves his little girl. He's making her a doll or ten.*

When the back door opens, I nearly shit myself until I turn around to find Evan standing there, wide-eyed and staring right at me.

I grin at him. "I knew you'd cave."

"Keep your voice down!" Evan hisses, looks to the left, then the right, then down at the table where he recoils. *"Oh my God, he's creepy as fuck."*

"He's got a little girl, granddaughter, name's Julia, he calls her Jewels." I step away from the table and move into the living room, scoping everything from the couch to the long coffee table to the *yikes-circa-1980-something* entertainment set complete with a turntable and a small yet impressive vinyl collection. "No pets, no siblings, no living parents. Just one daughter named Betty, through which he has the granddaughter."

"You can tell a lot about a person by the—"

"—layout of their furniture," I finish, eyeing him. "I remember. What can you tell about Hanson?"

Evan looks at the couch, then up at something on the wall, then off somewhere else. *"He's ... lonely."*

"You don't have to whisper."

"He has no taste for color," Evan continues to whisper, *"but he thinks he does. He's ... confused, or conflicted ..."*

"You're getting all of that just from his furniture?"

"Pretty much. Just an intuition. I could be wrong."

Evan follows directly behind me in my exact path, as if afraid to have a footprint left somewhere. I feel him softly gripping my waist as we slowly move across the living room. It's kind of sexy.

"What the hell are we doing now?" I tease him. "A conga line?"

"*Shut up.*"

"Salsa dance lessons?" I lean back toward him. "We gotta be facing one another for those."

"*Let's just get this over with quickly.*"

We pass a hall closet on our way to the door leading out into the garage, which I push through. The whole garage reeks of paint and sawdust. An unplugged table saw rests in the middle of the garage next to a pile of two-by-fours. Along the wall are leaned several full-size doors as well as what seems to be an unfinished cabinet.

Then I spot it by the wall. "Bingo."

Evan's right at my back. "*Bingo? Bingo what? What's the bingo?*"

"You can seriously stop whispering, and the bingo is *that*," I tell him, coming up to the wall where gallons of paint and spray paint cans rest.

Among them: bright bubblegum pink.

"Oh my God, it *is* Old Man Hanson!" gasps Evan, slapping a hand over his mouth.

I point at the can next to it. "It isn't exactly unusual to own black paint, I guess, but it's there as well. And it's opened, from the look of it." I glance at Evan over my shoulder. "The color of the dick on Stevie's garage door."

"Y'know ..." Evan shrugs. "I'm almost disappointed. I didn't realize it'd actually be the guy we all suspected it was from the start. The old man down the street ..."

I move away from the paint and scope the rest of his garage. In the corner is a half-made doghouse. On second look, it might be a very ugly attempt at a dollhouse.

"Hmm ... I'm not so convinced yet."

Evan scoffs. "We found bubblegum pink paint, the same color my mailbox was painted, same color as the word on Marcellus and Vinnie's driveway. What else would he *possibly* be doing with this color of paint?"

"He builds things, clearly," I point out. "And he *does* have a sweet little granddaughter."

"So? I'm also fairly certain I saw a *Hating Your Gay-As-Hell Neighbors* handbook in the other room ..."

"Not sure I noticed the handbook," I mutter, playing along, "but y'know what I *did* notice?" I stroll right up to Evan, then incline my head. "*No wife.*"

He frowns. "Uh ... would *you* marry that wrinkled, hateful, scowling old man? Of *course* he has no wife."

"Never been married," I carry on. "Used to live on the outskirts of Belleview four years ago ..."

"Oh my God, are you suggesting he's gay? No way." Evan shakes his head and waves a dismissive hand in the air. "He's *so* not gay. Not even *close.*"

I shrug. "Well, why else did he move onto a street notorious for being the gay part of town?"

"Uh, to antagonize us?" Evan suggests. "To make a statement? Any number of reasons! We live in a very politically *loud* time, Dane. Wake up. These haters feel *entitled* to their hate."

I crouch down to get a better look at the half-built dollhouse. The trim of it is painted bubblegum pink. *Hanson still could have used the paint for both purposes—the dollhouse* and *the vandalisms*, I reason.

"He has a *granddaughter*," Evan reminds me. "That means he has a *son or daughter*, too."

"Yes, a daughter named Betty. Who knows. Maybe he was married to a lovely lady for a while and lived a happy hetero life before realizing he needed a dingdong in his mouth and a man's wang up his hidey-hole."

Evan dry-heaves and turns away.

I come up to his back. "My point is, we don't have enough evidence here to know for sure."

"Well, *I* know, and that's enough for me to take back to Raymond and settle this whole thing, which is sort of the only reason you're here at all, if we're being honest. *Now can we go home finally?*"

His words slap all the fun right off my face.

After watching him fuss at the paints for a bit, I ask the question: "Is that what all this is actually about?"

Evan turns to face me. "What?"

"You just wanna impress Raymond."

"I ... huh?" Evan's eyebrows pull together, confused.

"You wanted me to solve this thing quickly so you can go to Raymond with the vandal's name, save the day, and look like the hero in front of your friends."

"I'm not ... I ... *ugh!*" Evan scoffs at me. "Really, you think that's all that matters to me? My image?"

Evan forgets how very easy he is to read. Especially when you were his boyfriend all your college years and learned every single in and out of his ample reactions, including when he's in severe denial, or when he's hiding something—*even from himself.*

I cross my arms. "Well, judging from what I've seen of you this past week or so, yeah, that's a fair theory."

"I'm not even ..." He huffs and looks away to gather a few words, then comes back at me with, "I'm not even sure what to say about that."

"Nothing to say," I decide, then head for the garage door back into the house.

I'm about halfway across the living room when Evan catches up and spins me around. "So that's it?" he blurts. "You think ... You think that I'm just another image-obsessed queen on Figaro Lane? Really?"

I shake my head, dropping it. "Never mind."

"No, no, you and I, we are going to finish this."

It might be the wrong time to note this, but Evan looks his sexiest when he's pissed. His expression goes stern and loses all the well-meaning inauthenticity of his politeness. All that's left when Evan gets like this is pure and unfiltered emotion, which is some days the only thing I can trust.

And nothing is sexier than trust.

"I don't like what you're implying, Dane."

"That you care more about what Raymond thinks of you than about me?" I offer helpfully.

"You think I'm a shallow image whore!"

"Hey, you said it, not me. I'd never call you a whore unless it's in the perfect context of having you naked, spread-eagle, and on your belly across my bed."

Evan rolls his eyes.

"But if I'm being honest here," I go on, "I'm not all that thrilled about your new set of values. This street? These fake friends of yours? That salon? You're living a lie, Evan. You're living a life *other people* have given you permission to have. What about the life *you* wanted?"

"Fuck you, Dane," he says so flippantly, it rolls right off my back like a stray breeze.

"Fuck needing everyone else's permission," I retort as glibly. "This isn't what I wanted for you. This isn't the Evan Pryor I was expecting when you first called me up to meet you."

"Well, I'm so sorry to have disappointed you."

I shoot him a look. "Evan ..."

Just then, a noise is heard at the front door.

Evan and I stare at each other. *Oh, fuck.*

The front door opens.

Since the back door is in perfect view of the front door, I make a split-second decision, grab Evan's hand, and dart for the hallway. Just as the front door shuts and Hanson's grumbling voice is heard, Evan and I slip right into the hall closet and gently shut the door, sealing ourselves away in perfect darkness.

"Don't fuckin' care, Betty, I don't fuckin' care. Have you seen how these fuckers pamper themselves? They're all a bunch of fuckin' *fairies*, not one of them givin' me the—Oh, you and your idealism! Get your head outta the clouds, Betty, I'm sick of—Oh, you, you, you." His voice carries him somewhere distant in the house, and then another door is shut.

"*What do we do?*" whispers Evan in the dark.

"*Wait,*" I answer him.

"*But it sounds like he went into a room. This is our chance to get out.*"

"*No. He just got home. We can't risk being seen until we know he's occupied for a while. If he goes into the bathroom, that's our best bet, otherwise we hope he's just home because he forgot something and will leave as soon as he gets it.*"

"*Am I really such a disappointment to you, Dane?*"

Neither of us can see each other's faces right now, it's so damned dark. He doesn't see my tightened jaw or my looking away.

"*Well?*" he prompts me.

"*We have to be patient and wait,*" I tell him.

"*I don't care about Hanson or Raymond or … anyone else. I was just impatient. I want this whole matter over and done with. I … I just want to be back at my house … with you.*"

Not forty seconds after the man's gone into some room, we hear him emerge again into the living room, still on the phone. "You're talking out of your ass, Betty! Not one of these fuckers here talks to me. They're all a bunch of prissy, judgmental, stuck-up …" He seems to listen for a moment. "I'm just tired of it, Betty. I'm a hot minute away from doing something about it, too."

I freeze every muscle and listen.

Fuck, maybe I was wrong and this is *the guy.*

Evan's hand touches mine. "*Dane …*" he whispers so softly, it's barely a breath.

"No, I ain't going out. Every dang bar in the area is tainted with them, too. Surrounded, I'm telling you. I'm fuckin' surrounded." Then Hanson marches off, a door is slammed shut, and with a squeak, we hear the distant noise of running water.

I push out of the closet and head across the house to the back door, Evan following. We slip out the door, gently shut it behind us, then hurry around the house to the side gate to let ourselves out. There's barely any light left in the sky, and the only thing that shows our way is a spill here and there of amber streetlight.

Evan's voice stops me at my truck. "I haven't turned into a shallow person. And my neighbors …"

"I don't think you're a shallow person."

"My neighbors aren't as shallow as they seem. It's just ... a different way of life here. Maybe it's all because of Raymond's obsession with image that all of us find ourselves ... *prioritizing* certain things. So yes, of course, I will feel *good* if—whether it's both our efforts or just yours—to be the one to solve this problem on our street. Why shouldn't it feel good? And while we're being all honest here, why did you take so much offense to what I said earlier?" he goes on, his confidence mounting the longer he talks. "This *was* the only reason I came to you. I needed your help. I just ..." His eyes drop to my chest. "I didn't expect ... *other* things to happen."

I watch his half-collapsed face for a while—and that all-too-familiar apologetic look he gets.

A part of me wants to have fun with him, toy with him, draw this out and really milk it for all it's worth.

Another part doesn't.

"Maybe I'm a little crazy to think this," I finally say, "but ... when you came to see me at that bar, and we had our almost-game of pool ... I was hoping you really *did* have ulterior motives for seeing me. That maybe you ..." I shrug. "Maybe you *did* want to mount the horse again."

He watches my eyes for a moment. "Do you really think 'mounting the horse' is the best euphemism for the intended context?"

I give him a look. "Evan ..."

"Sorry. Weird time for jokes." He lets out a forced huff. "See? You're already rubbing off on me again."

I glance back down the street. The last thing I need right now is a heavy talk with Evan, especially when the task at hand is still unfinished—*and I fear, by a longshot.*

"I'll set up surveillance of the street," I tell him. "I didn't think it'd actually go this far, but ... catching him in the act—whoever it is—might be the only way to go about this thing."

"Alright." Evan glances at me tentatively.

I nod, deciding it. "Alright." I open the door to my truck.

"Wait."

After hopping in the seat, my hand on the handle of my door about to shut it, I glance at him.

He takes one deep breath in, then lets it out. "Okay. Fine. Alright. Maybe I *did* have ... 'ulterior motives' that night." This is difficult for him to say. "When I came to see you. But ..." He eyes me. "But it's not quite the way you think."

"I'm listening."

"I don't honestly think my motivation was ever, 'I'm gonna get my ex back.' Maybe it might be more honest to say ..." He toys around with a few words. "... that I just wanted you to see me."

"You wanted me to see you?"

"For you to see what I am now. Like, an update."

"An update."

"Like: 'Here I am. Take a look. I'm still alive.' And I wanted you to ... see that I'm doing well."

I sense there's more. "And?"

Evan sighs. "And then I saw you. And I ..." He slaps a hand to his chest. "I started to feel things. Lots of ... of *confusing* things. It's been five years, but in a lot of ways, it feels like not so long ago at all. You get what I mean?"

Yeah, Evan, I do. I really fucking do.

"Why don't you get out of that truck and come in?" he offers. "You haven't eaten. And ... I don't know about you, but I could go for a nice and relaxing night after the crazy crap we just endured."

I find myself smiling down at him. "You were pretty adventurous tonight."

He comes up to the door. "You were, too."

"I miss that side of you."

Evan bites his lip, looking up at me. That look in his eyes makes me think of all the things we did earlier ... as well as the things we didn't.

My dick starts to swell at the thought.

But not tonight.

"Good night, cupcake," I tell him, shoot him a wink, then shut the door. And with a bewildered Evan staring after me, I crank the engine and pull out of his driveway.

Chapter 12.
Dane and his many, many eyes.

In the dead of night—*roughly three in the morning, to be less dramatic*—I fix a hidden camera under the mailbox of a Josiah Langley, aimed down the cul-de-sac.

Three minutes later, another camera makes a home in the knot of a tree, staring straight at the fat mansion of Raymond Havemeyer-Windsor III at the head of the cul-de-sac.

A twin camera faces his next-door neighbor's Prius.

It's adorable, by the way. The Prius.

Another camera is set at the lip of a sewer, staring up like a metal one-eyed zombie at Hanson's house, just in case he really is our guy—*which, by the way, I'm still not convinced.*

Four more trusty little guys keep tabs on four other spots, targeted specifically so as to give me full view of as many nooks of the street as possible, covering any place a vandal might need to go in order to access a house on the cul-de-sac.

With as many cameras as I've set out, he can't so much as take a piss in a bush without my catching it.

Since the activity has been relatively limited to one end of it, I presume that after my eleventh and twelfth cameras are in place, I'm able to legally declare myself to have "gone totally fucking overboard with it".

I sit patiently in my truck, now parked outside the neighborhood, just in view of a beautiful, sprawling lake cast upon by moonlight as well as a Starbucks. Now all I gotta do is sip on my coffee, stare at the screen of my laptop—*and the twelve feeds it helpfully lends*—and wait.

And think about Evan.

And wait some more.

And think about Evan some more.

I glance down at my silent phone, pucker up my lips in thought, then glance over at the entrance to the neighborhood. Evan's in there. And I'm not.

I could be watching these feeds from my home, by the way. Easily. Other than the twenty-minute drive, it'd be nothing at all to just hang out at my apartment, naked, kicking back some beers, and occasionally giving a glance at my laptops.

It's all recording anyway. Even if I dozed off, I could easily rewind and review what I'd missed.

See how fucking easy this is? I should have done this lazy shit from the beginning, then we'd have our spirited dick-painter in a jail cell downtown already.

But I'm not home itching my exposed balls on my couch kicking back a beer. I'm sitting here in my truck, staring at those nice, fancy houses, and thinking about a certain sexy man sitting in his house all alone.

I'm such a jerk for not staying.

Let's be real. If I stayed, we would have played nice, made up, then fucked twenty-seven times until morning. I wouldn't have set up these fancy cameras, I'd neglect the work I was brought here to do in the first place, and we'd wake up to some other delightful artistic addition to Figaro Lane.

I need to be out here in my truck, away from him.

The man I love.

"Hah ... 'the man I love' ..." I mock myself, my own voice filling the car and mixing in with whatever crap is playing on the radio, then take another sip of coffee.

The street that leads into his neighborhood is called Traviata Road, as in the opera *Traviata*. It runs like a heart vein right down the center of the neighborhood, branching off into such streets as Butterfly Lane, Tosca Lane, Isolde Lane, Boheme Lane, Mignon Lane, and even the adorable pair of Hansel Lane and Gretel Lane.

And then there's Figaro Lane.

All my thoughts, like all those winding roads, lead right back to Evan James Pryor.

Great. Now my dick's hard. I don't even know why. Maybe because I thought his name.

Evan James Pryor.

Evan.

My Evan.

That's all it fucking takes lately.

After a quick glance at my camera feeds, I close my eyes and lean back with a sigh, ignoring my wood. Some old 80s hit I can't identify is playing on the radio, and before I start trying to sing along badly to it, I force myself to go over the pros and cons of Evan and I getting back together.

Pros: A nice, tight ass.

Like, really, really nice, tight ass.

Also: Someone with a sexy body to cuddle up with who has the *perfect* dick to give blow jobs to.

My eyes flap open. "I should probably consider a few nonsexual reasons, too," I tell myself out loud.

Eyes close again, and I reorganize a few thoughts.

Pros: Deep down, Evan is one of the most beautiful souls I have ever known.

Evan makes me feel like I've already won the game.

He's also fairly stubborn at times, totally ridiculous in the most endearing ways, and can make me laugh so hard that I go blind with hysteria.

If that isn't a winning combination of a boyfriend, I don't know what is.

Cons: Evan might not actually be in love with me, but rather the fantasy of what we were, or could've been.

Cons: Evan might decide I don't fit into his new life, and dismiss me as a second-chance waste of time.

Cons: Evan ... might break my heart.

I don't think I'll be able to withstand that again.

With a huff, I pull out my phone, lift it to my face, and start to type out a text to him, asking if he's awake.

I stare at the text for ten long seconds, then roll my eyes and delete it.

Then I type it out again.

Then delete, delete, delete—and I toss the phone into the passenger seat with a groan.

I'm so fucked up over you, Evan.

Chapter 13.
Evan hosts a coup de théâtre.

A wink?

What the fuck does a wink mean??

It was the last thing he did before taking off in his truck. I haven't seen him in two days.

And nothing's happening on Figaro Lane.

No more garage door dicks. No more rainbow glitter. No more pink mailboxes.

And where the hell is Dane Cooper?

Every time I look at my phone and consider texting him, I feel weak and foolish, like I'm just giving in to his little game—if that's what this is at all.

So I decided to take a little action myself.

In the form of an impromptu movie night, hosted by yours truly, in which I invite all the usuals—plus one key guest.

"Hi, precious," sings Marcellus as he strolls past me into my house with his little black poodle Madonna in hand—who I didn't exactly invite. Vinnie follows with a meek nod my way, and I give the pair of them a warm smile and show them to the refreshments.

And then: "I thought we were canceling activities this week," coos Stevie on his way in, several moments later, carrying a hot pink vitamin juice with a straw, "but I'm *sooo* glad we're not."

Sluuurp.

"Me too," I reply briskly. "Finger foods are inside, beverages and wine in the kitchen, and, well, everyone's fighting over what to watch in the living room, so there's that if you want in on that fun foray."

"You had me at 'finger'." *Sluuurp*, and he's gone.

An impressive number of people show up. Josiah and his fair-weather attitude. Will and his twenty-four-hour sunglasses he always wears. Leland, Thomas. Hell, even Xavier shows up, much to my surprise.

But my key guest still has yet to show up.

He *has* to show up. *He's the whole fucking point.*

I invited everyone by way of a note I left on each of their doorsteps, which is pretty much how we always do it lately. There used to be a system of group texts or a special email list for organized neighborhood events, but on account of some virus or spam bot or something else dumb, we stopped communicating in all manners digital. Besides, Raymond insisted that it is *"seemly"* to receive a handwritten invitation to any event that *matters*. Ever since he said that, no one is caught dead sending an email or text to anyone about any sort of party. Are we surprised anymore?

Despite always getting (read: requiring) an invite to everyone's event, Raymond rarely shows up to any of them. I presume it's because he mostly deems only his own events worthy of his precious time.

So imagine my utter shock when I see Raymond Havemeyer-Windsor III sauntering up my walkway like a preened pelican with a big bottle of expensive wine, in a skintight polo, sleek designer pants, and a sweater tied over his shoulders.

"Oh, I wasn't expecting—" I start.

"We're all in need of a bit of *tipsy-tipsy* around here, what with all the chaos on our street."

"Yes, right ... though nothing's happened in a few days," I point out with a smile, accepting the bottle.

Raymond simply nods with a, "Mmm," then passes right by me, entering my house like King Figaro and I'm just renting the place or something.

I'm so stunned by his arrival that I just stand there at the door, watching as a wave of surprise followed by a chorus of fake welcomes and high-pitched greetings to Raymond rush across the room from all those here.

I should look at it as a good thing. But instead, I just find myself uneasy as hell. No one even realizes that this movie night is just another component to my plan—and to make it work, they *can't* know.

I really wish Dane was in on this with me.

This is a lot harder to stomach than I thought it'd be.

After bringing the bottle to the kitchen, I find Mr. New Homo On The Block Xavier standing aloof over a platter of cheese. In a black faded button-down and blue jeans, he looks up from his mop of messy, spiky black hair and says, "I still don't know why you invited me."

I did observe that no one's been socializing with him. "Why wouldn't I?" I counter casually. "I invited all the other guys on the street. Only a few didn't show, like Preston. You live here, too, so you deserve an invite."

"You know as well as I do, I'm not *one of you*."

I study him a moment. "And what are we, exactly? The ones of whom you're allegedly not?"

Xavier—*who may or may not be wearing black eyeliner, but who's noticing?*—shakes his head with pity at me. "If you have to ask, then you're already a lost cause."

I frown. "That's not nice."

He looks over his shoulder at the gaiety exploding in the living room as four men clamber over themselves to be the first to offer Raymond the best compliment about some flashy new watch he's wearing.

"Thank *Christ* I'm not one of you," he mumbles.

I bristle a bit. "Well, look, no one's asking you to be anything but yourself," I assure him, "so don't worry about who you are or aren't. Tonight is just ... a little fun movie night, that's it."

And also a bit of a ruse. Or a coup. Or a scheme.

Or whatever the hell I want to call this.

But that lovely last part is better left unsaid.

Xavier shrugs. "Whatever. I'm just sticking it out 'til the summer, then all these high-end bitches can fuck off for all I care." He tosses a cube of cheese into his mouth at that, chewing with conviction.

I eye him, then find hairs on the back of my neck prickling up. "Summer? High-end bitches ...?"

He glances my way, then rolls his eyes. "Shit, sorry. Not talking about you. I know they're your friends or whatever. I just mean ..." He wrinkles up his face, leans toward me, and lowers his voice. "Can't you be objective and sometimes think—*Wow, I'm surrounded by a bunch of pretentious plastics, what am I doing living in this hellhole?*"

I just stare at him, suddenly finding myself trying to picture him drawing a big dick on Stevie's garage door.

Xavier wears mostly black. He's half a resurrected goth-punk from my high school days. Black is his thing.

Could he ...?

"Come the summer, I'm gone. I can't care less what happens to these tarts. And before you ask it, no," Xavier blurts, "I don't feel bad about what's happening on this street. Serves them right. Yeah, I laughed at that big dick painting. So? It was funny."

"Well ..." *How do I say this?* "... if that ... *thing* ... was painted on *your* house, maybe you wouldn't have—?"

"I would've still laughed," he insists blithely. "Hell, maybe I'll paint one on my own door, just so I feel like part of something." Then he chuckles at himself, throws another cube of cheese past his lips, and heads to the living room to claim a seat.

I watch him, frustrated and unsure what to make of his words. Is he trying to throw me off, or accidentally self-incriminate himself? I pull out my phone by reflex, thinking I should text Dane about it to get his opinion.

Then suddenly I remember our last exchange.

And how we kinda haven't talked since.

I end up staring at my phone for a solid five minutes, going back and forth on whether or not I'm allowed to share my feelings with Dane. This just plain sucks.

Has this new, fancy life of mine really made me such a social icicle? Am I ruined now? *Was Dane right?*

The doorbell rings.

Instead of crossing through the busy living room where Stevie is in the middle of telling everyone a story about something funny his mother did over the holidays, I cut through the kitchen and dining room to the foyer where I stop at the door, steel myself to greet my next guest, plaster on a smile, then pull it open.

My smile falters.

Old Man Hanson shifts his weight from one leg to the other, clears his throat, then grunts, "You got some kinda movie thing here tonight or somethin'?"

In this little moment here on my doorstep, it never quite occurred to me that I've not seen Hanson up-close. He's surprisingly young-looking for a three-hundred-year-old man. I wouldn't put him past maybe fifty at the most, though his skin is a bit worn around the edges of his face, perhaps indicative of his drinking or smoking. He's wearing a decent sweater vest and oversized slacks cinched by a brown belt so tightly, they're dimpling and missing one or two of the belt loops.

He's my special guest, by the way.

The whole reason for this affair.

Let's call this: *building a bridge I hope we needn't burn.*

"Hanson," I greet him, forcing my smile right back into place. "Welcome! We're happy you showed up!"

"You Evan?" he asks.

His voice is brusque, but not rude. "I'm Evan, yes. You got it right. I invited everyone on the street over for a little movie night thing!"

Gosh, I sound so fucking chipper.

"Movie night thing, huh?" The man grunts and eyes me skeptically. "Ain't been invited to one of these things before. Why now?"

I feel a pang of regret. Or guilt. Or something else. "I apologize that ... I hadn't invited you sooner. I'm sorry if you've felt excluded. In all honesty, I ... never really gave myself the chance to get to know you."

Hanson squints at me, working it over in his head.

"Please." I take a step back and gesture inside. "I'm happy you came. Relieved, even. Come in! Refreshments are in the kitchen and ..." I already forgot the thing I've been saying to all my guests. What else do I have? Is there a cake? Topless dancers? "... and make yourself at home, please."

Hanson grunts, then gives me a tentative nod, lifts his wrinkled chin, says, "Alright," then moves past me.

I guess it didn't matter my greeting at all, because the second he steps into my house, everyone's eyes fall on him, and the entire party drops to dead silence.

Only the soft, unintelligible murmur of the TV in the background—and whatever random channel it was left on—is heard weakly in the living room.

Hanson stops short right there, staring at everyone staring at him, overwhelmed.

It's the strangest social stalemate I've ever seen.

I come right up to his side and make a proper intro. "Hey, everyone! This is the fellow from down the street, Hanson. He's come for movie night!"

Dead silence.

Insert: I crap my pants.

Then, from the sea of silence comes a single lame response: "Hi."

It's from Xavier, surprisingly, who gives a little lazy wave. Stevie glares at Xavier, I guess holding a grudge from having the dick on his garage door laughed at.

To my—and perhaps everyone's—surprise, Raymond faces the man, his stare like two icy needles, and he nods once, rigidly. "Hello there, Hanson."

His greeting seems to unlock everyone else's, as if giving them permission, and suddenly there's a flood of "Hi!" and "Hey there!" and "Hello!" across the room.

Hanson doesn't seem to know what to do with any of it. He just stands there and stares back suspiciously at the room awhile.

Then, as if coming to life, he adopts a weirdly high-pitched, light sort of voice, and says, "Well, then. Good evening, gentlemen. What movie we watchin'?"

His greeting is met by a few more hellos and a wave of tentative smiles. Then Josiah quickly points out an actor's name in one of the movies he wants to watch, Marcellus sighs and mentions a scandalous thing he read about said actor in some blog article, and at once the party is revived in a storm of mad chatter. Hanson says a few more up-close hellos as he shuffles his way to the kitchen to help himself to some of the finger foods I've laid out, and everything pretty much returns to normal.

Until my phone buzzes in my pocket, nearly scaring the hot sauce out of me. My heart jumps—*Is it Dane?* I reach toward my pocket to pull it out and check.

"Still no leads?"

It's Raymond whose voice stops me halfway. I look up, startled, and put on an apologetic smile. "Dane's hard at work on it. He's ... We've ..." I'm aimlessly drawing squiggles in the air with my finger. I slap my hand down to my side. "He's getting close, I'm sure."

"It's only a matter of time before something worse happens. My patience is *thinning*." Raymond shakes his head disapprovingly. "I'd hate to see someone's cat's fur dyed pink and purple."

My smile wanes.

Raymond notices. "Perhaps that was an ill-fitting example. I wasn't referencing your adorable cat. Where is she, by the way? Ally? Is that her name?"

"Anne. As in Anne Boleyn, except *with* her head. And she's likely hiding in my bedroom." I give a wince. "She doesn't like my social gatherings."

Raymond gives a microscopic, eye-scrunching smile of endearment, then tilts his head quizzically. "What *is* Dane doing to find the vandal, exactly? I haven't seen him conducting any interviews."

"Well, he's got his own ... *quieter* ... way of working. His work consists of ..." I'm not sure Raymond would excuse our activities the other night, so I paraphrase a bit here. "... gathering evidence ... and managing a sort of ... process of elimination, you could call it."

"Ah, his 'list' ... right." He quirks an eyebrow. "Any more names knocked off of it?"

"Not really," I admit, "but ... I do know he's noting a few specific things. Like who hasn't been vandalized yet,

and where everyone is at the time of each vandalism ..."
I shrug. "Stuff that would obviously implicate someone,
or otherwise clear them."

"I see. Smart. Oh ..." Raymond's eyes light up as he
turns my way. "Are you saying ...?" He inclines his head
toward me, leaving the rest of his sentence unfinished.

I stare at him, unblinking, and not following. I twist
my head slowly. "Am ... I ... saying ...? What?"

The tiniest hint of annoyance crosses his face. He
lowers his voice. *"Are you saying this movie night is a secret
ruse? Part of your and Dane's plan to catch the culprit?"*

I may never know exactly what crosses my mind the
moment he asks the question. I experience a wave of
worry. Then I think for a split second about Dane and
what he may be wearing tonight—*if anything at all.* Then
I think on if I should really be an interior designer.

Then my lips part and out comes: "Not at all."

Raymond quirks an eyebrow. "No?"

"Nope," I state more assertively.

After a moment of suspicion, Raymond shrugs and
speaks normally again. "I'm just assuming everything is
part of some *plan.* Sometimes, I wonder if I'm capable of
relaxing. For that matter, why did you invite Xavier?"

My phone buzzes again in my pocket.

I glance down and wonder if it's Dane trying to get
ahold of me for something urgent.

I've been waiting for this for days, and he picks now *...??*

"Oh, I don't know," comes Xavier's voice instead of mine, startling both me and Raymond. "Maybe because I live on this street? Y'know, like *you* do?"

Raymond slow-turns to the new guy, his eyes wide with insult.

The three of us are in my foyer in full view of the living room, and with just those few words exchanged, the whole house has drawn quiet again.

If Xavier was looking for a confrontation, he just got one, complete with an audience of half the cul-de-sac.

"Indeed, you do," replies Raymond coolly.

Xavier, ever so unafraid of the head bitch of Figaro Lane, takes a challenging step toward him. "And I'd like you to know—personally, man to man—that I think the letter you sent me about my hedges is complete bullshit."

Jaws drop. Hands are drawn to chests.

Raymond only purses his lips. "Everyone in this very room signed the same agreement as you when they moved into this *prestigious* neighborhood. I wonder what makes you feel you're somehow exempt from the same rules that all of us—including myself—must abide by?"

"You used the wrong P word." Xavier gets right up in Raymond's face—Raymond, who doesn't so much as blink or flinch. "Your *pretentious-as-fuck* neighborhood."

No one draws a single breath.

Even Hanson is watching this exchange with wide, scandalized eyes. All he's missing is a bag of popcorn.

Without a single change in his face, Raymond replies in a tone so genial, you might call it polite. "I'm afraid those are *three* words. Pretentious." He tilts his head. "As." He tilts it even more. "*Fuck.*"

Stevie from the living room chortles at that, perhaps proud of Xavier being humiliated in front of everyone.

Xavier rolls his eyes, then glances my way. "Is this really what you have to put up with, Evan? You actually take this shit from this polo-wearing fuck-wad?"

I feel a lot of attention turn my way really fast. All eyes turn my way—except Raymond's, which continue to slow-burn Xavier without a care for anything else.

I realize my response here is the difference between earning Raymond's respect, or earning his ire. And if I've learned anything about living on Figaro Lane, it's that you do *not* want to be on the receiving end of his ire.

On the other hand, Xavier has a point.

Raymond has hated the poor guy since the day he moved here. He's sent him copious letters for no reason other than to annoy and antagonize. No one knows why.

Well, other than for the obvious reason that Xavier isn't like Raymond in any way, shape, or form. Unlike any of us, Xavier doesn't play the game. To make it even worse, he avidly rebels against it, mocking the whole pretension of the game to its leader's face.

And now Xavier, all on his own, friendless, no one on his side, looks to me for support.

In a sea full of Raymond's guppy followers.

In a sea full of polo-wearing lemmings.

In a sea full of preening birds.

And now we find out what I'm made of.

"I'm sorry, Xavier," I finally say, "but ... Raymond's my friend, and I think ... I think you're out of line."

I'm made of wimpy, lemming, guppy shit.

That's what I'm made of.

My words don't hurt Xavier. He's like a sheet of iron against these machine guns of judgment blasting off in this room, audible only to those of us who care.

Me. Raymond.

And the whole rest of the damned room.

But not Xavier. He's impervious. And to my words, he just rolls his eyes, flips us all the bird, then saunters to the door with a, "Fuck this noise," and sees himself out.

The door does not shut gently.

Raymond turns to me, lips pursed, fussing with the front of his hair like he's afraid the confrontation disturbed a few unruly strands in the front. "I rest my case on *that* unfortunate fellow. I think I'm due for a bath." He puts on a fake frown. "I have to go, darling. I do appreciate you inviting me, and I hope you all enjoy your movie. Perhaps next time I'll stay."

"Don't leave just because of that *weirdo*," Stevie calls out from the living room. "We haven't even picked a movie yet!"

"So very sorry, my darlings," he goes on, facing the room now, "but I really must. I really only planned on stopping in, anyway. I have too much work to do for the Valentine's Gala still, anyway, and so little time." He gives the room a flattering view of his face, a lightly blown kiss, then turns to make his leave only moments after Xavier made his.

The door shuts gently after his departure.

It isn't long before the room is full of conversation, but with the departure of both Xavier and Raymond, the tone is notably more *gossipy*.

Ten minutes of half-assed socializing later, I retreat to the dining room and pull out my phone. It reads:

> **DANE**
>
> how's movie night?

I gape. *How'd he know?* Then I smirk, remember who the hell he is, drop my ass into the chair at the head of the table right by a front-facing window, and type away.

> **EVAN**
>
> Giving in to the possibility that we may not watch one.

A moment passes in which I glance out the window, curious if Dane is in his truck out there somewhere. A big smile crosses my face, thinking of him. I hadn't realized how badly I wanted this text until just now. I'm downright giddy.

Then my phone buzzes.

DANE

u girls can't choose a damn movie or what?

I snort privately, then gnash my thumbs.

EVAN

You should have witnessed the scene Xavier and Ray-Ray just caused. O. M. G. Poor guy got sassed and lost his shit.

Right then, my front door bursts open and in pours an out-of-breath, hair-tousled Raymond with a dramatic shriek that stops time itself.

"The vandal!" Raymond cries out. "He got me! He got my garden!—my precious fucking garden!"

Chapter 14.
Dane isn't exactly a hero, but ...

I frown at my laptop, which sits on the coffee table in front of me.

Why'd Raymond go running back to Evan's?

I check the other feeds quickly, but they don't reveal anything except a light on in Xavier's front room, and a cat sitting on top of Stevie's car staring at the big dick on the garage door, likely pontificating the intricacies and nuance of human communication. The sprawling front of Raymond's mansion reveals nothing either.

I glance at my phone where I sent a text asking what this "scene" was all about—figuring it might be pertinent to my investigation—but haven't gotten a reply.

My pad full of notes lying next to my laptop stares me tauntingly in the face. At the top, I have three names circled. I bite my lip, staring and staring at them.

Activity on the screen catches my eye, and at once, I watch everyone pour out of Evan's house and, with Raymond at the lead, head down the street to his mansion. As they march along, I find myself confused as to what's going on. Are they relocating the party?

I take another look at my phone. Still no text. *What the fuck's going on?*

I slap shut my laptop, tuck it under an arm, then swipe my keys off the counter. After flicking off a light and mashing a button on the TV remote, my cabin's dark with only light from the moon shining in through the big back window as I head out the door.

As I'm on the open road, wind slamming past my rolled-down windows, my phone buzzes in the passenger seat. Since it's connected to my truck via Bluetooth, I just tap my display screen and let the digital butler read the text to me:

"*From: Evan Cupcake,*" it recites in its soft male voice. "*The message reads: OMG. ARE YOU PARKED DOWN THE STREET? THE VANDAL STRUCK AGAIN. THIS TIME IT WAS RAYMOND'S GARDEN.*" *Beep.* "*Would you like to reply?*" Ding-ding.

Raymond's garden? I didn't see a damned thing on any of my feeds. "Reply." *Ding-ding.* "Stay put, cupcake. I'm on my way. Be there in thirty."

Beep. "*Message has been sent.*"

I get pedal-happy, gunning it down the road until I reach the highway, on which I recklessly zoom ahead of the slowpokes (i.e. people actually going the speed limit). After exiting half an hour later and tearing down Royal

Avenue, I pull into his neighborhood at last, turn onto his street, then park at the curb by his house.

After hopping out of my truck in a hurry, I do a quick look-over of the area, scoping for anything out-of-place as I head down the sidewalk to the end of the cul-de-sac where Raymond's house sits like a fat, brick bird's nest. Nothing catches my eye at first.

Until I spot Xavier on his front doorstep across the street watching me, arms folded.

I stop short, squinting across the way. I remember him as the guy who laughed at Stevie's garage door dick. He never struck me as someone who actually lives on this street, but rather as some dude's rebellious punk nephew who's here visiting, plays his stereo too loud, and refuses to do his chores.

I shoot him a chin-nod of acknowledgement.

Xavier does nothing but stand there and stare at me like a crow on a branch.

I'll file that away in a mental note cabinet for now.

When I arrive at Raymond's, I notice chatter coming from the side gate, left open. I follow my ears by the side of the house, passing a double glass door to the covered patio, which wraps around to the back. The ground turns into smoothed marble stone as I walk, which circles an enormous pool. On the other side of it rests a long stretch of a garden that ends at a greenhouse. It's right outside the greenhouse that everyone's gathered.

Not a head turns my way, everyone so engrossed in whatever it is they're freaking out about that they don't even notice my approaching.

Thankfully, they don't have to. I spot Evan standing apart from them all, some paces away, as if uninvolved. He's got one arm tucked under the other as his free hand holds his phone, into which all his attention is poured.

Is he waiting for me to text him that I'm here?

I stop a few paces behind him, forgetting all about the trouble at hand, and just thinking to myself how sexy he looks tonight. I don't think I've seen him wear those specific pants before, which fit him *so* invitingly. I have half a mind to walk right up behind him and give that ass of his a surprise squeeze.

But that's just my libido talking.

The mature, civilized part of me walks up to him like a gentleman and says, "Hey."

Evan turns, startled. Relief splashes over his face at the sight of me. "Dane, thank fuck you're here. It had to have happened while we were all at the party. Raymond had his garden—"

"You look good."

The words stop him short. Evan seems to remember himself suddenly, as if having forgotten how we left things. "Um ... thanks." He swallows, then gestures at me. "You, too ... a lot."

"Me, too, a lot?" *He's so fucking cute.*

Evan rolls his eyes. "You caught me off-guard, okay? I was trying to tell you what happened."

"Go on."

"Someone broke into his greenhouse and snipped all the heads off his roses, then arranged them on the floor to spell out two words."

"What two words?"

"The first one was HOA. The second was ... a four-letter C word."

"What's so bad about HOA *cock*?" I tease.

Evan narrows his eyes. "You know damn well that's *not* the four-letter C word I'm talking about."

I let on half a smile of amusement, then glance at the fences to Raymond's backyard, thinking it over. Each of them is made of stone, and fairly tall, maybe seven feet.

"Where've you been these past couple of days?"

I return my gaze to Evan. "Home."

"Home? You've ..." A look of disappointment falls over his face. "You haven't been watching over the street from your truck? Or—?"

"Of course I've kept watch. I set up surveillance—a few cams. It feeds to my laptop. I just didn't think it was necessary to camp out in my truck, so I took my work home and have been keeping an eye out from there."

"Oh." Evan's brows pull together, and he lowers his voice. "*Is that ... legal? Setting up surveillance like that?*"

"You want to find this vandal or not?"

Evan draws a zipper over his mouth and throws away the key.

Now I'm thinking of kinky shit.

Evan with a gag in his mouth. Evan in leather. Evan tied facedown to a bed while I lay my body over his, my dick hard and sliding right between his cheeks, slippery and throbbing and ready.

The sound of his muffled moans of pleasure when I finally enter him after hours of foreplay and teasing and driving one another crazy.

The sweat that forms over our bodies, turning our skin and muscles glossy as we make love.

"Where exactly *is* your home?" he asks.

I smirk. "Remember that bar I had you meet me at? You were about a stone's throw away from my place."

"Really?" he blurts. "You live in that tiny middle-of-nowhere lake town?"

"It isn't *that* tiny," I argue. "It's got its charm."

"Charm." Evan mulls it over, nodding slowly as he glances away, as if to check on the others. Only one or two heads have turned our way, the rest too wrapped up in their scandalized banter. Though, if my ears aren't deceiving me, a cluster of them aren't even talking about the scandal anymore, having moved on to discuss some mysterious new guy at their local gym.

I give Evan's hand a tug. "You alright?"

He glances down at our hands and doesn't pull away.

I notice.

"So ... did you ... see anything?" he asks, lifting his gaze to mine. In a whisper, he adds, "*On your cameras.*"

My thumb gently rubs over the top of his soft hand. "Last thing I saw was your party squirting out of your house and racing across the lawn like *Braveheart.*"

"You didn't see anyone approaching Raymond's?"

I shake my head. "Nope."

He sighs with frustration. "Really? No one at all? Even with the—" He whispers again. "—*the cameras?*"

"Not a peep of anything, which tells me one of two things." I lean in close to him. "Either the culprit hopped over one of these fences, or he was inside Raymond's house already."

Evan takes a glance at one of the walls himself, then returns his dubious gaze to mine. "You actually think someone climbed one of these big stone fuckers?"

"No other explanation."

I'm still holding his hand, my thumb still soothingly rubbing across it.

How can such a simple act make my heart drum as excitedly as some dumb teenager discovering his crush for the first time?

"Do you wanna get outta here?" I ask him suddenly.

Evan lifts his eyebrows. "What?"

"Let's take you away from all this drama, all this ... homo this, glitter that, pink mailbox crap."

Evan's eyes narrow, that defensive look creasing his face at once.

Then something beautiful happens, like a light that flicks on in his eyes, and suddenly the world is full of magnificent possibilities. He faces me. "Where would we go?"

"To my tiny nothing lake town," I tell him.

His lips part, but he says nothing, staring at me with this curious, mystified expression.

"It's called Brady, by the way. The lake town."

"I know." Evan glances down at my hand, finding it really fascinating for a second. "You went and moved all the way out there after college?"

"It's more of a recent thing," I clarify. "After I left the force. Went there a few times on some investigative work, and the place kind of grew on me. I got a cabin near the water."

Evan's eyes snap to mine. "A cabin?"

"Yep. Think it over. You work half-days Saturdays, so I could pick you up after work, take you out to Brady, and we could spend the night and Sunday there. Think of it like a little mental getaway. I'll take you out for a little dinner, show you the town, and—"

"Done," states Evan with a smile.

Chapter 15.
Evan takes an adventure with the ex.

On Saturday afternoon, after I leave the salon in the capable hands of Gary and the others, I drive home with a smile on my face and a heart that races both with excitement and fear.

I trust Dane. I really do. I'll be in good hands when I'm with him. But I'm also scared of what might happen during this getaway with Dane.

What if I really, truly fall in love with him again?

Is that a good idea at this point in my life, when I've got everything going for me, and my career is exploding with business at the salon, and I've got this nice house in a wealthy part of the city?

All Dane had to say was "cabin on the lake" and my figurative legs were spread in a hurry for him to have his way with me.

So predictable. *And pathetic.*

Here I am, packing a small overnight bag, ready to risk it all.

Somehow, I can't make myself say the words: *Dane Cooper is worth risking it all. Dane Cooper is worth making a fool out of yourself for. Dane Cooper ...*

Dane Cooper came back into my life for a reason.

And maybe this is it.

When I hear the loud, throaty rumble of an engine, I quirk an eyebrow at my bay window. Ditching my bag, I cross my room and take a peek outside.

My stomach drops.

No fucking way.

And five minutes later: "There is *no* fucking way I'm getting on the back of that."

Dane Cooper straddles the seat of a motorcycle.

A sleek, smooth, metal sex-bomb of a bike.

"Yeah you are," he growls, then revs the engine with two quick twists of his wrist.

I let out one bark of disbelieving laughter, then take a glance to the left and right at all the houses of my neighbors in view. I am absolutely certain that no less than twenty of them are at their windows right now watching this spectacle.

Dane extends a helmet to me. "C'mon, cupcake. Or are you afraid you might *sprain an ankle* climbing on?"

His taunt does the trick. I straighten right up, lift my chin, and tug my bag over a shoulder with gusto. "Punk, I'm not afraid of *anything*."

With that, I grab the helmet and slap it right on.

Dane, with a smile he's trying to hide, reaches out and fastens the helmet to my head with the strap and buckle under my chin.

I frown at him as he does it. "I was getting to that."

He finishes, then slaps the side of my helmeted head. "Get on up, then."

After a moment of uncertainty that I'm trying not to show, I mightily swing a leg over the seat. Never having been on a motorcycle, it takes a moment of shifting to get myself comfortable.

"There's no bitch bar, so you're gonna have to hang on to me," he orders.

Mmm, the way he says *"bitch bar"* ...

Do I have to make everything so sexual lately?

I throw my hands around to his front, locking them like a second belt around his waist. He's in his sleeveless denim jacket—the same sexy one he was wearing the night I met him at the bar—and his muscled, tatted arms are gloriously exposed and flexed.

"Your house locked up? Got all you need?"

My head rests against his broad, strong back. It isn't lost on me that my crotch is digging into his backside. "Now I do," I answer.

I don't need to see his face to know he smiles at that.

Then his engine rips a big wide hole in the space-time continuum as the bike rears around, and off we soar, blasting down the street.

Okay, we're not going that fast yet, but when you've never ridden a motorcycle before, any speed at first is pretty much fast as fuck.

Also, with your legs wide and straddling the bike, your skinny jeans tightly clenching your cock and balls, and your ass kinda spread by your legs, your experience of riding becomes an unplanned lesson in ball vibration, cock overstimulation, and ass awakening.

Think of it like a surprise sex toy that's stuck on one goddamned setting: max.

And you can't get away from it.

And you kinda don't want to.

"You always wanted one of these," I call out to him when we stop at the exit to my neighborhood, waiting for traffic on the cross street to pass.

Dane chuckles, then looks over his shoulder. "Yep. Saved up my money for a while. It was the first thing I got myself when I quit the force. And yeah, you bet your ass I rode one as a cop. When I want something, *I get it.*"

Something about riding a bike makes you feel brave. With my arms locked around his waist, I reach a hand to cup his crotch firmly. "Me too," I growl back.

"Careful there," he warns me. "You might inspire a whole new idea for gettin' road head."

The moment he takes off again, I let go of his crotch, losing both my grip and my nerve, then lock my hands around his waist and hang on, heart racing.

Just before we hit the highway, Dane turns his head and goes, "Ready for this, cupcake?"

"Stop calling me that!" I shout back.

He twists the throttle, and we take off ripping the road so fast, I literally shriek out in excitement. Up the onramp we go, and it isn't long before I'm certain we are going three times over the speed limit.

Of course we aren't, but perception is everything.

And there is something downright magical about the moment Dane and I are sharing right now. This is the very last thing I expected to find myself doing on a lazy Saturday afternoon. I was fairly certain the trip to this little lake town of Dane's was going to be a leisurely one in his truck with the windows down, radio blasting, and wind cutting through my hair.

Instead, Dane has me riding down the highway on the back of a motorcycle at the speed of light. My heart is racing so fast, I can't stop smiling. I don't even notice the crazy vibrations between my legs anymore. They've become something second nature. I'm not even focused on the fact that I'm gripping the waist of the hottest man in the world right now.

All I know is the thrill surging in my heart like the brightest, bravest, boldest storm crashing waves against beach rock, like thunder ripping across a brilliantly blue and flashing sky.

I feel absolutely fucking invincible.

Out here on the open road, no judgmental looks from Raymond even exist. I don't give a shit whose name I'm wearing or who's looking. It doesn't matter if a vandal paints my whole house in unicorn poop.

Out here, I'm fucking alive.

"I'm fucking alive!!" I scream into the wind.

I feel Dane laugh against me, then he lets out a howl.

In theory, it should have taken us fifty-three minutes to get to Brady. But it feels like less than twenty before he takes an exit off the highway, and we gently slow down as he turns us onto a side street off the feeder.

Slower now, we go down a long road lined with tall thickets of trees. The sun sneaks peeks at us through the legion of crisscrossing branches, its light filling the sky with a deep-orange, golden glow.

The air out here feels strangely cool. I close my eyes, lay my head against Dane's broad, denim backside, and breathe it in. I smell the fresh, crisp, young oxygen of the woods—as well as Dane. Nothing compares to his very specific scent.

Maybe that's the thing I should have noticed first, but didn't have the chance to. When we met at that bar, reconnecting after five years, I was robbed of the chance to remember his smell, what with the air being so thick with smoke and alcohol and other sweaty bodies.

Dane has this scent that takes me home, no matter where I am. We spent so much time around each other back in the day, I grew absolutely accustomed to him. Maybe even neurotically so. I wouldn't be surprised if, like Pavlov's gay dog, I became conditioned to feeling totally at ease whenever I was around Dane Cooper.

There's something Dane doesn't know.

About the breakup.

I sat in that apartment for hours and hours and hours after he left. I was even beyond crying. I felt dead. Worn to the bone. Confused. I was full of these doubts that kept playing our argument over and over in my head. One minute, I was certain that I'd overreacted. The next minute, I was certain I hadn't, and knew Dane deserved every last ugly word he got from me that night.

Then I went to the closet to get myself a sweater, because it was unseasonably cold for Texas that year, and I felt strangely shivery.

And I saw the two remains of his favorite shirt that I had torn in half. They were on the ground like two grey pools of soft fabric, just lying there like nothing at all.

I must've stared at them for ages.

Then I crouched down, picked them up, and buried my face into them. I didn't cry, I was all out of tears. All I did was keep them in my face.

And I breathed.

In, then out.

Two hours later—and yes, it was nearing sunrise at this point—I sat at Dane's desk in the corner of the room by the window that overlooked the street, and I had my only needle and thread out, and with a color that totally didn't match the shirt, I slowly started to sew the halves of the shirt back together.

I didn't like seeing two halves torn apart.

Especially when those two halves belonged together, and there was no other half of a shirt—none in the whole lonely world—that would belong to the other.

I didn't finish the job. My eyes grew heavy when the light of morning started to touch the sky, and in that chair with a needle in one hand and my Frankenstein's Monster of a shirt bunched up in the other, unfinished, I fell straight asleep.

Dane doesn't know that.

He thinks I threw the shirt away.

And even crazier: I still have that unfinished sewing project in a closet somewhere in my house.

I wonder why I'm thinking of that just now.

"Almost there," Dane tells me.

I squeeze him a bit tighter as we take a sharp turn, and then we're riding down a quaint street of some out-in-the-sticks town lined with little storefronts. Despite the apparently small size, there seem to be a lot of people walking around, maybe because it's a Saturday.

"How about a bite to eat before we hit up my place?"

I'm already smiling, looking at all the people. "Sure," I answer, inspired to just go with the flow.

Dane parks his motorcycle in the parking lot of a sweet little diner, its metal roof positively blinding from the angle of the late afternoon sun.

I let go of Dane, ending the longest back-hug ever.

Dane leads the way onto the long wooden porch of the diner, and I follow clutching my shoulder bag. There hangs two porch swings on which a couple old ladies are sitting. He seems to know them as he gives them each a nod, and the nod is returned with a pause in their little conversation and two knowing smiles.

"After you," he says like a gentleman, holding open the door to the diner.

Inside, it's a blast of home-cooking aroma, wooden tables and chairs everywhere, and soft country music. After him meeting me at that bar before, I didn't expect to be taken somewhere so family-friendly.

We get a booth by the window. Our server, a sweet girl who can't be older than twenty, takes our order and is off to the kitchens cheerily, stopping by two other tables to make sure things are alright, but also to ask some Loretta about her baby, and Georgina about that leak in her roof, and a Paul about his missing dog.

"Goodness, this place has a vibe," I mutter.

"It's kind of infectious," admits Dane, then taps on the window. "That place look familiar?"

I peer through the glass and stare dubiously at the bar across the street. "Looks different in the sunlight."

"You owe me a game of pool," he reminds me.

I catch myself smiling, then shake my head. "I have to admit, this place *does* have a pretty welcoming feel. I mean, I wouldn't have been caught dead saying that a few weeks ago at that bar across the street, but maybe that was on account of my mood and ... purpose."

"Purpose," echoes Dane, staring at me.

I look at him, then web my fingers together on the table in front of me. "It's funny what life does to us, isn't it? There has to be a reason for all of this. It can't just be blind chance that we're in each other's lives again."

"Maybe. Maybe not. All I know is ..." He puts up his elbows on the table, leaning forward, then recites: "It's highly probable that something highly unprobable will happen to each of us in our lives."

"I don't believe 'unprobable' is a word."

"Well, the fellow who told me that profound little gold nugget didn't speak English as his first language," Dane points out, "and I prefer to keep the saying exactly the way he told me, untouched, uncorrected—pure."

"It's 'improbable'," I say anyway, being snarky.

"Hey, don't sass me or the old wise man's saying."

"I'll sass you however, wherever, whenever I want."

"Is that so?"

"Oh yeah," I growl, smirking playfully. "That's so."

Dane bats at my feet with his own under the table. I kick back a bit, then it grows more playfully aggressive

162

as we leg-wrestle. After a few labored efforts and one timely kick that sends our whole table rattling, suddenly we've stopped at once, laughing, our legs in a pretzel.

Our food is brought out: a fat, juicy, loaded burger with a large side of home-cut fries for each of us.

"I haven't eaten a burger in *ages*," I confess.

"Sorry this isn't a filet mignon with a glass of wine, but this is the good stuff that feeds your fucking *soul*," he growls at me as he lifts his burger up to his face, then takes the biggest juice-dripping bite out of it. His eyes rock back as a deep groan issues from the cavern of his throat as he chews and chews.

Just watching him is gift enough.

He stops chewing and stares at me, just his eyes visible over that mountain of a burger. "Go ahead," he grunts, his words muffled. "Sink your teeth in."

I pick up my huge burger, then stare it down like a conquest. It's an effort just to hold it with two hands. Already, I feel grease dripping down my wrist.

"Gonna be honest," I blurt. "I'm ... slightly scared."

"Dive in before it runs away from you."

"The grease is already doing a good job of that."

I chomp down on my burger. *Holy fuck.* Flavor bursts across my tongue in droves. At once, my desire to eat turns into slow motion, and it's my eyes that rock back as I savor and relish in every little bit of magic happening in my mouth right now.

"Holy ... *fuck*," I moan through my mouthful.

Dane's already halfway through his burger. He takes a few fries and shoves them into his mouth, then shakes his head and masks a laugh. "It's something else, isn't it? You're ruined for life, now."

"RUINED!" I practically sing, then go for another bite before I've finished the first. I'm in fucking heaven.

I honestly wonder if I could eat two more of them by the time I take the last, juicy bite.

"You've set me back on my carb count about six or seven months with just that one meal," I tell him awhile later when we're finished and our plates are clean, save for a few fries and a stray pickle slice.

Dane shrugs. "Worth it."

"Hey, what's that?" My ears perk up and I turn my head in search of it. I listen carefully.

"What's—?"

"Shh!"

Then I start to hum along, and it's just a few seconds more of the melody before I realize they're playing it.

"Is this—?" Dane starts.

"That one country band that came to our campus. Remember?" A few lyrics of the song go by as our eyes lock across the table. "It was a totally spontaneous thing. We scored tickets last minute and went, and somehow, against all odds, we got put in the front row. We hadn't heard a single song of theirs until that night."

Dane nods slowly, a faint reminiscing smile creeping on his face as he stares at me. "So what? You gonna get up and dance or something?"

I snort. "In front of all these people?"

"Thought so." He sneers tauntingly. "Chicken."

I'm out of my chair the next instant. "Get up."

Now it's Dane who looks startled. "Uh, what?"

"Chicken? Get up!" I order him.

"What? No," he says at once when he realizes what I'm trying to do. "I was kidding. We aren't gonna—"

"Yeah, we are. In front of everyone. Now get up!"

"Nope."

I grab his hand, then yank him right out of his seat. He's helpless to resist as I pull him across the restaurant between tables and past all the other booths. We end up right smack in the middle of the restaurant under the big TV—an open spot with no tables.

It probably serves the purpose of facilitating traffic, this little spot. But right now, in this moment, the only purpose it serves is as our dance floor.

"You remember the dance?" I ask. "Everyone in the audience started doing it during this song."

Dane stares at his feet as if expecting them to move themselves. Then he glances at mine, clueless. "Uh ..."

"Follow my lead." I get in front of him and, from the best of my memory, start the line dance by moving right with the beat four counts, then left.

Dane trips when I change direction, and suddenly his hands slap onto my waist to keep himself steady.

I smile. "Good. Follow my lead."

"I remember the damned dance. I can do this."

"Can you? Don't get saucy. Just follow my lead."

"Easier said," he grunts. Then he starts to move, his hands on my waist for a guide.

It's like we're on the bike again, except standing, and this time, I'm the one driving.

"Back four counts," I guide him over my shoulder. "Forward four. Kick your boot this way, that way, hop, turn, and *repeat* ..."

He struggles to keep up, staring at his feet the whole time.

It's cute, really, watching him try. I kinda expected him to be better than this.

"C'mon, you remember the steps," I coax him.

He's so damned focused on getting the steps right, he doesn't even hear me. He trips whenever the direction changes, and once kicks me on accident with a muttered, "*Fuck, shit,*" under his breath.

People are watching us with smiles (or confused and squinty-eyed looks) on their faces, several of whom have stopped eating entirely to pay witness to this (hopefully) adorable display of two men trying to dance.

Well, one of us at least. I'm a total natural.

"Look into my eyes," I tell him.

Dane scoffs at that. "If I look at you, I'm gonna step all over your feet. This is hard enough as it is and I'm staring *right* at what I'm doing."

"I said look into my eyes."

He obliges with a frustrated huff, looking up at me. His face is slightly flushed, I'm guessing from all of the attention and clumsiness, but his eyes are full of desire and determination.

It's like he wants to commit to this to impress me.

Something about his expression, his commitment in this moment, his spirit ... it steals every bit of me away.

My breath.

My sense.

My soul.

"Five, six, seven, eight ..." I count.

And then, eyes locked, we do the moves in sync.

He doesn't once look down at his feet as we go right, then left, then back ... on and on, the line dance never ends, its life spent only when the song is.

Just like that, he gets the gist.

Like his body remembers it, even if he can't.

"Well, look at you," I tease him, and he just gives me a smirk and one cute, brusque laugh.

Suddenly, someone else is out of their chair—an old woman who came with her friend—and she's doing the dance along with us. A man and his wife nearby rise from their booth, the woman letting out a light spray of laughter, and they're joining us too. Next, a couple kids. Then the old woman's friend, who gets all the steps wrong, but laughs as she does it anyway.

And Dane looks into my eyes, his lids heavy with something that transcends anything he's said to me in the past few weeks.

In this moment, he looks like the sweet-hearted guy who invited lost, bewildered me to sit next to him in a psych class so many years ago.

I remember that moment like it just happened.

I *feel* that moment in my bones.

Under all those tats and muscles of his, Dane Cooper is just a boy who, like all of us, is desperately looking to belong somewhere in this confusing, sometimes harsh, and oftentimes unexpectedly beautiful world.

I see that boy right now in this moment.

His eyes are pouring into mine, and deep in them, somewhere, he looks thankful that I'm here right next to him, sharing this makeshift dance floor, thankful that I exist, thankful that I'm his ...

Thankful that in a world of highly *unprobable* things that could happen, we broke the odds and—*unprobably*—came into each other's lives again.

Chapter 16.
Dane considers love at second sight.

Strolling down Main Street holding hands with my Evan under the setting sun feels so surreal, I'm not even sure I can quantify it with any amount of words.

So instead, I'll try to quantify it with moments:

Evan pointing up at the sign of a store with this look on his face that made his eyes twinkle like stars, his lips slightly parted and curled up and kissable.

Evan trying on a hat in a thrift store across the street from the diner, batting his eyelashes at me and making some comment about *"country couture"*.

Evan resting his head on my shoulder when we sat at a bench, and our after-dinner ice creams were eaten down to the cones, which we each were still holding.

Evan on the swing set of the playground, kicking his feet up to get as much height as he could, and that one swing that made his eyes flash with surprise when he got so high, it looked like his heart leapt out of his throat.

"Ready to see where I live?" I ask him.

We're back at the parking lot of the diner after a lap of the town, my bike patiently awaiting us. Evan bites his lip, positively giddy, then gives me an eager nod.

My bike roars to life, then takes us down Main Street, away from town, and down a dark road through the woods.

I feel Evan hugging me tighter from behind.

His embrace makes me smile despite myself.

I turn down my street, up my driveway, and then come to a stop right next to my truck. My modest little lakeside cabin sits waiting for papa to come home, but maybe didn't expect him to bring a visitor.

"I'll give you the tour," I tell him, hopping off my bike and taking his helmet. "It won't last long."

"Wow, it's dark out here," he murmurs from behind as we head toward the porch.

"Pretty amazing how dark it gets when you're away from the blinding city and suburb lights, huh?" I push open the front door, then gesture inside. "After you."

Thankfully, I had cleaned up the place considerably before leaving to scoop him up from his house. I wanted him to see all my best sides tonight, from my cleanliness to my thoughtfulness to even the way I got his favorite snacks and put them in a bowl.

"You got my favorite snacks *and put them in a bowl!*" he exclaims when he discovers it on the coffee table.

I smirk, following him in. "Of course I did."

"You didn't have to do that." He looks up and his eyes catch the view through the big back window. "Oh, wow. You can see the lake from here."

"I'll show it to you after the tour," I tell him.

The tour, as promised, isn't very long. I take Evan into my bedroom, which has a wall of windows that face the lake in the back, and a king-size bed, on which Evan tosses his overnight shoulder bag. "Hey, who says you're sleeping in here?" I taunt him. "I've got a nice, cozy little doghouse out in the back for you." Evan just throws me a look as he walks around my room, inspecting things and humming that country tune from the diner. Next, I take him into my bathroom, which is a modest size, not too big, but has a decently-sized bathtub and shower. "I am bathing in *that* tonight," Evan announces, inspiring a chuckle from me—and a score of dirty thoughts. Then we pass back into the main room, the other side of which opens to a kitchen and dining area, which is a semicircle windowed inset, giving something of a panoramic view of the woods and, if you squint, the road.

"Wow, we're having breakfast in the morning right here at this table," Evan decides, continuing to make all our plans for his whole stay here.

I shrug. "I rarely use that table. Usually I take my breakfast to the couch where I do most of my work."

"Do you have your laptop with you?" he asks at once with a start. "The one with all the camera feeds?"

"We're not looking at the camera feeds tonight."

"Why not?"

"Because the whole point of this is to get you *away* from all that crap. Come here." I grab hold of Evan and pull him into a tight embrace, crushing his face into my chest. "This is *our* special fuck-off weekend. Alright?"

"*Got it*," he mumbles, his words squished.

"What was that?" I tease him. "Couldn't hear you."

"*Because your big man-boobs are suffocating me.*"

I squeeze him tighter. "Still can't hear you."

Then he grabs me aggressively in some sad attempt at a tackle, and squirms to break free from my grip. I let out a laugh as I pretend to lose to him, just like way back when we play-wrestled in our old apartment.

Suddenly, I feel my grip on him *actually* breaking, and with a quick twist of his body—and a deep grumble from mine—Evan tackles me straight to the ground.

"You *have* been working out," I blurt out, grunting as I struggle to regain control.

Evan's atop me, straddling my waist and fighting to pin my wrists. "You look sexy when you're losing."

"You look sexy when you're trying feebly to beat me," I retort with a smirk.

"Nothing '*feeble*' about this. Especially when I *have* beaten you."

"Oh yeah, big boy? You think you won?"

"I *know* I have."

The next instant, a surge of strength fills me, and in one breathless maneuver, I flip him right off of me—he yells out something unintelligible in surprise—and then I'm atop of him just as fast. I look like I weigh twice as much as he does in muscle alone, so the poor guy isn't going anywhere. My thick, toned thighs hold him right in place like a vice grip.

I pin his hands easily to the floor, but I do so with an ease and a gentleness, staring down at his helpless form.

All the aggression comes from *him* now as he fights and struggles and grunts. He tries—*feebly*—to break free from my hold for exactly ten exhausting seconds before giving up in a fit of heavy, labored panting.

He stares up at me now with half-lidded, defeated eyes. And I stare right back down at him ...

Down at my beautiful ex-boyfriend Evan.

He is so sexy right now, in the way that he's all mine to do whatever I want with. We have always had this pseudo-dominant-submissive energy between us when we get all hot for each other. He fights to prove himself to me. I let him for a bit, amusing myself, then take back control at once, putting him in his place. And he looks up at me from the floor with that defeated part scowl, part knowing smirk, and we both know we're exactly where we want to be: me in control, him at my mercy.

Whether the cocky, cute little bastard ever admits it or not. This is the way he likes it—*and I know it.*

Taken by an impulse, I bring my face down and put a thick, tight kiss on those lips—those soft lips that just looked like they were waiting for me.

And they were. Evan receives the kiss with an eager force, kissing me right back, even while I still keep his wrists pinned to the ground. They might as well be bolted there with metal plates for as heavy and certain as my grip is.

"*Oh, Dane ...*" he breathes after I end the kiss.

A breathy chuckle comes out from me, and then I let up on him, getting off the floor. He looks up as I extend a hand down to him to help him to his feet.

After a moment of him staring at me challengingly, he finally takes my hand. Then he's up too fast and falls against me. I look down at his face, feeling his firm, slender body against my own.

Something comes over his face.

Something comes over mine.

Then we kiss again. Then we kiss even harder. And without warning, he's peeling off my shirt. I peel off his, and when we hear a seam rip, neither of us pay it mind. We start moving as we kiss and fumble to get every bit of our clothes off. Buttons clank against themselves as our pants work their way to our ankles, then kicked away with our shoes, rendering us both naked.

Flesh against flesh, Evan's hand comes down to my cock and grips it tightly.

I moan from his touch, then kiss him more fiercely as he starts to stroke me.

It's an on-switch that makes every part of my brain focus on one goal, and one goal only: *put it inside him.*

And now.

My hands slide down this toned, taut new body of my ex-boyfriend, desperate to feel every inch of his skin, and more desperate to enter him. I find my greedy palms cupping his ass like it's mine, pulling so hard I've spread the cheeks apart, hungry and forceful.

"*What is it with us,*" pants Evan, "*not ever making it ... to the bedroom ... before we ...?*"

I growl as I kiss him, then pull away. "Good point."

Then, like a fucking caveman, I throw Evan over my shoulder and march to the bedroom. I give his bare ass one tight spank, making him yell out, "Hey!" before I dump him onto my big soft bed.

He doesn't even have time to breathe before I crawl over him, my hungry eyes bearing down upon him.

Evan stares up at me excitedly.

"It was grabbing your dick that did it, huh," he then concludes like a scholar as his warm brown eyes pour like syrup into mine.

I press my lips together as I gently grind my swollen hard dick against his body.

"You know me too well," I retort, my voice low.

Evan's eyes flash.

Then I flip him over like meat on a grill. He lets out a sound between a groan and a whimper as I swipe the bottle of lube out of my nightstand drawer like a ninja. I squeeze a Dairy Queen swirl of it onto my palm, then work my steel-hard dick for all of two seconds before easing my hand between Evan's tight cheeks, slickening it up down there. When I lay atop him, I let my dick sink and slide between those sweet cheeks of his, gently teasing and taunting his hole as I glide my whole length back and forth over it.

"*Oh my God ...*" he moans into the pillow, biting it.

I lay myself on top of his back, our bodies pressed together now, as I continue slow-fucking his cheeks to milk every last sensation I can before I blow my mind, but not yet entering him. I hook my hands under his arms and grip him tightly for leverage as I gently thrust.

"*You're mine,*" I whisper.

"*I know,*" he whispers back.

I kiss the back of his neck, then behind an ear, then finally his cheek, which is the key as he slowly turns his face to bring his own lips to mine.

When we kiss, my cock finds purchase at his hole, nearly by accident, and slips half an inch in.

Evan's lips break from the kiss as he gasps out.

I grin against his mouth, then pull out, and slowly start to grind my cock up and down his crack again, sliding up, sliding down.

"The hell you doing back there?" he breathes at me, his eyes rolling back drunkenly without having a drop of alcohol in his system, his lips parted, his face flushed.

"Jerking myself off with your butt cheeks."

He snorts at the way that sounds, then reaches with his mouth and playfully bites at one of my fingers, clung under his arm. "If you don't put it in me soon ..."

"Then what?"

"Then I'm gonna *fuck* a hole in your nice, big, pretty king-size bed, that's what."

Evan loves acting tough when I've got him totally under my control. He also craves the way I objectify him like this, throwing him to my bed facedown, then using him like my personal toy.

I unhook a hand from his arm, reach back, and give his ass one firm, flesh-popping smack.

Evan gasps.

"You're gonna do *what* to my bed?" I throw at him.

He half turns his face to me—as best as he can in his position—and his eyes are narrowed insolently.

"Don't speak like that about my lovely bed," I taunt him, playing my role. "Bad language doesn't suit you."

"Oh? You think one *spank* is gonna set me straight?"

"Nah."

I give him another loud, ass-cracking swat on his tight ass. He gasps once and shuts his eyes. Half a smile breaks over his flushed face.

Sometimes, I think he taunts me to punish him as much as I taunt him with the punishments themselves.

I bring my lips to his ear. *"But maybe a few more will,"* I growl, my voice deep.

"You can try anything you want," Evan says back.

"Watch it. Those sound like fightin' words."

"They are." His tone runs low. "You gonna fuck me sometime tonight? Or are you just a big dumb bag of muscles who's confused about what to do with that big dumb dick of yours?"

I could either laugh or play along with this "horny dirty boy" act he's putting on.

But even between his jokes, there's truth.

Namely: *get the fuck on with it.*

"I know exactly what to do with my big dumb dick," I growl at him.

"Yeah? Other than buttering it up between my—?"

It gets stuck at the hole again and slips right in like it meant to, this time a little over an inch.

Evan winces, yelps, "Oh, God," and then claws the pillow.

I feel his biceps flex when he grips the pillow tighter, clinging to his arms as I am.

"You ready for this?" I taunt him, the tip of my dick still inside him, stretching him, and only a thrust away from filling him right up.

Evan looks at me sidelong. "I dare you."

And *he* was the one who accused *me* of playing too many games.

I smirk, then lean in close. *"Sorry,"* I whisper, *"but I'm so hungry for you, I don't have time for fucking romance. I just need to get inside you right now."*

And then I slide the rest of the way in.

Evan gasps so hard, I think I see tears in his eyes.

I start rocking his body gently at first, then with mounting force as I feel his ass let go and embrace all of my dick with little resistance.

Evan's starting to moan.

That's when I know I've got him right where both of us want to be.

It feels like I'm driving in deeper and deeper with every thrust. The rhythmic slapping of my body against the smooth, taut flesh of his ass fills the room.

It won't be long before I'm hitting his prostate, and then if he's gonna play his usual long game, it'll take a hell of a lot more for him to keep from coming all over my sheets underneath his panting, rocking body.

This boy will be a puddle of sweat by the time I'm done.

His moaning turns into unintelligible whispers and words that sound suspiciously like, *"Fuck,"* and, *"Please,"* and, *"God."*

That tells me he's ready.

Normally, I'd keep this going for a lot longer, since I like to drive myself crazy as much as I'm driving him.

But when you've gone this long without seeing each other, smelling each other, or touching each other ...

And the circumstance arises that you've gotten him on your bed, in your remote cabin by a big grand lake, all to yourself ...

And nothing in the world can possibly come between you two other than an act of God ...

You kinda can't help but just get to the point.

After all, I'm pretty much seeing this as round one of five, minimum, tonight.

We're only just beginning.

I bring my lips to his ear, just close enough to make him sigh with delight. "I'm gonna come in this tight ass of yours. I'm gonna come *so hard.*"

Evan lets out another exasperated moan, then turns his head and shoots me his eyes as best as he can. "So much for romance, huh?"

"Fuck romance," I growl.

"I dare you to do it."

My heart jumps excitedly at those words.

That's basically more than permission: *he's downright asking for it.*

Still clinging to his body, my front against his long, smooth backside, I plant kisses on his neck over and over as I up my pace, pumping him even harder and deeper.

Evan feels it, grunting and whimpering and grunting again, taking it all.

He's as hungry for it as I am.

Unexpectedly, I reach the tipping point.

"*Fuck!*" I cry out.

Evan shouts out too, sighing vocally, right there with me in the moment.

Bliss ripples through me like a warm, crackling drug as I shoot my whole load inside of my Evan.

I don't dare stop pumping or slow down.

And Evan feels every bit of it—my cock throbbing and flexing and pumping within him, my breath and my involuntary moans all over the back of his neck, my squeezing fingers still hooked under his arms like I'm hanging on for our precious lives.

Then I've spent my last.

And it's over just like that.

I let my dick slip out and convert into just a lump of meat lying on top of Evan while tiny fingers of pleasure still tickle through my whole body as I come down from that insane high.

I feel like I just touched Heaven in that moment and did little to nothing to deserve it.

I feel like I'm embracing (*or crushing, more accurately*) the most beautiful man in the world, and I did little to nothing to deserve him, either.

And yet here I am, enjoying the afterglow of the best damned orgasm I've had in years.

Thanks to Evan.

I'm almost embarrassed to think on how short the whole thing lasted. It feels like it ended before it had a chance to begin.

I guess I was just that eager to get inside him—to feel him again, to know him intimately again, to listen to his moans of feral ecstasy I've become addicted to.

I wanted it too badly to make it last.

Grunting under my weight, Evan murmurs, "Oh my *God* that was intense."

I give his ear a little bite. "I would have pounded you all night," I tell him, "but didn't want to wear you out this soon."

Yeah, I wouldn't be caught dead saying I came earlier than I meant to.

Evan smirks knowingly. "Sure. If you say so."

I frown at him.

"Or maybe ..." he starts, gently flipping himself over underneath me as I do half a pushup to let him, "you were just *so* excited to see me that you couldn't contain all that pent-up man juice inside you any longer."

I wrinkle my face. "Man juice?"

"Hey, we should go down to the lake!" he exclaims excitedly.

I think I might have just unleashed the inner Evan that Figaro Lane and all the haughtiness of his fancy new life had locked up like a prisoner.

"Now?" I let out a little laugh. "Like, right now?"

"Yeah! Why not?"

I feel his cock flex against mine. "You sure you don't want me to do something about ... *that?*" I move my hips a little bit, like a dance. "Because it seems to me like *he* wants some attention."

"I like to enjoy the high," he tells me. "You can just leave me pent-up for now. Who knows? Maybe I'll stick it in your face while you're peacefully sleeping later, see if something happens."

Evan always plays this game. I get off first, and then he draws out his own horniness until he's insane with the desire to let it all out. It's his thing.

With viper swiftness, I reach right down between our bodies and grip his dick tight.

Evan gasps.

"If that's how we're gonna play," I tell him, "then this dick of yours is now mine. You want to stay all pent-up and horny for me?"

"*Mmph,*" is his response.

"Good. Because it sounds like you don't know how to take care of your own dick anyway. You need me to do it for you."

"You can't just *own* my dick," Evan protests—but it's all part of that role he likes to play, pretending to resist my attempts to take control. "I come when I want."

"You come when *I* want," I growl with a teasing half smile in his face.

Evan smirks all defiantly, then looks up at me with two lazy, no-big-deal eyes. "Fine, whatever you say. You gonna show me this big amazing lake of yours, or are we just going to lie on this bed sharing taunts all night?"

"Of course I'm gonna show you the lake. But if you want to see it with your clothes on, you're gonna need to catch me."

He lifts an eyebrow. "Huh?"

I'm off the bed in the next second. I rush out of the bedroom, swipe his clothes right off the floor, and while Evan shouts a protest, I dart out of the back door, racing for the lake.

I don't have to look over a shoulder to know he's trailing behind me, just as naked as my crazy ass is.

Chapter 17.
Evan ... or whoever this new idiot is.

Don't worry.

I haven't officially lost my mind.

There's still a tiny bit of restraint somewhere in this loose and totally over-horned brain of mine.

"Dane!!" I shout out, racing through the trees as I chase him toward the big moonlight-glimmering body of water ahead.

"Slowpoke!" he throws over his shoulder, several paces ahead.

He might be fast for a big guy.

But I'm faster.

Right when we break through the trees, I tackle him, and both of us (and my clothes) go crashing to the soft ground in foolish, sputtering laughter. After it subsides, suddenly we're wrestling each other again on that dirty, damp bank, him laughing and throwing his taunts, me grunting as I struggle underneath his muscles.

This is pretty much foreplay for us.

Except he already came.

But soon enough, he'll be ready to go again, and maybe by then, I'll decide to let my own torment off the hook as well.

The thing about Dane is, he can go four times in a night. There is something insufferably *unrelenting* about his libido. As for myself, when I finally come once, I'm so spent after the long, drawn-out buildup and torture that I'm through and zonked out. We've learned this and developed this dynamic over the years we were together, and it seemed like some oddly perfect sexual symbiosis.

Also: we both like wrestling each other like a pair of locker room idiots, even though he always wins.

Is this true love?

Soon, the pair of us are settled on the bank, naked as fuck, a pile of my clothes somewhere nearby, and staring ahead at the expanse of mirror-calm water. The bright waning gibbous of a moon watches us twofold: overhead, and reflected across the water, giving pale light to our otherwise dark world.

"I can't believe you live out here."

Dane chuckles. "Sometimes, neither can I."

"It's like ... the perfect woodsy paradise here."

"There's a billion paradises all across the world," he tells me like some wise old man. "This is just the one that happens to be mine."

I smile, then lean my head on his shoulder. "I can't believe we're sitting out here naked."

"You've said that already."

"Seven times at least, I know. It's just ..." I have to laugh at it all. "I don't ... chase my boyfriend naked through the woods at night. I mean, this is *so* not me. I don't do these sorts of things."

"You used to."

His words carry weight. I let my eyes drift across the lake, lazy as a bit of debris floating in that water with nowhere to go, with no plan or purpose, just floating and seeing where the current takes it.

Then: "Did you just call me your boyfriend?"

I flinch, then look his way. "What? No."

"Yeah, you did. *'Chase my boyfriend naked through the woods at night.'* You called me your boyfriend."

"I didn't mean ..." I scoff and shrug it off. "I meant, I mean ... you *were* my boyfriend. It didn't—"

"You're so fucking cute."

He may not be able to see it well, but my cheeks are flushed now. A part of me doesn't even know if I want to deny that I said that word.

I know I said it.

And maybe I meant it.

Maybe it revealed some hidden part of my psyche to me I've been knowingly or unknowingly blocking out.

Maybe I really do want my boyfriend back.

Then Dane says, "I'm willing to give it a try."

I don't look at him. "Give what a try?"

I know damned well what he meant.

Why did I say that?

Dane humors me anyway. He leans into me, lips just short of kissing my ear, and in his gentlest, softest tone, he says, "I'd do whatever it takes to be your man again."

I close my eyes.

Goddamn, those words.

"I'll take you out to dinner every night." He touches his lips to my ear. "I'll bring you to this lake every day." He puts his lips on my cheek. "You really ought to see the sun shine off of it in the morning. It's ..." A kiss on my cheek, lower. "... the most beautiful thing."

His lips find mine.

We kiss.

There is something different about this kiss. Even in my horny state of mind, I don't feel pulled along on a string with the way he seduces me. This isn't one of his usual ploys or playfully manipulative tricks.

I can hear it in his voice. And I can feel it in this soft and meaningful kiss.

He truly wants me back in his life.

And I'm a fucking liar to myself if I don't say the same.

"Take me back, Evan," he whispers between kisses.

I lift a hand to his cheek, caressing it. He brings one to mine, so gentle you'd think I was made of brittle glass.

And then it happens:

"I already have," I whisper back.

That's how two naked ex-boyfriends on the bank of a lake turn into two naked boyfriends: with just a kiss, three whispered words, and nothing else between us.

The magic is still well alive an hour later when we're back inside, and I'm leaning back against him in his tub full of warm, sudsy water. He embraces me and, now and then, puts a kiss on the back of my neck.

I'm also bone-hard between my thighs under the water, but let's forget that detail for now.

Dane is in the middle of telling me a story. "And to be fair here, the department wasn't full of liars and lazy pricks. Like any office, you got one or two bad seeds. I'd just been turned down too many times by my chief. And I saw too many people get promoted ahead of me, all on account of who they knew and nothing else."

"Politics," I mumble sympathetically. "It's a game that seems to be anywhere you go. Managing people, and their expectations, and their judgments, and where your role in all of that madness is."

"And no matter how hard you fight to be good, you will inevitably be seen as the bad guy to someone else."

I rub his legs under the water thoughtfully. "Maybe I'm someone's bad guy, somewhere."

"We all are."

Leaning back against him as I am, I'm not looking into his face, which perhaps makes this next bit a little easier to say out loud. "You were my bad ex-boyfriend."

One amused, breathy chuckle shoots out his nostrils. "Oh yeah?"

"For years. It's all I'd dare to call you. Bad. That was your adjective. My *bad* ex-boyfriend. It ..." I scoop some soap suds my way, hugging them like a blanket without substance. "... helped me cope, I guess."

Embracing me as he is, one of his hands gently slides up and down my front, rubbing me. It keeps grazing my nipple, and I wonder if he's aware of how crazy-horny that's making me.

Bad timing, I know.

"We all have our coping mechanisms and shit," he says back. "If seeing me as the bad guy got you through a tough time ..."

"It helped me stuff away a lot of feelings," I confess. "But ... I don't think it really helped me in the long run. It wasn't honest, to call you 'bad'. You weren't all bad. You were very good to me, too."

"I was also an immature shit."

"Well, so was I," I catch myself saying.

His hand gently runs along my nipple again under the water. It's so sensitive now that I'm getting chills, and with each time he touches it, my already-hard-as-sin cock flexes more.

"How were you immature?" he asks.

"I ... think I might've ... expected the world from you without giving it in return."

"You gave me the world, Evan."

"We might have different ways of looking at it. I did a lot of soul-searching over the years after we broke up. I didn't realize how much I had relied on you for simple comforts, like a hug when I was sad, or a guy to cuddle with during a movie ... or a storm. Sexual urges, you can satisfy that with a right hand and half an hour, but—"

"Debatable."

"—when you really pare it down, you discover that having someone in your life is a lot more than having a guy to stick your dick into. It isn't just the cuddling, or the kisses, or the sex. In a relationship, the whole really *is* greater than the sum of its parts."

His fingers go over my nipple again. A wave of ill-timed pleasure shoots through me.

I blurt out, "Can you stop doing that?"

His hand freezes in place. "Doing what?"

"You know what."

The breath of a signature Dane chuckle hits my neck, and then he starts to rub my abdomen instead, well below my sensitive nipples.

"Just living up to my name," murmurs Dane. "*Bad.*"

"So as I was saying," I go on, ignoring his taunt, "the longer we were apart, the more I started to question everything I knew. And my mind just went ... *dark.*"

Dane puts a kiss on the back of my neck.

"Are you listening?"

"Yeah, babe, go on. I'm listening." Another kiss on my neck. "Your mind went dark?"

"Yeah." I settle against him again, letting my head rock back onto his chest, staring at the opened bathroom door and the window of his bedroom beyond it which, from here, shows nothing but black. "So the only way I could cope with that dark part of my mind was to build my life around something else ... something that wasn't us. I got my cosmetology license, poured myself into my work, and never looked back."

"And the rest is history," he murmurs, hand sliding farther down my abdomen. "You've had a lot of success. Starting your own business in a part of town like yours is no small thing, Evan."

"It's funny, I don't even see it that way. It just ..." I shrug. "It just happened. I was working nonstop, with no focus on anything else. Not dating. Not friends. Not my parents. Then I woke up years later and ... I owned and ran my own salon."

Dane kisses the top of my head. "Do you notice that dark part of your mind anymore? Is it still there?"

"Funny you ask," I tell him. "I ... stopped noticing it recently."

"How recently?"

"The day you came back into my life."

Right at the moment I say the words, I feel his evil, knowing fingers graze my hard cock under the water.

I close my eyes under his touch, enjoying it for one passing second, then turn my head. "Did you hear me?"

"So I'm pretty much your savior."

I blink. "My what?"

"I'm saving you from the darkness. It came when I left, and it left when I came." His fingers wrap softly around my cock. "And maybe it'll be gone for good ... once *you* come."

I can't even keep a straight face with that one. I let out a laugh and shake my head. "I'm trying to be all deep here, having this meaningful conversation about life and love, and you can't keep your hand off my cock."

"Maybe you can't keep your cock off my hand."

Then he starts stroking me.

Everything is slippery and super sensitive and out-of-control good down there under the water.

I slap hands to the rim of the rub with a gasp.

His other hand locks around my body like a seatbelt, holding me firmly against him.

"*Slow down ...*" I breathe.

"I'll jerk you however fast or slow I want to."

"Did you ever think of me as your ... *oh, God ...*" I'm already so close to the edge and he's barely stroked me for thirty seconds. "Did you ... ever ... *fuck ...*"

"Can't even form sentences, huh?"

While jerking me underwater, his other hand slides up my stomach and stops right at my chest.

"*Fuck ...*"

His fingers start exploring without abandon, teasing my pec, then dancing down my stomach and abs, then back up to cup and massage my pec—and then instantly, like it was his evil plan all along, he pinches right on my nipple like a clamp.

He hit my self-destruct button. "*Dane! Oh my fuuuck, Dane, stop, stop, oh my God ...*"

"What were you asking me?"

"I can't fucking think while you're—"

"C'mon, cupcake," he taunts me. "Don't tell me that something's distracting you from asking a question."

I start to squirm, getting way too close. Then Dane hooks his feet around my legs, locking me in place, and now there's about nothing I can do to get away from the ecstasy he's forcing me to enjoy.

Well, he's not "*forcing*" me, per se. Let's be honest: this is exactly the kind of thing I fantasize about.

But maybe his timing could be better.

He pinches more on my nipple.

"*Dane ...*"

Then the bathroom fills with the noise of my hollers and moans as I explode under the water with my long, long awaited release. I feel like I'm literally melting against Dane's chest behind me as I sink and sink, all of my pent-up frustrations pumping out of me with each of his slippery, underwater strokes.

But he holds me in place, right against him, right above the water, right where I know I'm safe no matter what—and I'll always be safe.

I'm out of breath by the time it's over. I'm sweating all over my forehead. With the coolness of the air on my wet skin, and the hot bathwater, and my heart racing in my chest after that powerful orgasm, I feel like I'm twenty-seven different temperatures.

"You and I," I finally breathe, "are the only people who need to take showers after our baths."

To that, Dane lets out a hearty laugh, which I soon find myself joining.

Moments later, the bathroom's full of a new wave of steam as we shower off quickly. His towels are rough and less fluffy than mine, but I find it endearing; even his towels are so Dane-like. He dries my backside, and I dry his, and then together we slip into his bed, the sheets of which feel so crazy soft.

Or maybe it's just my skin that's so sensitive after such a strong orgasm.

And that was one strong fucking orgasm.

This place is so peaceful, I could just fade away in its gentle embrace. All the lights in the cabin are out, save a nightlight in the bathroom, which holds its blue glow like a little precious treasure. The only other light comes from far away through distant trees where the moon still watches, knowing the shameful stuff we did at the lake.

The air is temperate, yet cool enough to make the sheets and Dane's warm embrace feel necessary.

Our cuddling feels so ideal and perfect right now, like it's exactly what my body needs. The comfort. The protection. The security.

He's always known exactly what I needed.

He still does.

Dane cuddles me so closely and tightly, it feels like ninety percent of the bed is going unused. We're just two tiny people on this enormous mattress. It's strange, how a bedroom can feel so big, and yet the cabin itself be a fairly modest size.

It's like my heart, in some regards—big at times, yet so little of it occupied.

Like this cabin.

And this bed.

"I was trying to ask this question earlier," I murmur in the quiet semidarkness, "but ... did you ever ... think of *me* as your bad ex-boyfriend?"

Dane puts a kiss on my cheek, then my lips, and he whispers: "*Never.*"

Chapter 18.
Dane wants to make up for lost time.

Evan looks like some relaxed, almost-intoxicated version of himself from the way he can't stop smiling, even as he sleeps.

I hope he still likes his eggs over easy.

He's a brick in the morning, and I'm an early bird, so I'm out of that bed the second the sunlight strikes into my cabin like a million molten gold spears. I whistle as I cook up some brown sugar bacon in the kitchen. Fresh-squeezed orange juice is something I'm used to making for just myself every other Sunday or so—and on a few choice occasions—so it's quite the treat to know someone else will get to enjoy it with me this morning.

And it makes all the difference that it's Evan Pryor.

Because I am sure as fuck not sharing my fresh-squeezed *nothing* with just anyone.

It isn't long after I start frying up the eggs that I hear him padding across the living room behind me. "Well, well, look who just woke up," I taunt without looking.

"Oh my *God*, that smells heavenly." He comes up to my side wearing a pair of blue boxer-briefs. His voice has that thick just-woke-up gravel to it. "Are you making—?"

"Bet your ass I am. You still take your coffee sweet?"

"So sweet you can't taste coffee anymore. Is that—?"

"Fresh-squeezed. It's gonna knock your balls with every gulp, so better be ready."

Evan shoots me a look. "Are you gonna let me—?"

"Finish asking a single question before I answer it? Nah. I'm feeling feisty this morning."

"Well, I'm feeling ... fantastic."

He hesitated. I notice.

I look his way. "Something up?"

"Nope. What could possibly be up?" He gives me a firm swat on my ass—my bare ass. "My sexy boyfriend's cooking me Sunday morning breakfast, naked."

I know when Evan's got something on his mind, and I know when he's acting a little too perfect.

Also, this is the first fucking morning that we woke up after (maybe?) declaring ourselves boyfriends again. I'm not gonna press the matter and make him tell me what's going on like I used to.

Today, I'm learning from my mistakes, and I'm just gonna let him have his space to work out whatever it is that's in his head.

And we'll do it over his favorite eggs. "Hungry?"

"*Famished*," he answers. "Where do you keep—?"

I pull open a cabinet, revealing the glasses.

He eyes me, probably because I didn't let him finish another question.

Is that annoying him? Or does he think it's cute? Should I quit reading his mind in that weird we've-been-boyfriends-for-too-long kind of way?

"I'll ... quit answering your questions too quickly," I tell him.

"No, it's okay," he insists.

After he pushes away from the counter and settles at the table, only the sound of frying eggs and hot, sizzling bacon fills the room.

Minutes later, I have us each a full plate of breakfast set before us complete with mugs of coffee and glasses of my specialty orange juice. We're seated across from each other, the morning sun spilling all over us through the window, which faces east and, therefore, the rising sun.

And neither of us make a sound as we eat.

Well, except for the fork-scraping, or the coffee slurp now and then, or even the occasional, "*Mmm*," from Evan when he takes another bite of my eggs, cooked just the way he likes them—and with a sprinkle of garlic salt to give them a kick.

Finally I can't stand it. "Is this weird?"

Evan swallows his bite of bacon, wide-eyed. "Huh?"

"This." I gesture between us with a fork.

"Weird? Is what weird?" He stuffs his mouth with another forkful of egg.

"Never mind." I finish my last bite of bacon, then start to drink my orange juice.

He points at his glass. "I didn't know you make—"

"I do. Fresh oranges from the market, a little honey. You can say it's a habit I picked up."

"Oh? Like cutting me off all the time?"

I look up and meet his eyes, confused for a second. "I did it again?"

Evan forces a chuckle. "I'm just teasing, anyway. It doesn't really bother me."

I stare at him unsurely. "Does it?"

He keeps chewing for a bit. Then, as if arriving at a thought, he swallows, sets his fork down, then says, "It's a little weird."

"Thought so."

"I mean, that's to be expected, right?" Evan crosses his arms and wears a worried expression. "We'd be crazy if we didn't feel a little ... *anxious* about all this."

"Anxious?"

"You know what I'm saying. Nervous. Like it's just too good to be true. Like this can't possibly last. Like it's only a matter of time."

I sigh and put down my fork, then eye him across the table. "Do you gotta set your doomsday clock on things all the time?"

His back goes rigid. "I'm not setting a *doomsday*—"

"We only just woke up a bit ago and sat down for a nice Sunday breakfast ..."

"There you go, cutting me off again."

"Why is it so *impossible* to believe this might work?" I fire back at him. "We're used to each other. We finish each other's sentences—a quality I don't perceive as *bad*. We complement each other's antics. We're both able to supply what the other one lacks. We're—"

"And what do I lack?"

I shrug and search (delicately) for which answer to give him. "You lack honesty, sometimes."

"Honesty??" he spits out in disbelief.

"With yourself," I clarify firmly. "I think you're in the situation you're in now because you weren't honest with yourself for the past few years."

"Situation??"

"And now you've got a big salon, and you're living among a bunch of self-preening parakeets, and you have completely abandoned your interior design dreams. You never would have pursued a different path had I stayed in your life, because I'm *honest* with you."

I'm pretty sure that halfway through that spiel, Evan blew a gasket and somehow defied physics by containing himself until I was out of words. "You were a *dick* to me back then. Let's get it straight. There's a huge difference between being honest and—"

"Being honest means telling the truth," I state, "and that includes telling the truth to yourself."

"Well, my 'truth' right now is wondering what the hell I was thinking, coming all the way out here and—"

"No, your truth is something closer to: you were horny, you were unsatisfied, I am able to satisfy you, and last night, you and I both realized that there's a lot more to this than just our insanely perfect chemistry, and now we're a bit freaked out and don't know what to do with ourselves."

Evan stares at me for a while after I say all that. His eyes lose some of their fight, and I can't tell yet whether or not that's a good thing.

"That's ..." he finally murmurs, deflates a bit, then finishes, "rather accurate, I suppose."

"Honest," I mutter, then pick up my fork and dig in for another bite of egg.

He watches me, but doesn't pick his fork back up. A hundred thoughts seem to be passing over his eyes—or at least a single troubling one.

I set my fork down again. "Listen. I don't want to fight with you."

"Me neither," he returns calmly.

"We got kinks and awkwardness and crap to figure out. This isn't easy for either one of us."

"You're right, it's not."

"But we both still want to try, right?"

"Yes."

That one-worded answer might be the most relieving one-word answer I've gotten in my life. "That's good." I let myself have my first real breath since all this tension and awkwardness began when he woke up. "That's great, actually. Really fucking great."

Evan smiles at me across the table, then finally picks up his own fork, and we're back to eating breakfast.

In silence.

I expected today to go a lot easier than this.

When I'm rinsing dishes off and putting them in the dishwasher, Evan is in my bathroom. I can't quite turn over in my mind a few things he said. In a lot of ways, it's just like some of the arguments we used to have.

And in some ways, it's new territory completely.

Something over the past few years has put this odd rigidness in Evan he never used to have. It's like his backbone has become as stiff and plastic as the men he's surrounded himself with in that neighborhood.

When I finish the dishes and I'm pulling clothes out of my closet to wear today, I stop with a pair of pants clutched in my fist and wonder if I'm being unfair.

Am I judging his new lifestyle too harshly?

Am I wrong about all his new friends?

Maybe he genuinely likes his new neighbors. Maybe they're all decent people caught in a self-esteem game of cat and cliquey, terrified mice.

Maybe without the game, they'd be people I would even make friends with.

Evan comes out of my bathroom fully-dressed in a cute pair of jeans and a fitted red t-shirt that somehow makes the red overtones in his russet hair pop. He also fixed it exquisitely, that perfect sweep, which just makes me feel worse about criticizing his hairstyling career.

He really does have a talent for it. He always has.

Maybe I really am the big prick here.

"You look great," I tell him.

He glances my way, then lets on a smile. "And you look absolutely stunning."

I peer down at myself in confusion. "I'm ... not even wearing anything yet."

"Exactly," he teases, coming right up to me, pushing me into the closet and planting a kiss on my lips.

We fall against my clothes, but the weight of them keeps me from falling all the way back, and I wrap him in my arms as we kiss deeply.

He pulls away. "I'm sorry about this morning."

"Don't be. We need chats like that," I reassure him. "We need to keep our eyes open, and our mouths."

"Our mouths, you say ...?" His eyes trail down my body and arrive at my cock.

I put a finger at the base of his chin and bring his attention back up to my face. "If we get started this early on, I'll never get to take you out on the town today."

"If you say so," he teases, then his face turns serious as he reaches down and grabs a big handful of my dick.

I grunt, then eye him admonishingly. "Evan."

He ignores me as he drops to his knees and, without any warning, takes the whole tip of my dick into his mouth.

I close my eyes, melting into the sensation. "*Evan ...*" I breathe again, my hand instinctively going to the top of his head.

Then I let go as fast, having a sudden and strangely timed concern about messing up his hair.

"Evan," I try again, staring down at him.

A moan is his response as he swallows another inch of my dick, then another, his mouth twisting up and down it, teasing it as skillfully as a wet, warm hand.

Soon, I'm just putty for him, and my hands, with no purpose, reach up and cling to the clothes hangers and the shelves.

In another handful of minutes, it's over.

Evan's back in the bathroom washing his hands, and I'm a sweaty mess who still can't pick out a shirt. But after a realization that most of my shit is basically the same, I just grab the first thing I can and pull it on with a pair of jeans.

The next thing I know, we're strolling down a path that cuts through the forest and edges along the lake. Evan keeps making these cute comments, talking about how magical the sun looks across the water. Then he wonders when the last time we went to the beach was, "because it's been, like, forever," he adds with a laugh.

I take his hand suddenly.

Evan glances down, surprised by it, then accepts it with a smile, peers up at me, then stares off at the lake.

"Just under an hour isn't a bad commute," I point out some time later when it's just the woods around us.

We're walking very slowly, leisurely. He scuffs at something on the path before wrinkling his face up and asking, "What do you mean?"

"To your salon in the city."

"Why would I need to commute?"

"If you were to ... oh, I dunno ... stay here overnight during the week sometime."

"Oh, yeah. Right." He lets himself chuckle. "It's not too bad, you're right. I'd just have to get up early to make it in time."

"Pssh. You're the boss, you can show up whenever you want."

Evan snorts with a smile and shakes his head. "I wish I could be as laidback as you are sometimes."

I smirk and squeeze his hand knowingly.

After a few more paces, Evan tilts his head. "Did you check the feeds this morning, by the way?"

"Nope. This morning is all about you, and us."

"Yeah, that's true."

Evan smiles, and we walk along some more.

His smile is short-lived. "But ..." he starts.

"Yeah?"

"What if the vandal struck sometime last night?" He turns his head my way. "Wouldn't it be irresponsible to not keep track of what's going on?"

I shrug. "If something happened, I'm pretty sure you would've gotten ten texts about it from your neighbors."

"Oh, that's true," he reasons.

Then we walk along some more. Birds chirp over our heads. A breeze passes through like a ghost, stirring up the front bangs of Evan's hair.

"I just wonder ..." he starts again.

"What?"

"What if something happened that no one saw? The vandal might've scoped out someone's house, preparing his next big thing, or poked around a few front doors, seeing who's home, being suspicious and weird and *vandally*, and maybe—"

"You're worrying too much."

"You just cut me off."

"The whole point of us being out here together is to get your mind *away* from all of that," I remind him.

"Why does it have to be *me* commuting from here?"

His abrupt shift in topic throws me. "Say what?"

"Is that your endgame?" He stops in the middle of the road and our hands separate. "To *rescue* me from my life on Figaro Lane? To *rescue* me from my salon? To whisk me all the way out here and show me some life I could have had with you, had I kept my temper that one night and not thrown you out?"

There are too many questions there to address all at once. "I'm not trying to rescue you from anything."

"Is this a punishment because I dumped you?" Evan spreads his hands. "Is that what all of this is?"

"Where's all this coming from?" I ask, exasperated. "Did you hit your head on a branch or something?"

"Just tell me. Did I make a huge mistake? Do you resent me for ending things?"

"No." My answer is firm. "No, I don't resent you. I think we were younger and maybe we made mistakes, but I don't hold a single one of them against you. I made my fair share of mistakes. I think we've learned a lot."

"We've *changed* a lot." Then his eyes detach as he arrives at a thought. "Well, I've ... *I've* changed a lot."

His anger is gone in an instant. Alarmingly so. His eyes search the ground as he works over a thought in his head. I don't like the look in his eyes.

I get close to him. "What's wrong? Tell me."

"I ... I think *I* was the problem, Dane."

He still isn't looking at me, even while I'm right in front of him. He's staring straight ahead, but is focused on something far away—as if he's looking through me.

"The breakup wasn't any *one* of our faults. It was—"

"No," Evan cuts me off gently. "It was mine. You haven't changed because ... because there was nothing wrong with you. You've always been carefree. And you chase your heart. And you're shamelessly immature at times. You're ..." He lets out one sad chuckle. "You're totally yourself."

That sad chuckle doesn't comfort me in the least. "Evan ..."

"Do you remember that fight? The one that broke us up? The one where I kicked you out?" He glances up into my eyes. "I was studying for my final exam, and—"

And I saw how stressed out he was. I had noticed for days that his studying had made him irritable, nearly crazy. Over and over I tried to distract him with my humor, with my body, with sex. One time, it worked.

That night, it didn't.

And it became something else completely.

"I exploded," he goes on. "And so many ugly things came out of me that night. I called you nothing but a—"

'Distraction!' he'd screamed. *'Always needing attention! No care for anything but yourself! Have you ever studied for a single test in your life, let alone a final exam? Have you ever worked hard for anything, ever? I can't stand to even look at your face right now, that* look *you're giving me, that stupid, stupid fucking look!'*

His explosion that night inspired my own firing of a shit ton of heated words. "And I yelled a lot of stuff back at you," I remind Evan, remembering every word. "We both said things. Myself included."

'*You are gonna turn into a soulless shell, walking in line with the rest of the high-achiever idiots boasting straight-As and fat bank accounts. But you know what they don't tell you? There's a price to all that supposed success, and when you're out of this college game and doing what you love, Evan Pryor, I want you to still love yourself, too. At this rate, you won't even recognize your own fucking reflection.*'

He was standing by his desk, breathing so heavily, you'd think he just ran a marathon. I was right by the bed wearing just a pair of boxers after having humiliated myself by trying to coax him into a sexy-time break.

But the humor and the sweetness was gone, and all that was left were two young, furious men, squared off across a hot, stifling apartment that, with every drawn breath, seemed to shrink.

Here in the woods, however, there is more air than either of us will ever need.

And more space.

"I was the problem," Evan states again, then meets my eyes. "*I'm* the bad ex-boyfriend."

I bring a hand up to caress his face, a whisper of, "*No you're not*," on my lips, but Evan flinches away before I can even say that much.

His flinching away hurts worse than anything.

"And I don't deserve you, or this."

"Evan, stop."

"You were right, Dane." The worst part is, there are no tears in Evan's eyes. He looks as blank and dead as a stone. "You called it. I'm just a soulless shell now. I'm a soulless, designer-wearing, HOA-abiding puppet."

He moves past me suddenly, cutting through the woods toward my cabin.

I let out a sigh and follow him, calling out, "Evan, you're not a shell. C'mon. You're overthinking this."

He doesn't say anything, no matter what I shout at his back as we cut through the woods. He trips twice over a root, but never stops. "Evan," I keep saying over and over. I must say it a hundred times.

We make it to the cabin, and Evan goes straight for his things, throwing his clothes from last night back into his shoulder bag.

"So what is this?" I ask him quietly. "You're going?"

"I'll call for a ride."

"Evan ..."

"This won't work, Dane."

The words stop me cold. Evan turns and faces me. His beautiful, brown eyes are full of emotion, but not a single tear drops from them. I don't know if that's because of how deep he is in his wounded mind, or just indicative of that Evan-brand strength he's always had.

It's hard to admire that strength when it's the thing that's made him so determined to leave.

"In the long run," he says, "I won't be able to change for you. I can't give up this life I have, and I mean that in more ways than just where I live or who I live with. I am a very different person now. I ..." His eyes move to the window, as if every sweet moment from yesterday just came rushing to that window to stare him in the face with sad, droopy eyes. "I can't be the guy who keeps you company in this cabin. I'm not that guy."

"Yeah, you are," I fire back with force. "You already were. You don't have to change a damned thing about yourself. You're overthinking it. This can be the easiest fucking thing, Evan. It's easy. Just *free* yourself, Evan. Give yourself the permission to live your life the way you want. The way *you* want."

"Easy ..." Evan echoes, then shakes his head. He lifts his gaze to me, sad and faraway. "Always so 'easy' with you, huh?"

I reach out, take his shoulders, and bring his face to mine for a kiss.

It's a short kiss. Shorter than I wanted.

And when we're apart again, he meets my eyes, and there's nothing in them but resolve. He doesn't say a word. He merely takes his shoulder bag off the bed, then gently, calmly makes his way out of my cabin.

The door shuts at his back.

I find myself staring at that door a lot longer than I ought to be. I want to be angry at him, but I can't.

Do I blame him?

Do I blame myself?

The feeling in my gut right now, it's something I've not felt since that fateful night so long ago. I know it so well that instantly, I feel twenty-two years old again. I can vividly recall leaving that apartment, going down the hundred damned stair steps, and sitting in my truck in that parking lot. I sat in that truck for hours staring at my dead odometer and the steering wheel, and far away, unbeknownst to either of us, a thunderstorm was getting ready to make its grand entrance.

I'll never forget that first boom of thunder, and the tumult of rain that swallowed my ears.

And the voice in my head that, over and over, kept asking the same stupid question: *What could I have done differently?*

I'm asking that question now.

Finally, I open my door and step out onto the porch. Halfway down the wide gravel path that serves as my driveway, Evan stands there with his phone out.

I come up to him, knowing he hears me several paces behind, with my loud, gravel-kicking footfalls.

"Come," I tell him. "I'll give you a ride home."

He glances at me, a lost look in his eyes. Then, with a sigh of surrender, he pockets his phone, then walks with me to my truck.

Chapter 19.
Evan sleeps in the bed he made.

The ride home is long.

"I'm just a call away, Evan."

I don't say anything the whole way.

The windows are down, but I'm not finding as much thrill in the wind blasting over my face as I did on the back of his motorcycle.

"If you change your mind and want to talk ..."

He keeps saying these little things.

And all I keep seeing is that night we fought and it all fell apart.

That night will happen again if we get back together. I know that even if he doesn't. *Honest*, he kept insisting. *Be honest.*

We will never work as a couple.

How's that for honesty?

"Evan, will you just look at me?"

After a while, he actually lets me have my peace, and neither of us say anything at all on the long ride back.

When we pull onto Figaro Lane, I half expect to find everyone's houses painted in glitter and rainbow slime. Instead, it's boringly just the way it was left yesterday.

"Thanks for the ride, Dane," I tell him softly, the first thing I've said since we left his cabin in Brady.

"Can I come in for a minute?" he nearly begs me. "Maybe we can just ... relax for a little bit? Have a little drink? Chill? We don't even have to talk."

I don't want to look at his face. Because then I'll see the man I fell in love with. And I'll see all those sparkly, inviting, devastatingly beautiful things that happen in his eyes when he's emotional. And I'll be amazed all over again at how such a big, tatted, muscular brute like him can have any sensitive, vulnerable emotion in him at all. And then I'll be stuck in this truck, and in this life, and in this tragic ending forever.

"Dane, please take the cameras with you."

He flinches. "What?"

"I don't want you to investigate this whole ... dumb thing anymore. It's just a big waste of your time when you could be investigating something real ... and with substance. Like a murder or something."

"If you only knew what kind of cases I've taken ..."

"Just take the cameras, okay?" I sigh. "I don't want you skirting any laws on my account. Not for these *self-preening parakeets*."

I feel him shift uncomfortably. "I didn't mean that."

"Yeah, you did. And ... you're totally right. And I'm one of them, too." I open the door and hop out.

"Evan ..."

I close the door, come around the truck, then pass my hot pink mailbox on the way to my front door, where I stop and fish through my bag for the key.

I hear his truck door shut, and then he's at my side at once. "Evan, I'm not gonna give up on this, or us. What we have ..."

I keep fishing and fishing. *Where is my damned key?*

"... it's more than I'll ever find with anyone for the rest of my life. And I know that. I hit the jackpot with you, Evan. I just ..." His voice lowers. "I hit it too soon."

The key finds my fingers. I pull it out and push it into the lock of my door.

This time, it slips right in.

"I'm gonna win you over one way or another."

I push inside my house, then turn to close the door.

But my eyes catch his before I do.

He watches me intensely. Every bit of his beauty is on display in this fleeting moment of doubt. The power of his beard and those lips, parted, anticipating a reply I may or may not make. The strength in his jaw. The light in his eyes that burns me down to my core and reveals every little bit of me that sits in the dark. He knows me. He feels every part of me. He loves me without abandon.

Then I shut the door.

You might expect that I go to my room, cry, then relocate to the kitchen for a glass of wine, then call up a friend and pout while I mourn the loss of love.

Instead, I sit in my living room with my shoulder bag—still packed—tossed onto the couch next to me. And the turned-off screen of my flatscreen is the only thing I stare at for an entire hour.

It doesn't need to show anything, because my mind is replaying the last five years of my life like some tragic documentary I'm not enjoying, yet can't stop watching.

And I'm anxiously trying to remember a moment— even just a tiny moment, even if it barely exists, even if it's a moment I might not immediately recognize—when I truly felt proud of my life.

I've come up with a list of moments.

The list is short.

There's three of them.

First moment: I opened *Blown Away*, my salon. My dad was there with me giving me his buttery, mustached smile. My mom was pouring every customer a sparkling glass of champagne and helping the receptionist with the point of sale system, as she is quite computer savvy.

Second moment: I threw down a signature that made me the owner of this house I'm in right now, and I felt like a goddamned adult for the first time in my life. My dad and my mom were *not* there, but a nice bottle of wine was, as well as two giant, puffy pillows, both of which I squeezed to my face as I leapt onto my bed and squealed with excitement.

Third moment: I rode on the back of Dane Cooper's motorcycle without a damned care in the world.

That third moment somehow seems to surpass the others.

By a lot.

I'm sadly not afforded much more time to figure out my little love conundrum, on account of an inconvenient knock on my door.

I rise off the couch, drag myself to the door, then yank it open. "Arry," I greet him.

He pulls down his shades and eyes me over them. "Honey, you and I need to talk."

I sigh. "I'm sorry, but it's really a bad time for me. Can we—?"

"Well, it's a bad time for it to be a bad time."

Arry saunters right by (if I hadn't moved, he would have steamrolled over me) and plants himself on my couch with a, "Do you have some *daytime wine* we can partake of? This is a *wine* sort of conversation, by the way. Red wine, preferably."

With a hidden eye roll, I shut the front door, grab a couple glasses and a bottle from the kitchen, then join Arry on the couch after pouring us each a glass.

He takes a sip, makes some under-the-breath remark about my wine which I choose to ignore, then sets the glass down and faces me importantly. "Alright, I'll cut to the chase. I'm pretty sure I know who the vandal is."

My eyebrows shoot up in surprise. "You do?"

"Yes. Before I arrived here for your movie night, I noticed something ... *across the street*."

Across the street would be Josiah, the one who had the word 'HOMO' written across his driveway, or Stevie, the one who still hasn't painted over the dick on his garage door, or—

"Preston's house," Arry then clarifies.

He's across the street and up two houses, only one house away from Raymond himself. "What did you notice?"

"That night, I saw *Preston* out on his *driveway*. Now, I know that he walks his dog around the cul-de-sac a few times in the evenings, but ..." Arry bites his lip, leans in close to me as if he might be overheard, and whispers, "*but he didn't have his dog with him that night.*"

I'm paying full attention now, nothing else on my mind but his words. "He didn't?"

"Evan, I swear on my Gucci shoes, I saw him in a black hoodie and ... well, you might recall, he *didn't* show up for your movie night."

I nod. "So you're saying he might've done it?"

Arry lifts his hands innocently. "I'm not accusing anyone. I'm just stating facts. It's what I saw."

I frown in thought. *But Dane's hidden cameras would have caught him, and they didn't. Unless ...*

"He only lives a few houses away from Raymond," I ask, to be sure, "right?"

"Yes."

"Hm." *That's only two backyard fences he'd need to hop.*

"You're probably asking yourself *why* he would have done the thing he did to Raymond's garden. *If* it was he who did it."

Really, this conversation could be happening on a far better day than this. My emotions are still so raw after my time with Dane that I feel downright *unreal* at the moment, like this is all some vivid dream I'm about to wake up from with a start. It might actually very well be, and I might wake up in Dane's bed Sunday morning.

"Are you paying attention?" mumbles Arry dryly. "I don't want to rehash any of this tea."

"Yes, I'm paying attention. Preston is a guy I've ... never really gotten to know much about," I point out.

"Him and Leland both," Arry adds with a nod. "And I hope you realize that, while Preston *seems* super close and friendly with Ray ... there's bad blood there, too."

That, I didn't know. "What's the bad blood?"

"Preston once wanted to be head of the HOA."

I gasp. "So you're saying the garden thing was some kind of retaliation?"

"I'm not saying anything. Just presenting facts."

I mull it over for a second. "But why would Preston do ... all the other stuff?"

Arry shrugs. "Either he's just screwing with Ray and his obsession with having the perfect role-model street in the neighborhood, or those were done by someone else, and Preston's only responsible for the garden. Maybe Preston's capitalizing on the *real* vandal's glory by doing this to Ray's garden now, and figuring the vandal will be blamed for it. Who knows? I sure don't."

I shrug. "Well, I wish I could say this conversation was helpful, but it's just made everything all the more confusing." I sit back in my chair and make myself take a sip of wine, which fast turns into two hearty gulps.

I'm going to be a regular wino by the end of next week.

Thanks to this mystery vandal. *And Dane.*

"Well, you're the one with the big strong private investigator ex," sings Arry as he rises from the couch, "so I reckoned the information to be most useful in your hands. No, I'm not chirp-chirp-chirping to anyone else about it. Just you. Just little ol' you. Is something wrong? Are you alright? I noticed your ex leaving a bit ago."

He tacks those questions right on the end of his parting words, as if I have any bit of desire left in me to have it out about my personal problems right now.

So I just lift my glass to him. "I've got this lovely glass of wine in my hand and it's barely afternoon on a lovely, sunny Sunday. What could *possibly* be wrong with me, Arry?"

He winks. "You're turning into a mini-me. Careful there," he teases before heading for the door. He stops just short of opening it. "Oh, and this should go without saying, but I was never here, and if I *was* here, then we were just talking about the Academy Awards and how very *snubbed* dear Bradley Cooper was."

I give Arry a short nod and another lift of my glass. "You got it."

"I know." He sees himself out.

The second he leaves, all the feelings rush back in. All over again, I'm a numb and very confused mass of emotion.

Of course, the very first thing I want to do is call up Dane and tell him everything. It's an instinct as strong as an addict's. Every time something happens lately, he is the first (and only) person I want to tell about it.

Not my neighbor Stevie. Nor my neighbor Josiah.

Nor Gary at the salon.

Nor my mom or dad.

Just Dane.

"Jesus, do I even *have* any friends?" I blurt out loud to my empty house.

Anne Boleyn, as if summoned by my despair, rushes out of my bedroom. Her tail goes way high in the air, like an antenna, and then she hurries up to my feet in a fit of purrs and head-butts, walking circles around them.

I crouch down and scratch lovingly behind her ear.

Well, I guess I have one.

It's not until the evening after I've had some dinner, taken a long, thought-filled shower, and am curled up on my couch with Anne by my side that a flash of lights run past my front windows.

I look up. Then, perhaps by sheer boredom and a lack of motivation to do a damned thing on account of my wrecked emotions, I get off the couch and go up to the windows, curious.

Josiah's backed his car into his driveway, and he's getting out of it now. He glances down at the ground for a second where the faint remains of the word 'HOMO' still linger. He gives it the finger, then lifts his hand up toward the cul-de-sac in general, then heads into his house after that strange fit of anger is out of his system. I watch his door shut.

I'm about to pull away from the window when I spot Xavier sitting on his doorstep and having a smoke, lit gently overhead by a single front door light. He seems to have observed the same thing I did, except he's shaking his head and chuckling about it. Then he presses out the butt of his cigarette on the ground, rises up, and disappears into his house.

I frown, staring after him.

I don't have Dane to call to share these observations with. I don't have him to bounce ideas off of, either.

I need to be my own detective now.

Nor do I have him to cuddle with when I'm feeling shitty.

Or kiss him when I'm feeling naughty.

Or laugh with when I'm feeling silly and stupid.

"Anne Boleyn," I announce with due drama, "please look after the castle for a moment. I need to step out and engage in a little *private investigating.*"

I open my door, then step outside and start my way across the street.

My cat probably ignored me.

When I arrive at Xavier's doorstep, however, that stroke of save-the-world boldness is gone, and all that's left is doubt and a healthy slathering of *awkward.*

I lift my finger to the doorbell, but don't press it.

What you're witnessing, by the way, is Evan Pryor slowly chickening out.

I was so certain I could do this on my own, and now I'm just an idiot standing in front of someone's door, and I'm totally not a private investigator or a detective or whatever it was I thought I could find within me.

I don't want to disturb the peace.

I don't want to wreck anyone's idea of perfection.

I just want to go back home and finish that bottle of wine with my cat.

With a sigh, I turn around to leave.

The front door whips open. "Evan?"

I stop cold. *Fuck.*

I put a smile on my face and turn around. "Xavier!"

He stares at me suspiciously. "What're you doing?"

"I was just ..." I cough suddenly, take a step back, then change my mind and take a step forward. "I was just stopping by to ..."

Xavier lifts an eyebrow, waiting.

Then it hits me. "I was stopping by to apologize."

He squints at me as if wondering if I've lost my mind. After apparently deciding I haven't, he crosses his arms and cocks his head, waiting for more.

So I give him more. "I should've maybe spoken up at my movie night. On your behalf. I could've defended you a bit to Raymond, had I the nerve. I don't think it's fair, how you've been treated since you moved here."

"And that's supposed to be news?"

My gaze turns hard. "I'm trying to make amends."

"Too little too late. I already have plans to move out as soon as a new place is secured by the summer. Earlier, if I can manage."

He's being pretty hard on me, that much is obvious. What isn't obvious is why he came to my movie night at all, if he was already so keen on leaving Figaro Lane.

I keep my tone gentle. "Can I ask a question?"

"You just did by asking that."

I chuckle. "Yes. Seems I did. Well, I guess I'll ask it anyway. Why did you move here in the first place?"

Xavier's answers are quick, as if he reads minds. "I liked the area. It's the perfect distance between my work and the clinic, where I take care of my dad. I wanted a house that was big enough in case my dad needed to move in. He's injured," Xavier adds in a lower voice. "He's injured and may need round-the-clock care until he heals. My mom left when I was three, so it's just us."

"Oh, I'm so sorry to hear that about your father."

"Well, it's not ideal, but this house sure was." He gives a sidelong look at either of his next-door neighbors. "Too bad this perfect house comes with *extra baggage*."

I wince, sharing his glance from left to right. "Too bad, indeed," I mutter sympathetically, staring off at Raymond's big mansion.

I feel Xavier looking me over. Even without seeing him, I know the skepticism is still alive and strong on his shadowed face.

Still staring off toward Raymond's, I finally arrive at my true purpose for visiting: "Hear what happened?"

"I know something happened that night after I left. Don't know what it was."

"Raymond's garden was vandalized. All the roses clipped, and they were arranged on the ground to spell out a few obscene words."

Xavier lets out a chuckle at that. "Serves him right."

I turn to him, and in a soft, unassuming voice, I ask, "Why do you get a thrill out of all these things that have been happening?"

He rolls his eyes. "Wouldn't you, if you were me?"

"If I was you," I say before I can stop myself, "I'd probably be the one *doing* all the vandalisms."

At once, Xavier steps out of his house, and he's right in my face. "I *wish* it was me who was doing them," he growls. "I *wish* I cut up his garden. I *wish* I'd painted that mailbox, and wrote that word, and drew that big dick, and poured glitter into every car on this street. I *wish* it was me." He pulls back. "Because then you'd all have a *real* reason to hate me—a reason I could *respect*."

My heart's racing from his outburst.

And it breaks at the same time.

I don't know what it is about Xavier's rage, but it sounds like my own pain.

About living on this street. About this new life I've made out of glass that surrounds me.

About all the things Dane was trying to tell me.

The things I wouldn't hear.

It sounds just like every time Raymond out-sasses yet another poor soul on this street, and how everyone quivers in fear.

It sounds like the watchful eyes of all my neighbors, and how they all carry equal parts dread and *pride* in living among these big, fancy houses.

In Xavier's little eruption, I recognize every bit of buried frustration that every member of Figaro Lane must be feeling deep down inside.

And in an instant, I know the vandal isn't Xavier.

I consider, in a sudden tangle of exciting thoughts and notions, what brave and reckless thing *younger* Evan might do in a situation like this—the Evan who was a bit more daring, a bit more dangerous, a bit more ... *clever.*

And after a moment's thought, I have a plan.

At once, my whole tone changes, and I'm as light as air when I tilt my head. "Will you be going to the annual Valentine's Gala at Raymond's house this week?"

For a second, Xavier seems to be assessing whether or not I'm royally fucking with him. Then, in one burst of half a scoff and half a laugh, he exclaims, "Uh, fuck no, I'm not."

"Fuck yes, actually, you are," I return lightly.

He looks me over with a smirk. "No offense, but I ... don't think we're each other's types."

"Agreed. That's why we're not going as dates. We're each going alone."

"Hmm." He nods slowly. "It's that ex of yours, huh? He's still fucking you up, isn't he?"

The mention of Dane sits heavy in my chest. I fight the urge to get all sad and frustrated about it. I have all night to waste feeling sorry for myself. "It is what it is," I mutter bleakly.

"I saw him show up the other night after that whole thing at Raymond's," says Xavier. "He stared me down from across the street. He's a protective one, that guy. I could tell."

I nod. "He is."

"So why am I going to this stupid Valentine's Gala? You know as well as I do that no one wants me there."

I swallow away thoughts of Dane. "Well, you got an invite just the same, didn't you?"

"Yeah. Like everyone did. So?"

"So you're going to come. It's rude not to answer an invite, didn't you know?" I taunt him.

Xavier narrows his eyes suspiciously.

"And," I go on, "you will bring your own beverage—perhaps one of those energy drinks in a big tall can, the most obnoxious thing you can find at the corner store."

"I hate energy drinks."

"Not on Valentine's Day, you won't. And it'll be the *only* beverage you consume all night. But," I add with a lowering of my head, "*don't* drink it all."

Xavier is absolutely mystified by me. "Uh, why ...?"

"It's part of my plan."

I'm suddenly beside myself after saying that. *Wow, I have an actual plan. I'm planning things. I'm scheming.*

This is detective-level shit.

"And why in homo hell would I even go to this gala thing at all?" he asks.

"Because I think I just figured out who the vandal is," I answer him, "and I'll need you there to prove it."

Chapter 20.
Dane is not a quitter.

For the first time in a long while, I drive in my truck with the windows up.

So as not to fuck with my hair.

It took me about an hour to get it to do (almost) the thing Evan got it to do after he cut it. Then I freaked out because I barely had any hair product to get it to stay, since I'm not really a hair-styling kind of guy, usually preferring to just let it do its thing. I even enlisted a few opinions from the gals at the store, which I had to visit to pick up this tux.

Yeah, I'm in a tux. It's a nice fucking tux, too.

Complete with a pink bowtie.

A pink pocket handkerchief.

And a cummerbund.

I'm just one fancy motherfucker in a pink and black tuxedo tonight.

I've also got a big bouquet of pink roses, which I had grabbed at a florist along the way, figuring I ought to not show up empty-handed. I also picked myself up a heart-shaped box of chocolates, because if you're going to show up in a tux with a pink bowtie and a bouquet of roses, why not fulfill *all* the Valentine's Day stereotypes?

Besides, Evan is worth a thousand overpriced heart-shaped boxes. That man is worth more pink roses than this whole damned city can grow.

And he's worth seeing my hair at its best.

And not totally wrecked by the wind.

Hence riding with the windows up.

When at long last I'm pulling onto his street, I feel like I haven't been here in months. I've done so much thinking these past few days that I've damn near driven myself insane.

At first, I convinced myself it was a lost cause, and considered adopting a rescue dog to keep me company in my cozy cabin. Their faces on the website alone had me nearly in tears, and I never cry.

Then I decided I would just get a ton of side jobs to distract myself from the past few weeks. But all the clients I'd turned away had found other investigators to take on their jobs, and to be frank, I didn't really care to help solve who was shorting the register at the local buffet, or whether Ms. Deena's aunt lived a second life in Las Vegas. None of it mattered anyway.

Then I thought, maybe I'll just jerk off four times a day until I'm too spent to feel emotional about anything.

None of those things worked.

Every time, all my thoughts and feelings aimed like a stubborn compass right at my true north:

Evan Pryor.

He owned my heart, whether he knew it or not.

And I suspected at least a tiny part of me still owned his.

And before he lets go of that tiny last part of me forever and officially declares me his bad ex-boyfriend for good, I needed to appeal one last time to him. He has to realize by now how fucking perfect we are for each other. He has to get over the past, let go of his mistakes, forgive me for mine, and see our future together.

Because if I can't have Evan Pryor, I know for a fact I'll never fall in love again.

There's something deeply relieving about that idea, knowing I've found the one.

And deeply terrifying.

I park at a spot I find on the curb, as there are a lot of cars parked all along the street. All the houses on this street are dark and lifeless, save the one at the end, the biggest one, Raymond's mansion, which bursts with light and color and music.

I get out of my truck, stare at that house, take a deep breath in, then blow it all out through my teeth.

With my bouquet and box of chocolates in hand, I march for the front door. With every footstep, the music grows, and the noise of a hundred people chatting and laughing grows, and the pounding of that desperate heart in my chest grows. I might pass out before I reach the damned door.

I've never been this nervous in my life.

So much is riding on this moment.

I reach the door, plant my feet, then give a hearty knock on the door.

It swings open to reveal a guy in a bright pink suit.

"Um ..." is his greeting.

His eyes, wide and unblinking, scan down my body like a laser beam. Behind him, a blender full of chatter and music is swirling into a berry smoothie of a hundred suited, dressed-up, or otherwise fancy faces.

"Hi," I greet him, breaking the guy from his trance.

His eyes flick to mine. "Are you some exotic dancer Raymond hired for the evening?"

I blink. "No."

"Can you be?"

At once, a familiar face spots mine, and he rushes up to the door to come to my rescue. "Well, hello there, Mr. Dane," sings Arry. "I didn't know you were coming!"

I smile and give him a nod. "Until a moment ago, neither did I."

"Are you here to sweep Evan off his feet? He's been a mess about you. Well, I mean, he hasn't said a word, and no one's gotten a word out of him, but we all sort of *know*, if you know what I mean. We just *know*."

The pink-suited guy flicks his eyes back and forth between me and Arry, as if he's twenty steps behind and playing conversation-catch-up.

I smile ruefully. "Well, I'm hoping to rectify that."

"He's been acting really *strange* ever since that movie night." Arry gets close and lowers his voice. The pink-suited guy leans in, too, unnoticed. "Are you trying to win him back? Is that what this is? Are we all in for some super big Valentine's Day romantic gesture? The only appropriate answer here is yes."

I give my bouquet a wiggle. "This." I give my box a wiggle. "This." I spread my arms. "And me is all I got."

Arry bites his lip in thought, staring me down. "No flash mob?"

"No fancy fireworks show, either," I add forlornly, playing along.

"I guess you can't always have the world. Want me to take you to him? He might be anywhere. This house is a bit of a labyrinth, and it's packed to its limit."

"I can always pick him out of a crowd. I think I'll manage if you just let me in."

It's perhaps only now that both Arry and the pink-suited guy realize their bodies are barring my way in.

At once, they separate and gesture inside. "Please. After you," says Arry. "If you are in a hurry, I'd check the library or the wine room. Raymond was giving one of his tours to some friends who've never been by."

"Thanks, Arry," I say with a nod.

"You remembered my name! Swoon!" Then he lifts an eyebrow. "Don't even *think* about going for a beer before trying Raymond's signature punch. Every year—"

"*Ooh, his punch ...*" moans the pink-suited one.

"Shush, you're interrupting!" Arry faces me. "Every year, Raymond makes his signature punch for the gala. It is his pride and joy. It sits in the center of the main table on an ornamental glass structure, pouring like a fountain straight from Venus's Temple. And it tastes *exquisite*. Just enough sweet. Just enough pucker. Looks like sweet, pale pink champagne with rose pedals and strawberries floating in it. You'd wear it's a goddamned love potion."

"*A goddamned love potion ...*" moans Mr. Pink.

Arry slaps me on the arm. "Have some for good luck before you face off with your man."

I give him another smile. "I appreciate the tip, but ... I'm pretty sure Evan's my own special brand of love potion—*and he's the only damned thing I'll drink tonight.*"

Arry and the pink-suit man sigh against each other.

Figuring my first trial in entering Raymond's house to be conquered, I step inside. Only five more paces and I'm cutting through a crowd of fancy suits, corsages, and a fuck-lot of fragrances. I get several looks, which I try to return with a polite nod or a straight-lipped smile here and there, but my mind is pretty one-tracked now, and until I find Evan, I don't give a shit about anything.

When I'm out of the foyer, I get my first breath of air at the foot of the gigantic living room, into which you must step down two steps, as if entering some grand court. And considering the breadth of the room, I half expect to find a throne at the end of it with Raymond seated, awaiting all guests to kiss his ring or some shit. Evan wasn't kidding when he'd joke that this place was Raymond's palace, and Raymond was King Figaro.

I haven't stepped down into the room yet, so it's a bit like standing atop a hill right now, scouting across all the heads and wine glasses and punch glasses in the room. I don't even pay mind to the giant punchbowl display, too focused on finding my man to care about anything else.

I give up and, with a few apologies and a grunted, "*Excuse me,*" I make my way to the library, which I had assumed was a joke to refer to his study, but it is no joke, and this *is* a fucking library. Books from floor to ceiling in bookshelves built into every single wall, with just a tall slit of glass for a window here and there, as it's in the corner of the house.

With no trace of Evan, I turn to check another room, and come face-to-face with, of all people, Raymond-the-King himself. "Why, Dane," he says for a welcome, his eyes wide and taking me in. "You actually came."

"Sorry, I know I didn't RSVP ..." I start, attempting to anticipate his words.

He stops me with a hand. "I'm happy you're here."

I give him a tight nod. "Thank you, Raymond. You throw quite a party. This whole thing is really very ..." I'm not sure I have the words. I'm not the best at this whole pleasantries thing. "... very nice," I finish lamely.

"*Nice*, is it ...?" He's amused by my word. "'*Nice*' is what you call a fancy gold watch, or a perfect manicure, or a ceiling fan imported from Italy. *This* ..." He spreads his hands grandly. "... is a fucking *masterpiece*."

As if part of some brainwashed cult, a batch of men within earshot all cheer after he says that, lifting their glasses—*tink, tink, tink*—and then kick back their drinks.

Raymond brings his hands back together. "But I'll take 'nice' from you, since you've been lovely in sorting out the trouble on our street. You *have* sorted it out by now, haven't you?" He squints his eyes curiously.

I suspect he knows the answer already, judging from the way in which he asks the question.

Evan wasn't kidding. Something about Raymond's demeanor—amplified by all the ears and eyes around us, who all hold Raymond in some weird kind of demigod regard—is intimidating.

I would say I couldn't care less what he or anyone here thinks about me, but the truth is, with Evan still living here, I have a motive to stay friendly with them all and not rock any boats, so to speak.

So I give him a slight nod and, vaguely, answer, "I'm well on my way to sorting it out once and for all."

"Pity. I thought you'd be a master at putting all the pieces together. I mean, you should take a waltz around this very house and you're bound to turn up at least a few clues, from the way people ... *talk*." Raymond gives me a quick once-over. "Unless you really are just that. All talk. No action. Maybe Evan was wrong about you."

I'm not fazed one bit by that comment. I just stand my ground right there, unmoving, unflinching.

Raymond, apparently out of steam himself to have any more fun at my expense, gives a flippant shrug, says, "Enjoy your time, Dane darling," then saunters back into his throng of perfect men who, like the walls of a cocoon, close in on him and follow him away.

The second he's gone, I've already forgotten about the pompous bastard. I slide through the crowded room, seeming to cut between couple after couple, and make my way into what appears to be a large dining hall with a long line of expensive-looking fancy catered crap.

On the other side of that table, I see two men. They are, among all this uppity bullshit, the two realest people in the room. For a second, I wonder who the hell invited them. They look like they wandered right off the set of some romantic film, these two. They are both handsome, but approachably handsome, not over the top. They look into each other's eyes, and it's beautiful, not annoying.

These two are clearly madly in love.

And it looks like they have been for a long time.

One of them brings a chocolate-dipped strawberry to the other's lips, then misses and touches part of his cheek. It's hard to tell whether it was deliberate, but the lover laughs as he chews off the end of the strawberry, drops of chocolate on his chin and cheek. The men are laughing, but it isn't a show of laughter to attract attention. This precious little moment only belongs to them, no one else.

I'm standing over here, halfway down the room, on the wrong side of the table, and I'm seeing it all.

It's my moment, too.

When the other man brings another strawberry up to feed his lover, something shimmers, catching my eyes.

A ring on his finger.

Husbands.

The strawberry is gone, and the men exchange a soft, nothing kiss. The love in their eyes is infinite. It burns with something far deeper than passion, something that resonates, that sticks ... something unconditional.

When I look away from them, it's like fucking magic that my gaze turns up, and I discover the balcony of the second floor, which overlooks both the dining hall and the main room.

Standing right at the balcony, staring off somewhere, distracted, is my man. But as soon as I see him, his focus is stolen away by something else, and he's gone.

And so am I, going after him—*in a hurry.*

Chapter 21.
Evan hates Valentine's Day, by the way.

Yep, I'm a regular Sherlock Holmes.

I walk around the party with a purpose, but no one knows what it is. I give a nod to some random douche friend of Raymond's. I give a smile at someone else who seems friendly.

And inside, I'm feeling immune to all of it.

I had watched from the top of the stairs when Xavier came in. He was wearing an eighth grade dance outfit. That is, an outfit that's too-cool-for-school and tragically out of style. He picked the drabbest non-Valentine-color dress shirt (picture maroon but one shade darker and ill-fitting, like a burnt tomato submerged in a questionable fluid) then slapped a black tie to it. His sleeves are rolled up. He's sipping a (huge) green Monster energy drink in a can. His shoes are brown. His slacks are black. It's a gay tragedy of operatic proportions.

He's basically the hook of my vandal fishing line.

And he's about to place the bait.

Right after I place mine: "Hey there, Raymond!"

I find him showing off a collection of china to a few of his friends. He turns at the sound of my voice, then gives me a plastic, cheek-to-cheek smile. "Mmm, Evan," he sings. "I'm just so glad you're here and not moping at *your house.* Did you see who's downstairs? I just spoke—"

"You mean Xavier?" I cut him off.

Raymond's eyes flash, whatever he was going to say swallowed up by the mention of that name. He doesn't even move or draw a breath, as if that simple name was the mirror to cast back Medusa's own stare.

"I just saw him walk in," I say innocently.

Raymond moves to the banister at once, peering over at the crowd. His eyes track Xavier as he struts through the crowd with his beverage, lazily scoping the room.

Then a little smirk creases Raymond's face. "Well. I didn't expect him to make an appearance after how badly he embarrassed himself at your movie night."

I chuckle, playing along. "Who knows? Maybe he's curious about your infamous specialty punch?"

Raymond eyes me at once. "Did you convince him to come? Are you two in cahoots again?"

My mouth goes dry in an instant. *Did he see me?* I put on my most innocent expression. "No. Why would you think that? I don't really know him that well."

Raymond's face wrinkles up. "I didn't mean Xavier."

Now I'm confused. "Who?"

241

"I meant your ex-boyfriend Dane, obviously."

My heart stops.

Now it's my turn to stare at Raymond like I didn't hear a damned word he just said.

"He's downstairs looking for you," Raymond ever so flippantly enlightens me. "He's carrying a heart-shaped box of chocolates and a bunch of pink roses, the lost little puppy he is."

There's nothing *lost* or *little* about Dane Cooper.

But the last thing I expected was for him to actually show up to the gala.

What's he doing here?

"I'm sure he's just here to ... to wrap up some loose ends with the investigation." I shrug. "Dane has his own way of conducting his business."

"Without interviews." Raymond sighs. "I was really hoping for some heated *interrogations*. It just sounds fun. There's a few people I'd love to see ... squirm." He keeps anxiously glancing over the banister.

I think I can call the bait officially planted. "It's nice to see such a diverse crowd of people here. Not only the few from our own street, but many from the rest of the neighborhood, and beyond."

"Oh, darling, people come here from other *cities*. My Valentine's Gala, you will come to learn, is the talk of every year. You'll hear people still talking about it come the fourth of July. This is your first, isn't it?"

"My second," I correct him. "I was still pretty new to this neighborhood last year, but never quite got the chance to fully appreciate all the work that goes into this whole Valentine's Gala."

Raymond looks proud of himself. "Oh, last year's is *nothing* compared to *this* year. You're quite lucky." Then he shoots me a little happy look. "You're one of my favorites, you know that?"

I was glancing off toward the stairs, worrying about what I'll say if (or when) I run into Dane downstairs. But Raymond's words hit me, and I turn to him. "I am?"

"Always been. You just ..." He shrugs. "You're so ... compliant. Cooperative. And intelligent."

The first two words are very strange words to use in complimenting someone. *The third* ... "Well, I did score top of my class since I was a kid," I point out with half a chuckle.

"Then you'll put those smarts to use and help rid this neighborhood of its *trash*, won't you, Evan?" He eyes me meaningfully.

I stare at him, unsure how to respond, my lips trying to form even the first word of a sentence, but I can't.

Thanks to the Prince of Bad Timing, I don't have to. "Evan," comes his deep, sultry voice.

I flinch and turn to face him.

Dane Cooper. In a stunning tuxedo complete with a pink bowtie and cummerbund. Pink bouquet of roses. A

243

heart-shaped box of chocolates wrapped with a pink, silk ribbon. And his hair is styled and swanky and dark. His eyes are burning with passion and confidence.

The second I look into his eyes, I'm enslaved.

"Dane," I return.

And it feels like letting out a breath at long last after holding it in for days.

He extends the roses. "These are ... well ..." He peers down at them uncertainly. "I wasn't sure if—"

"Oh, you two lovebirds," coos Raymond. "I'll let you two have your Valentine's moment. Evan, remember what I said." He eyes me again, then gives a scornful glance over his shoulder at the banister. "*Trash.*" Then he turns on his heel and fades into another crowd of men who greet him and swallow him up in all of their cool-mannered banter.

And I turn on Dane at once, my voice low. "*What're you doing here??*"

He doesn't seem sure what to say. Maybe he's just juggling between twenty different lines he'd rehearsed on the long trip here from Brady. "I ... I want to win you back, Evan."

"I'm not a prize at the *fair.*"

"You're the best prize at the fair. You're the gigantic stuffed teddy bear at the top that everyone wants, but the games are all rigged and no one ever wins him." He extends the bouquet toward me again. "I want you."

244

My eyes descend to the roses.

They're stunning—the softest, liveliest, most vibrant roses I have ever seen.

"This is just the *worst* timing," I let out with a sigh.

"Fuck timing. Just be mine," he states. "I'm nothing without you, Evan. I'm a lost dog in the middle of the woods with a big lake covered in stars every night, and it means nothing to me without you at my side to enjoy it, without you to make me laugh, without you to fill up my heart, to make me feel free, to better me."

I meet his eyes, and I'm trapped again.

"Dane ..."

He rushes forward and puts a kiss on my lips. I close my eyes and just stand there, rendered paralyzed by the touch of his soft lips against my own.

When our lips separate, he keeps his face close, and in the quietest voice, he murmurs, "I love you."

Before I can reply, a wild shriek of madness thunders across the room, inspiring silence from one end of the house to the other as everyone perks their heads up in search of what happened.

And in a room full of astonished faces, I'm the only one that just figured out exactly what happened.

I face Dane. "*I'm in the middle of something here,*" I whisper, "*and I am so sorry, but I have to see this through.*"

Dane turns very serious. "*What are you in the middle of, Evan?*"

"*WHO DID IT??*" cries a voice—Raymond's voice—from the main room downstairs. "*WHO??*"

I bite my lip and look up at Dane. "I'm sorry, but I need to do something, and it's going to get quite ugly. I recommend calling the police ... before some blood is spilled, possibly mine."

Dane's eyes flash. "The police? Y-Your blood?"

"I've found the vandal," is all I tell him before I rush toward the stairs to enter the fray.

The party guests, when all of them are staring wide-eyed and openmouthed at Raymond in the center of the main room, are far easier to cut through. I push my way to the front of a clearing where Raymond stands, furious and glaring accusatorily here and there at different faces in the crowd. In his hand is one solitary item, which he holds up like it's the culprit itself.

Xavier's tall, obnoxious energy drink can.

"*WHO??*" cries out Raymond again, that single word stabbing through the room like a steel blade. He looks to his left, and a guy shrinks away. He looks to his right, and two men clutch each other and wither.

I look across the room and, right where I expected, I find Xavier standing by a window. His eyes meet mine importantly, and he gives two slow, certain nods at me.

And now I know for sure.

"*SOMEONE. RUINED. MY PUNCH!*" Raymond exclaims, then wiggles the can. "*WITH THIS!*"

Also among the crowd, I see Stevie, whose lips are attached to a straw poking into his glass of punch.

Next to him stands Will and his tall, perfect wave of blond hair, into which his designer sunglasses rest, for once lifted off his face as he shows his surprise.

I glance the other way and see Marcellus and Vinnie, the husbands with the poodle, and they look completely beside themselves at Raymond's outburst.

I even see Hanson, who is surprisingly dressed up in a fancy suit, his normally-greasy hair slicked back, and it seems he was enjoying a conversation with another fifty-something male, which has now been abruptly cut off.

I see Preston near the fireplace, and his eyes don't seem to reflect much emotion at all as he watches and waits, glancing around at others in the room.

Josiah stands near the punch, and a hand is on his chest as he stares at Raymond, then glances at the punch, then glances at Raymond again.

I notice Arry in the crowd too, and he wears a smirk as he watches the spectacle, detached yet curious.

Raymond, after allowing for some time for his words to burn, then brings his voice down, turning it into a nearly polite question. "Perhaps one of you would like to tell me whose beverage this ... *vile, overpriced canister of battery acid* ... is?"

Some eyes move about the room, confused, looking. A notable few turn toward Xavier, knowing.

Xavier simply stands his ground by that window without a word, staring with stony eyes at the scene.

"Anyone?" prompts Raymond again, ever so sweetly as he looks around.

I was with him upstairs when he saw Xavier coming into the house. He saw him holding the drink. Raymond knows exactly whose it is.

He just needs someone else to say it.

"I ... I think I saw ..." comes a meek voice.

Raymond, like a spotlight to movement, turns on the meek man at once. "Yes?" he prompts him quickly.

The man clears his throat, adjusts his too-tight white bowtie, then finishes, "I believe I saw ... the fellow in the corner ..." He lifts a trembling finger and points it at the window in the corner where Xavier stands. "... h-he had a c-can of ... of ..." The man backpedals suddenly, too afraid to call someone out so directly. "But I don't know if it was that exact can. Maybe it's someone else's."

Raymond seems satisfied enough with that. He looks toward the corner of the room. Like Moses and the Red freaking Sea, the men back away, creating a direct path between Raymond and the accused: a totally nonchalant, arms-folded, smirking young man named Xavier who couldn't give any less of a fuck about anything.

"Well?" prompts Raymond. "Is this your doing?"

Xavier doesn't say anything, staring ahead.

My heart is pounding so hard, I could sweat lava.

"Are we playing the silent game?" asks Raymond, as if talking to a child. "Did you pour the contents of this filthy can into my punch or not?"

Xavier, at last, quirks an eyebrow, lifts his chin, and says, "That's what I was drinking, yeah. But I didn't spike your stupid punch. In fact," Xavier goes on, "I've been nowhere near it."

A hush of whispers spread over the room. Whether it's inspired by his tone, or his answer, or his use of the adjective "stupid" in regards to Raymond's prized punch, it isn't certain. But he gains no friends from that remark.

Raymond narrows his eyes at him. "So smart, you think you are. So, so, so smart." He looks around at a few others, observing their reactions. "If he's so *ballsy* as to ruin my punch ... who's to say he isn't *ballsy* enough to do ... other things? Other things such as ... putting a glitter bomb in someone's brand new Lexus? Or painting an obscene picture on someone's garage door? Or ..." He turns his narrowed eyes onto Xavier. "*Chopping up my precious passion roses in my beautiful garden and spelling out the words: H.O.A. CUNT.*"

The hush of whispers turns audible as people start to talk to one another, wide-eyed. Scandal and shock are on everyone's lips, and they keep stealing glances at Xavier, some as if afraid to look, some as if disgusted.

Xavier does nothing but stand there defiantly, not a trace of anything at all on his face.

Just as I told him to.

My heart is beating so hard, I can feel it in my neck.

And then: "It was me."

The quiet little words come from the last set of lips Raymond was expecting.

Mine.

Raymond turns toward my general direction, his big eyes flashing as he searches for who just spoke. "What?" he asks, annoyed. "Who said that? What?"

"Me," I state again. "It was me."

The men standing in my vicinity back away in shock, as if I'd just announced that I drink wine from a box. It isn't long before I've created a clearing in a radius of at least five feet around me.

When Raymond's eyes zero in on me, he doesn't at all look angry; he looks downright confused.

"No," he blurts. "It wasn't you. It ... It was him." He points a finger distractedly at Xavier without looking (resulting in his pointing unintentionally somewhere at the fireplace instead), then squints at me. "Not you."

"It was me," I repeat, fighting the terror that tries to creep up my spine at what I'm doing. *And I better know what the fuck I'm doing.*

"No, it was *not*," Raymond asserts, firmer.

I step forward bravely (read: just one and a half steps away from completely shitting my pants). "All of it was me. Not just the ruining of your punch tonight."

Raymond can't blink. He can't close his mouth.

He can't even move.

I glance over at Stevie, who is similarly stunned. "I painted that big cock on your garage door, too."

He gasps at first, then squints in thought, trying to work it out in his head.

I look over at Josiah. "I wrote 'HOMO' on your driveway. I guess I just got bored or something."

People are starting to murmur and gasp and look at one another.

I'm really stirring up the room with this.

"I put that glitter in your car," I throw at the married couple. "And," I say with a dramatic gesture at myself. "I painted my own mailbox pink."

"N-No, you didn't," Raymond stammers. He looks like he might pull out all his hair. "You couldn't."

"And ..." I fast eliminate all the rest of the distance between his stunned, rigor mortis body, bringing myself right up to his face. "I destroyed your garden with my own two hands."

"You can't have! You were at your own movie party! You're—" Raymond points an accusatory finger over his back. "You're covering for Xavier!! It was Xavier!!"

"And I'm ever so sorry I did it," I go on, playing my violin. "I'm just a lonely boy crying out for help. I'm the biggest eyesore on this street. I'll pay for all the damages I've done, and I'll sell my house, and I'll—"

"You can't leave!" cries out Raymond.

"What I have done is unforgivable." I turn to face all my friends and neighbors, some of whom look horrified, some of whom are still confused and trying to work out the logistics in their heads—Stevie, mostly, who's gone back to sucking hardcore on his straw, his face screwed up with bafflement. "I don't belong here on Figaro Lane. I am a fraud and a fake. I don't deserve your forgiveness, any of you, and I understand if you want to go and press charges against me. I am an awful neighbor, and a—"

"YOU CAN'T LEAVE!" screeches Raymond.

I stop short, turning to Raymond with wide eyes.

"*Why* can't anyone *see* that it was *obviously Xavier?!*" Raymond shrieks, shaking with rage. "He clearly *hates* this street! He *hates* me! He's—" Raymond turns on him now, aiming all of his wrath on the poor guy by the window, who still hasn't even so much as flinched. "He is *obstinate*. He is *unfriendly*. He is *mutinous*. No matter *how many times* I've tried, he will *not* follow in line with our rules, nor stick to his promises, nor return any of my calls! He is *exactly* like Ivan was!!—Stubborn, asinine, and *totally fucking gorgeous!!*"

The room falls to absolute silence.

Even I gape, not expecting that.

Who the fuck is Ivan?

But Raymond, oblivious to even his own words, is not finished. "And *why* won't any of you on this *stupid* street just get the fucking hint?? I want him gone! I can't stand to look at him every day! It kills me! And I tried, I tried the nice way, I tried every way I could to get Xavier off our street, but then YOU—" He points furiously at Stevie. "—made that comment about hoping he has a big dick when he first moved in. Well, how did you like that *big dick* on your garage door? Or is it too big to *suck* on for your liking? And YOU—" He points at Josiah. "—didn't even think he was gay. Well, he is! He's a *big, guy-liner-wearing* HOMO! And YOU TWO—" He points at Marcellus and Vinnie both. "—thought we should throw the new guy a glitter party! What the fuck is wrong with you? Did you enjoy the glitter party *I* threw you? It was NOT Evan! None of it was Evan! It was all *him*—It was all ... It was ..."

Raymond stops.

His hair's a mess. His bowtie is askew. His forehead is full of sweat.

He turns his face one way, then the other. He takes in everyone's faces.

"I ..." As if coming out of a psychotic trance, he at once finds himself as he straightens his tie and gives a quick wipe of a hand across his slick forehead. "I was ..." He swallows, then clears his throat. "I meant to say that I think ... I think Xavier should ... should go."

No one says a word.

All eyes are on Raymond Havemeyer-Windsor III.

The one who just self-incriminated himself for every crime that happened on our street.

Raymond starts to breathe funny as his eyes resume their flicking around the room. "What are you looking at?" he blurts suddenly, looking at a man near him. Then he hugs himself and looks at someone else. "Did anyone hear what I just said? Xavier did it all. Xavier—"

"Uh ... I think *you* just confessed to doing it all," says Stevie, "and totally sort of lost your shit."

Raymond's eyes flick to him coldly.

But no one in the room is intimidated by his hard, indignant gaze at the moment—least of all Stevie.

"You put the glitter in our car?" asks Marcellus in a quiet, disbelieving tone, clutching his husband's side as the two of them stare at him, hurt.

Raymond bristles. "I ... I didn't say ..."

"You're the one who painted that word across my driveway?" Josiah scowls at him. "Why?"

Raymond shakes his head. "No. There was a ..." He shakes himself out of his stunned state. "You are all very clearly misunderstanding my words. I didn't say—"

"Who is Ivan?" I ask.

At the sound of my voice, all eyes turn to me.

The look that Raymond gives me is full of pain. I'm not quite sure whether he's hurt that I outed him in such a public way, or that I said the mystery man's name—whoever he is.

To my surprise, it's Raymond's *frenemy* Preston who speaks. "Ivan is his ex-boyfriend. He's the one who got away. The one who—"

"*Preston!*" hisses Raymond, his face turning red.

"—he loved. The one who couldn't put up with his sick obsession with image. The one—"

"*Preston!!*" he growls again, mortified.

"—for whom he throws these galas." Preston crosses his arms, then looks out at the rest of us. "They broke up on Valentine's Day. He thinks one of these years, Ivan is going to come back for him."

Raymond throws up his palms and buries his face in them, then proceeds to sob quietly.

In front of the whole room.

At his big fancy gala.

"*What a hot mess ...*" whispers someone nearby.

No kidding.

Men all around the room start to look at one another, some of them touched, some of them looking bored, and some of them still puzzled and trying to work out my dramatic fake confession earlier.

From the back of the room, Arry's distinctive scoff is heard. "Uh ... are we seriously going to ignore the fact that the head of the HOA himself just confessed to vandalizing all of your houses?"

With that, Raymond opens his hands and cries out, "I'm sorry!" Tears burst from his eyes as he looks around the room at all his guests and friends and otherwise. "I'm sorry! I'm ... I'm *diseased* with a broken heart! I'm broken by love! I'm loved by no one ... not truly, not since *him*." He sniffles very unflatteringly, wipes his nose, then spreads his hands like a confession. "I'm sorry! I don't know what to say! I'm a fraud. I'm a jealous, wounded, hateful fraud of a human being. I hate Valentine's Day. It is the worst fucking day in all of humanity. But worse than this stupid holiday, *I hate myself*."

With that, Raymond charges ahead and cuts through the crowd. It isn't obvious whether this is just another performance, or if he's truly going through some kind of public nervous breakdown, but after he makes his way up the stairs (where from the banister, a whole other mass of men were watching this spectacle), there is one definitive slamming shut of a door, and he is gone.

No one seems to know what to do for a moment. Then, as if this whole scene was just a minor *interruption*, people start to chat among themselves. Some decide to leave. Some decide to stick around in case anything else interesting happens.

But a key selection of men come my way at once. Namely, my neighbors.

"Oh ... muh ... *gah*," exclaims Stevie as he approaches with wide eyes. "What ... *the hell* ... just happened?"

"That was a pretty messed up thing to do," says Arry to me with a smirk, which turns into a smile. "*Good job*."

"What about my driveway?" whines Josiah.

"Ugh, girl, I *told* you I know a power-washer," comes in Will with a roll of his eyes before setting his shades back in place over them.

Marcellus and Vinnie share a look, then glance at the others. "So are we not pressing charges against him, or what?" asks Marcellus. "Yeah," mutters Vinnie. "None of this is sitting well with me now that I know it's *him*."

"He only did it because his heart's broken," puts in Stevie, then frowns. "So sad. And Xavier reminds him of his ex."

"Yeah, 'so sad'," sings Arry sarcastically. "Oh, and meanwhile, you have to repaint your garage door. And Evan here has to repaint his mailbox."

"Speaking of," murmurs Will thoughtfully, turning my way. "Why *did* Raymond vandalize you first? He never gave a reason."

The boys all turn to me expectantly.

I shrug. "Maybe because I was the one with the cop ex-boyfriend, and he wanted to make sure someone was personally involved who could take some serious action against the vandal."

"Cold-blooded, that Raymond," mutters Arry with a sneer. "Setting up Xavier like that."

Just as he says the words, Xavier appears among us, having drawn forward from the window. For a moment, no one seems to know what to make of him, each person

257

in our little circle looking to the next to do something or say something.

Then, unexpectedly, Arry throws an arm around the back of Xavier, pulling him in for a side-hug. "Welcome to the neighborhood, you *not*-vandal, you."

Xavier smirks with amusement, then eyes everyone in the circle. "So ... you guys *don't* hate me now?"

"We never did," Marcellus insists. "We just ..."

"... thought you were a little off," finishes Vinnie.

That earns a smack in the arm from Marcellus. "No, we didn't!"

Will sighs. "The power of suggestion from Raymond is *strong*, and as soon as he got a foul sniff of you, I felt compelled to dislike you and distrust you along with him. But ... secretly, deep down ..." Will squirms. "... I'd always thought you were pretty much a bad-ass."

"That is *sooo* the truth," agrees Arry with a relieved sigh, then a look at Xavier. "If I wasn't so chicken shit, I would've high-fived you for speaking your mind all this time. You've got guts."

"And you totally *do* look like him," adds Preston, who shuffles up to our little group as well. "Ivan, that is. You even have his hair."

Xavier glances up, as if to acknowledge said hair, then shrugs.

It's now that Xavier notices the one person who hasn't quite acknowledged him yet: Stevie.

"I'm sorry about laughing that one night," Xavier tells him. "Y'know. About the big dick painting."

Stevie wrestles with the apology for all of a second. "Well, I guess, like ... um ... maybe it was a *little* funny." Then he gives a tiny smile, which Xavier returns with a breathy chuckle.

"Wait." Arry turns on me suddenly. "I just realized this whole thing had to have been your plan all along. How the hell did you think to set up Raymond like that, tricking him into confessing?"

With everyone looking at me, I shrug. "Honestly, I wasn't completely sure it was him. But, thanks to the hard work of my ex Dane, I knew that the vandal was someone *looking* for attention, and it wasn't just random acts of a bored idiot. They were intentional and directed. And ... I only had a *suspicion* it might be Raymond."

"So he had me bring a can of Monster," Xavier picks up, "of which I barely drank a sip, then left it near the punch bowl. Evan pointed me out to Raymond right as I arrived. Considering Raymond's suspicious mind, it was just a matter of leading him right into the trap, and then letting the truth free itself."

"I wasn't sure he'd even do it," I confess.

"Me either," agrees Xavier. "That was a big huge risk we took right there."

"Wait," cuts in Arry yet again, his eyes wide. "You mean Raymond—?"

"—ruined his own punch and tried to frame me for it all?" finishes Xavier. "Yep. That's exactly what he did."

Stevie looks like his eyeballs might fall out of his head. "How did he even do that without anyone seeing?"

"I watched him," Xavier explains. "He distracted his friends by making one of them tell a story, then sneakily poured the whole can into the bottom bowl of punch."

Arry shakes his head, half appalled, half impressed. "You scheming bitches."

Everyone in the circle laughs, the tension broken by Arry's dry humor. I only give a halfhearted chuckle, all the excitement and terror of the scene giving way to a lot of ignored emotions and nerves that now rush to the surface of my mind.

Ignored emotions, like my own broken love life.

Like wondering where Dane is.

Like figuring out whether it's even a good idea that I try to find him in this insane throng of men.

He looked so fucking adorable in his tux. And with that bouquet of pink roses. And with that heart-shaped box with the ribbon.

"I think I'm gonna go talk to him," says Xavier.

I lift my gaze up to him, confused for a second, since he nearly took the thought out of my head. "What?" I blurt in my bafflement.

Xavier shrugs at the others. "What can it hurt? He hates me because I remind him of his ex. Maybe he just needs to be talked to like a human being instead of stared at like some *magic gay god* or something."

Arry gawks at us, then turns to him. "You *do* realize he just tried to frame you for a couple thousand dollars' worth of damage to your neighbors' property, right?"

Xavier shrugs. "I've had worse experiences. Besides, isn't forgiveness a virtue or some shit?"

And with that, punk-boy Xavier saunters off, all of us watching him go.

Forgiveness is a virtue, he said.

If I don't forgive Dane, I'm lost. And even worse, if I don't forgive *myself*, I'll turn out just like Raymond.

Hosting a Valentine's Day Gala for a man who will likely never show up. Resenting every love I witness that passes me by. Hating anyone who looks remotely happy.

Despising even the notion of love.

I can't let that happen to myself. And I'm a fucking idiot if I let Dane slip away from me for a second time.

"Evan, are you alright?" asks Stevie. "You look, like, *majorly* distressed about something suddenly."

I look up at each of my friends. "I need to find him."

Stevie squints. "Find who?"

Arry nods knowingly. "His man. He needs to find his ex—"

"Boyfriend," I state. "I need ..." My heart jumps in my chest with excitement. "I need to find my *boyfriend*. I need to find *Dane*."

Chapter 22.
Dane's good ex-boyfriend.

The lawn outside Raymond's mansion becomes a steady stream of groups of guests leaving.

Especially after that fiasco inside.

After watching my brave Evan take on the mighty beast that is Raymond, I figured I didn't need to call the police after all.

Thanks to my ex-boyfriend Evan who clearly had the *"dangerous"* situation handled like a boss.

I stare at the mansion, all these emotions coming back to me, emotions I haven't felt since college when I was looking ahead at my career as a law enforcement officer, full of hope and good intentions. I was with Evan then, and I felt like I was on top of the world.

Tonight, I feel like I could be there again.

Before I know it, Evan emerges at the front door of that giant mansion, looking one way, then the other way with urgency on his face.

Then his eyes find mine, straight ahead, waiting.

And all that urgency melts away as he comes across the lawn, a vision in a snazzy suit with a cute red tie and a modest corsage pinned on his lapel.

I feel like a kid at the school dance, and my crush is walking across the dance floor to take my hand.

My heart's racing just the same.

When did I become such a sap?

Evan stops in front of me, his hands in his pockets. "Hey there, Dane."

"Hey there," I return softly.

We're looking into each other's eyes far too long to be natural. Clearly we both have something very heavy pressing on our minds, yet neither of us are able to put it into words.

So I—*for the third time this evening*—extend my roses toward him, in lieu of a perfectly worded sentence.

And for the first time, Evan actually takes them. He buries his nose in the pink, pillowy petals, closes his soft and adorable eyes, then smiles.

"They match your cheeks when you blush," I tease him lightly.

Evan opens his eyes, then hugs the roses. "They're beautiful."

"Not as beautiful as you."

He studies my face, as if discovering something. He assumes a faraway, thoughtful look as he murmurs, "I'm always surprised by you, Dane."

"Surprised?"

"Yeah, surprised. No matter how much I think I have you all figured out ..." He shakes his head. "... you just go and surprise me."

I chuckle, then shrug. "It's just a bouquet."

"It's so much more than that."

"You're right. It *is* more." I lift up the heart-shaped box of chocolates. "Nearly forgot about these, too."

When Evan laughs, his eyes scrunch up and a ton of adorable, heart-crushing things happen on his face.

There's no way to put all of my feelings about Evan Pryor into words.

"Sometimes, you ... fill me up with your beauty so much," I tell him, "that it terrifies me."

He stops laughing, but the tears of glee still sit in his eyes as they sparkle, curious, gazing upon me. "How?"

"You are that dream boy you only meet when you're asleep." Here goes my big romantic thing. "And while your brain is still playing tricks on you, making you believe the dream boy's real, and the love is *perfect*, and every intimate part of you is known and revealed to him, and every part of him to you ... it's terrifying, because some still-asleep unconscious part of you knows ... that if you realize you're dreaming, your body will start to wake itself up, like an automatic response. And the dream boy, the perfect boy, the love that—for a short moment—felt so fucking real ... it'll all start to fade."

Evan comes right up to me at that, burying his face in my chest with the roses and the heart-shaped box, and I wrap my arms around him at once. The noise of the fading party from the house, and the people still pouring out of its doors, are so far away suddenly. The only thing I hear is the soothing nighttime breeze, Evan's slow and deep breaths, and our hearts beating between our bodies.

"I won't fade," Evan promises, the side of his face still pressed to my chest.

Holding him against me tightly is the most secure feeling in the world.

I don't want this embrace to ever end.

But in the interest of allowing my favorite person in the world some oxygen, I let go and bring my face close to his. "Evan, will you be my Valentine?"

"No."

I quirk an eyebrow. "No?"

Then he lifts his eyes to mine. "I want to be your boyfriend again. Not just an overnight trial-run at your cabin, but your real, actual, devoted, loyal boyfriend."

Those words.

Are music.

To my ears.

I don't even give him a reply. Once again, words are not my friend. I just grab hold of him at once, bring his face to mine, and plant my lips on his.

Every broken part of me is fixed in one soft instant.

Every misgiving I had is vanquished like a fire under a deluge of storm water.

Every loathsome particle of sadness and loneliness I had just a day ago is squashed out by this kiss.

And now all that grows in me is love, and it's just as disastrous a contagion as the bad stuff was, infecting each and every part of my being, from my mind, to my hands, to my lips.

I love this man so fucking much.

In another hour, the vast majority of the guests of this year's Valentine's Gala have cleared out, leaving just an intimate twenty or so still dwelling in the house. To my knowledge, Raymond was coaxed out of his room by none other than Xavier himself, and the once-rigid King Figaro was force-fed a serving of humble pie as he then formally apologized to each person whose house he, in one way or another, vandalized. Each and every person—from Josiah, to Marcellus, to Vinnie, to Stevie—forgave him, contingent on the obvious understanding that Mr. Ray-Ray would pay for all the damages incurred. He agreed outright.

Then, in an unexpected gesture, Raymond formally stepped down as the head of the HOA in front of those who remained at the party. He announced that he really needed to rethink some things in his life, and therefore would campaign for his "excellent, close friend" Preston to be elected the next head. Preston's eyes lit up like two full moons at the good news. Apparently he's wanted the position for years, Evan later had to fill me in. Without the jealousy in the way, both Preston and Raymond seemed light as air as they started re-mingling with all the remaining guests. Continually, Raymond played off the whole big scene as "a temporary bout of insanity".

By the time Evan and I returned to the party, we were old news. I guess everyone kind of assumed the two of us were undoubtedly going to fall right back into each other's arms once all this vandal drama cleared away.

Evan made a point to approach Raymond. When the two faced off, I worried for a split second that it was a mistake, all things considered. After Evan said his piece, however, Raymond said, "There's no apology necessary. You did what you had to do. Though, maybe it might've been more polite to confront me in *private* ..." After a scolding look from Preston, he amended his words. "But yes, of course, right. I deserved to squirm. I'm happy to have come to my senses about all of this nonsense. Perhaps I'll be better off without the stress of the HOA sitting upon me, don't you think? Thank you, Evan."

And like that, fences were mended, and there existed no bad blood between the neighbors. It was like the ugly incident wiped out all their problems, and the men, for once, just had a relaxed, good time among each other, laughing and talking and gossiping about the other half of the guests who had left the party.

By the time Evan and I make our exit, it's just a few minutes short of midnight. "This was probably the most entertaining Valentine's Day I've ever had."

I agree with a chuckle and a nod.

We're strolling ever so leisurely down the sidewalk from Raymond's to Evan's. The stars are sprinkled over our heads, and crickets chirp in all directions.

"I'm shocked we both still have our lives," says Evan with a sigh. "It got pretty intense in there earlier."

"And no police were involved," I point out.

"I'm glad you made that call to not involve them. I am pretty sure they have much more important things to spend their time on. It's funny," Evan adds, "I think, in retrospect, they made the right call in the first place. A glitter bomb? Paint on a driveway? A pink mailbox?" He sighs. "*Real* problems are happening out there in the city. There are gay, trans, and queer men and women every day who actually *are* in danger, who're targeted, harmed, or seriously threatened by vandalisms or violence."

"It's all relative," I throw in. "What's one gay man's crisis is another's roll-of-the-eyes."

"I just ... feel like I see things so much more *clearly* now. It's like Raymond's hold over us was some kind of all-consuming hypnosis, and now it's broken, and now I think ..." Evan lets out a chuckle. "I think Figaro Lane is never going to be the same, that's for sure."

We stop in front of his house. "We're here."

"Indeed."

Evan looks at me imploringly. "Dane ..."

I lift my eyebrows. "Yeah, cupcake?"

"I ..." He bites his lip, gaze detaching, unsure what to say suddenly.

Sensing where his mind just went, I take his hands in mine and bring his focus onto my face. "I know you probably have a lot of regrets from this past weekend. I do, too. I wish I hadn't emotionally pushed you the way I did. There was so much history between us we didn't acknowledge. Too much. I know I've been thinking a lot since we parted ways. You have, too, I'm sure. We both know the trouble we've gotten into, but there is clearly enough love here between us to overcome whatever it is we need to. This thing we got going, it's more important than some stupid fight we had five years ago. You mean more to me than where we live, or what career we're purusing, or what we plan to do with our days, or who we spend time with, or how little or much we care about our image. You transcend all of that. As long as I have you in my life, at my side, in my bed, I'm happy."

Then I give Evan a deep, impassioned kiss on his parted lips.

When we pull away, I give him a smile. "Does that cover everything you were trying to say just now?"

Evan blinks. "Uh ..." He gestures at his house. "I was just going to invite you in."

I stare at him for five solid seconds.

Then I reply: "Well, shit. Invitation accepted."

He takes my hand, and the pair of us go up the path to his house, our shoulders pressed together.

When that front door shuts, Evan says, "And yeah, I guess you covered everything."

"We have a minute left of Valentine's Day."

"Oh! That's just enough time for me to bring you my gift!" exclaims Evan, hurrying to his bedroom.

I frown, following him. "*Your* gift? You didn't even know I was coming to the gala. How do you have a—*oh, hey there, Anne Boleyn, you cute girl, you!*—gift for me?"

Evan pulls a box from his closet, then sets it on the bed. He stares at it for a while, something troubling or emotional taking his mind away. "Well, it's a sort of gift I've had with me for quite some time. I just never had the chance to give it to you. And now's that chance. It's the perfect night for it, really."

"For what?"

He pushes the box across the bed toward me, then lifts his expectant eyes at me. "Open it. It's yours."

I smirk, suspicious, then approach the bed and take hold of the box. It's super light. I look up at Evan, my eyebrows pulling together, then I finally set the box back down and lift its lid off.

What meets my eyes is a heather gray shirt with a gigantic police badge drawn across the front with the words "Protector, Lover, Buddy" written on it. It's a shirt I got from some thrift shop my freshman year, right around the time of our first date, just days after we met in that psychology class.

But that isn't the big, remarkable thing about this seemingly unimportant shirt.

It was once torn. The night we broke up. Evan tore this special, one-of-a-kind shirt in half.

And what sits in this gift box right now is that same shirt—stitched back together with red thread down the middle.

"Evan ..." I'm so overcome, my throat tightens. My view of the shirt starts to blur, thanks to my sudden tears. "Evan, I ..."

"We belong together," Evan tells me from across the bed. "Two halves, that don't have any other half in the world with which they belong. Two one-of-a-kinds."

The shirt feels so soft in my grip. I look up at Evan suddenly. "This ... This shirt ..."

"I know, I know. It's too sentimental. You probably thought I threw it away years ago. I didn't. I ... actually hadn't even finished sewing it together until just a day or so ago. It was left unfinished in my closet all these years. I started resewing that same night we fought and you left, five years ago."

I set the shirt down, then slip off my tuxedo jacket. I remove my cufflinks, take off my pink bowtie, undo the cummerbund, then start unbuttoning my shirt. It slips right off, and then I take his shirt.

"Uh, slow down there," Evan teases. "You're about six sizes bigger in muscle than you used to be."

"The shirt'll hold." I eye him. "It'll handle it. These threads aren't popping apart ever again."

Evan's lips press together.

He heard my double meaning.

When I pull that shirt on, it fits me snug, but the seams stay strong. I remember I used to wear it baggy when I first had this shirt years ago, so with my added muscle over the years, I just fill it out now.

I meet Evan's eyes. "Like a glove."

Evan comes around the bed, throws his arms around me, and says, "Happy Valentine's Day. I love you."

I smirk at that adorable face of his. "You just wanted to show up my wimpy box of chocolates and roses, showing off with this big romantic gesture that almost made me cry."

"It *did* make you cry. And that's all the more reason I'm so fucking in love with you, Dane Cooper."

"Nah, I just got something in my eye."

Evan kisses me right then, shutting me up, and then I'm out of breath as I grab hold of him and tackle him to the bed with a laugh. Our lips lock, our hands clutch, and we're lost in each other's kisses for hours.

This man is mine. *And I'm never letting him go again.*

Epilogue.
Evan's favorite time of year.

Dane wakes me up with a kiss.

I blink, rub my eyes, and the first thing I see is a big fluffy cupcake on a plate, complete with pink icing and a huge red candy heart sitting atop it.

"Happy Valentine's Day, cupcake," he murmurs.

This is a year later.

I sit up in the bed and stare at the giant thing. "Holy crap, is this my breakfast?"

"Just a treat. A cupcake for my cupcake. Get out of bed and maybe your day will vastly improve."

With that, Dane leaves me with the cupcake and hops off the bed, strolling out of the room—naked.

I watch those big, tight buns of his as he goes, biting my lip and wondering if we should even bother with any of the plans we made for today, or just stay home and fuck twenty times.

I mean, how the fuck else should we celebrate our anniversary?

I take the cupcake with me out of the bedroom and into the living room, where the light from the sun pours in through the back and kitchen windows. Even from here, I can see water glimmering off the lake through the trees, the sun is so bright.

I may never get used to that view in the morning.

Dane has been busy cooking up an impressive spread of breakfast, which we enjoy over a light chat—and a tasty, adorable cupcake, which I graciously share half of. I feed him a fork of it, and he feeds me a fork of it, and when I say, "Happy Anniversary," he smirks at me and dabs some of the frosting on my nose. "Our anniversary is in *July*," he says defiantly. "*This* is *Valentine's Day*, which is our anniversary of when we got back together."

I just shrug. "Can't a boy have two of them?"

"No. That's greedy," he teases me. "But if you can't help yourself, then fine, we can claim Valentine's as our own as well. We gotta make up for last year's *catastrophe* somehow."

I fork another bite of the cupcake, then stop and say, "Y'know, cupcake really doesn't go well with eggs and bacon and your Dane-brand of orange juice."

He shrugs. "Call me impulsive. I saw the cupcake, I said—*I'm getting that cupcake for Evan*. So I did."

And so he did. I can't help but smile, then glance down at my hand.

And the ring on it.

That's pretty much exactly what he said not a few days after that Valentine's Day fiasco last year when we got back together. It was the morning of the sixteenth when we woke up together in my old house on Figaro Lane, cuddled up in my bed, that he said it. He told me when he saw me walk into that bar and we *almost* played that game of pool, he said, '*I saw you, Evan, and I said to myself—I'm getting Evan back. So I did.*'

Then he took me for a little trip out to Brady. He got me to go back into that bar full of smoke and leather and bearded men, and he took me right back to that same damned pool table.

He said, "We're gonna finish what we started."

I smirk and replied, "I'll break."

And I did. And when we were down to just the eight ball, I stared him right in the eye as I pulled back my stick, sent it flying, and the eight ball flew right into the pocket I'd called—right where Dane stood.

Then Dane pulled out a tiny black box.

I froze in place. "What's that?"

The whole bar had gone quiet. I spun around, feeling confused and overwhelmed at all the sudden attention. Everyone was staring at us, anticipating something, their faces lit up, even the leather-clad bearded men.

When I turned back to face Dane, he had come right up next to me.

And on one knee.

"Evan," he said, "I'm done searching. I don't have an interest in anyone else in this world. I knew it the day you first walked into that stupid psych class. I knew it on our first date. I knew it for the years we were together and studying our own passions. I even knew it when we first broke up," he added with a smirk. "And I sure knew it when I saw you come walking into this bar, walking right back into my heart like you owned it. And Evan, cupcake, you do. You own my heart, and now I want you to own it forever."

He flicked open the box.

A golden band with crisscrossing rope designs stared up at me, shining and artful and perfect.

"Be my husband already," he said, "and put me out of my damned misery."

It wasn't a question. He didn't need it to be.

He saw the truth through my overflowing tears.

I was already his when I said, "Yes. Yes, yes, yes."

"I didn't ask nothing," he joked as the bar exploded into applause and joyous hooting, but he took that ring and slipped it right onto my finger, then rose to his feet and put a big kiss on my face.

I've been his ever since.

"Well," I say at the breakfast table, "it was one very tasty cupcake, and I'll take it no matter what I'm eating it with." I wink at him. "Thanks, Dane."

"Anything for you," he returns, his voice deep.

There's a stirring under the table, and I realize with a start that our dog was sleeping underneath us the whole time.

Then I think the better of it. "What're you doing down there? Hoping one of us drops our bacon?"

The dog looks up at me with innocent eyes.

Yes, his name's Henry.

Right on time, Anne trots into the kitchen and plants herself at the foot of the table with a meow. She's gotten quite adjusted to the cabin life out here. She's downright happy without all those pesky neighbors dropping by all the time, in fact. And the best part is, she and Henry get along completely. She hasn't even lost her head yet.

Then Henry leaps out from under the table, Anne lets out a yelp of a meow, and the two are scurrying off, chasing after one another.

Okay, they get along *most* of the time.

Dane lifts his glass of orange juice to me for a toast. "Happy Valentine's Day."

I smile at him, then lift a foot underneath the table and gently plant it right on his big, bare dick.

"*It's about to be,*" I reply suggestively, "*a lot happier.*"

Dane lifts an eyebrow.

With that, the horny pair of us race back to our room and tumble onto the bed in a fit of kissing lips, grappling hands, and panting.

Henry and Anne sit at our bedroom door, confused.

This is our life.

And I'm so madly in love with this man that I am seriously considering the most socially suicidal move of all: blowing off Raymond Havemeyer-Windsor III's annual Valentine's Day Gala in favor of having sex with my husband twenty times today.

I'm sure he'd understand.

But seeing as I don't get out there as often as I used to—and I've been harassed by basically *all* of my former neighbors to come—I feel it's best we at least make a tiny appearance.

After maybe two rounds in the bedroom.

Make that three.

We decide to spend the afternoon down by the lake. When we hop out of the house, we pass by a table on the back porch where I was working out a design idea for one of my newest clients—a sweet old lady who just got a house out in Belleview after having moved away from a little town called Spruce. She had about a zillion ideas for her front room, and after one little meeting (where I learned all about her kind and adoring gay soccer player nephew Bobby, who was just heading off to college with his best friend Jimmy Strong), she decided to hire me to design the interior of her whole house. A tiny job became a big one, and I couldn't be happier.

Dane and I settle on the bank of the lake with Henry running around in the woods behind us, barking at about anything he finds, living, dead, or otherwise. Dane and I cuddle up on a blanket by the water, trading stories about the good ol' college days. I make fun of the way his hair used to be, and he makes fun of the sweater vests I was *obsessed* with back then for some reason.

"Do you think I should call the salon?" I mutter as I lie on my stomach.

Dane is knelt beside me giving my back the world's greatest massage with his strong, wide hands. "Nah. Gary has it all under control. Is he growing into his new position as store manager?"

"He stopped texting me every day in a panic a few months ago, so there's that. *Mmm,*" I moan, "*a little lower on the—yes, yes, God, yes, mmm ...*"

Dane leans down and puts a kiss on my ear as he works my lower back.

Then he works even lower.

And lower.

"That's my ass," I announce.

"Yes, it is," he agrees, then spreads the cheeks (and my legs) and buries his face right in it.

My fingers claw at the blanket and I gasp with such ecstasy, I literally hear my gasp echo through the trees and scare off a flock of birds somewhere.

Did I already say this is our life?

I'm saying it again. This is our fucking life.

Eating ass on the bank of a lake without a care.

We're a downright mess by the time we finally get in the shower to clean up early evening. (I did end up calling the salon—*just to be sure*—and Gary gave a lovely report on how amazing everything was running, and for once, I truly believed him. The guy has come a long way from the stiff-backed uptight receptionist, having turned into a warm and welcoming manager, swift on his feet.) The shower cleanses away every round of sex we had, as well as the filth we accumulated on the bank of that poor lake, and before our slippery bodies engage in yet another round against the shower wall, we decide we'd better force ourselves to exercise restraint, otherwise we'll never make it to Raymond's.

The ride in Dane's truck is shorter than I remember it. We keep sneaking glances at each other in our fancy suits with matching gold-and-red-striped ties, smiling, then stealing another kiss.

Those kisses never get old. Even a year later, and with a big history of stolen college-aged kisses, my heart still jumps and wiggles its toes with glee every time our lips touch.

When we arrive, we park along the curb of the cul-de-sac. Raymond scaled back his Valentine's Gala to just under fifty invitees, if you can believe it.

It's just about as intimate as Dane and my wedding last July, where we only invited our parents, our closest friends, and some select relatives. Several of my old neighbors from here had come, and there wasn't a dry eye in that chapel. The reception was an explosion of embarrassing dances and a lot of video footage shot on several phones that I'm sure will haunt me for years.

When we come to the door, we're met at once by Raymond, who cries, "Oh, heavens, I can't believe you two came! I'm so lucky!"

Please step aside for the *new* and *improved* Raymond Havemeyer-Windsor III:

He is basically exactly the same. Pretentious. Overly dressed, always. Looks with horror at anyone who wears clothing off a Wal-Mart rack (raising my hand: guilty).

But perhaps he's a little nicer now.

"Please, please, come in! My punch is in the main room." He leans into me. *"This time without any added Monster, thank you very much."*

We're led into the main room where all of my old neighbors are gathered around drinking punch, eating from tiny plates of exquisite-looking hors d'oeuvres, and chattering energetically.

Stevie is the first to catch my eye. "It's Evan!"

Then Marcellus and Vinnie turn, gasping. Arry even lifts his eyebrows with excitement, his arm hooked by his new beau—a similarly dry-humored stylist from my salon named Antonio. Hanson is with his boyfriend of eleven or so months, a sweet middle-aged man he met at the Valentine's Gala last year, and even his jaw drops at the sight of me. Leland, Thomas, and Preston all give a shout of excitement when they see us, as well as Will, who is without his shades tonight, but still has his tall and perfect wave of blond hair. Josiah gives a little wave from the couch, where he's sitting next to his boyfriend of four-and-a-half months, who I only learned about from a typo-riddled text from Arry.

Dane and I make our rounds, greeting everyone and, at once, being folded right into the latest drama everyone is discussing excitedly: *the new guy on Figaro Lane.* "His name is Frederico," Stevie tells us all, "and I'm pretty sure he's a serial killer. He's too handsome. Too polite. And he's filthy rich."

"Sounds like the perfect man," teases Arry dryly. "Why aren't you jumping on that, Stevie?"

"Because I don't want to be cut up into a hundred little pieces, that's why!"

"Maybe he's into kinky stuff," reasons Arry, then eyes his boyfriend Antonio with a knowing smirk. "There ain't nothing wrong with a little *kink*." Antonio reaches back and swats Arry's ass, causing him to gasp.

From the kitchen comes Xavier, who I'm shocked to say isn't dressed like a high school goth punk. He's got his same fuck-off demeanor in his eyes, but there's something wholly more ... *approachable* about him now. I'd daresay he even looks a bit sweet.

A year among folk you like can really do a number.

It sure has on Xavier.

And Raymond. "Xavier, honey, can you bring me a glass of bourbon? Since you're over there?"

Xavier shoots him half a smile and a nod, catches my eye, waves enthusiastically at me for a greeting, then goes back to the kitchen.

While Dane is absorbed in the conversation about Frederico, who apparently is the new guy in my old house, I pull away and turn to Raymond. "Some things never change, huh?"

He draws a hand to his chest, looking after where Xavier had gone. "Indeed. Everyone here still loves to make a fuss about people they don't know."

"Isn't it funny, how that can work out?" I lightly note. "How one's first impression of a person can be totally right—as in the case of Xavier, who I always thought was cool—and also how one's first impression of a person can be totally wrong—as in the case of Hanson, who is the sweetest damned man I think I know?"

"My first impression of Xavier wasn't so lovely," he admits, still staring off at the kitchen. "And now ..."

He doesn't finish his sentence.

I quirk an eyebrow. "Raymond ...?"

He flinches, then looks at me, annoyed. "What?"

"Are you ... and Xavier ...?"

Raymond gasps and slaps a hand to his chest. "How could you even suggest that? I can't even! Goodness, just the notion! I can't believe you'd just—! Yes," he answers, deflating. "Yes, we are. It's very new."

"Really?" I gawp at him. "You're seeing each other?"

"*Shh!*" Raymond leans into me. "No one knows. I'm terrified of anyone finding out. Everyone will talk about it. We're such opposites, Xavier and I. We have nothing in common, but ..." He seems to squirm. "When he puts his lips ... on ... on ... on me ..." Now he really squirms. "Xavier ... Xavier is a ... a *total animal*."

I smirk. "Sounds like a match made in heaven."

"I'll kill you, Evan Pryor."

"Evan *Cooper*-Pryor," I correct him.

Raymond slaps his own tall forehead. "Ugh, I keep forgetting! Why'd you do the hyphen thing? You should have taken his name outright. Evan Cooper has a *ring* to it. Oh," Raymond blurts suddenly, interrupting himself, "I have a room I want you to look at later. It's bothering me, and I'm at a *loss* for which shade of blue to paint it."

I smile at him, then give Raymond a big hug, which judging from the way his body went totally rigid, he was not expecting.

"I just want to say thank you," I tell him privately. "For being true. For letting yourself open up. For finding your heart and sticking with it."

Honestly, I'm not sure how I planned for him to take all of that, but after a moment, he pats me on the back, pulls away, and to my face, he says, "Thank *you*."

And there is deep, resonant significance in those two unassuming words.

I feel every bit of it.

Preston was elected the new head of the HOA, and the neighborhood has flourished ever since. He heads it with a much more laidback hand, ensuring that everyone enjoys living on any of the Operatic Lanes, and he even organizes and hosts events. Raymond always assists with his ample connections, and Leland and Thomas are quite inevitably roped into the planning stages, too. The fancy, party-planning quartet of them, no matter who the hell's in charge, are inseparable.

As it turns out, Figaro Lane and all of its neighboring streets are in good hands—*and among very good company*.

Later that night when Dane and I are driving back, we hold hands atop the gear shift, relaxed smiles on our faces. It'd been a long day filled with love and laughter and kisses, and now a spray of stars twinkle overhead, watching over us as we make our way back home.

Neither of us are ready for bed, and we're too spent for round six (or is it nine?), so we cuddle up on the couch and watch TV with Henry at our feet and Anne curled up on the ottoman.

I fit right into Dane's arms, snuggled up against his warm, muscled side, and feeling absolutely perfect.

"Did you enjoy your day, cupcake?"

I smile against his side. "More than you know."

"You ever miss your old neighborhood?"

I shrug. "Only the people. But I'll tell you this much: if given the choice, I'd pick living out here with you over anywhere else, hands down."

His hand rubs slowly up and down my arm, hugging me against him. "Love you, Evan."

"Love you, Dane. And you'd better tell me that every single day," I warn him.

"Oh yeah? That a threat?"

"Maybe. Maybe if you forget, I'll divorce your sexy ass, just so I can run around and tell everyone on Figaro Lane about my *bad ex-husband*."

Dane seems to find that so funny, he belts out with laughter so loud it makes Henry jump up, awake at once, and Anne perk up her head in alarm.

"Hmm," he growls. "I'm tempted. You know how I love the chase."

I bite my lip. "About that whole 'not being up for round six' thing ..."

"Round seven."

"I think I am, after all."

"Me, too."

At once, the pair of us are off the couch, fumbling to pull off each other's clothes as we back our way clumsily (and blindly) into the bedroom again.

I guess this is how you handle your bad ex-boyfriend you're secretly meant to spend the rest of your life with.

You take a breath.

You remind yourself of all the mistakes you made with his hot ass.

Then you stare at that hot ass like a goon.

Snap out of it, you're an adult.

You say fuck it and make all those mistakes again.

You marry the rotten, no-good, sexy bastard you just can't get enough of.

And then, every Valentine's Day, you make sure you keep down all those walls you're so good at building around yourself, because what's the use in a wall when life is all about connecting with other human beings?

We don't build walls. We build bridges.

And Dane Cooper built one right into my heart.

And on that special Valentine's Day, with all your walls down, you let him see the truth that's so eager to get out of you: the truth that, with him, you're a more complete version of yourself than you'd ever be without him. With him, anything is possible. With him, you can truly understand what love is, and what love means.

Grab your husband. Push him into your room. Kick shut that door.

And never let him go.

The end.

Printed in Great Britain
by Amazon